BOONIE

BOONIE

RICHARD MASSON

HOT
KEY
BOOKS

First published in Great Britain in 2013 by Hot Key Books
Northburgh House, 10 Northburgh Street, London EC1V 0AT

This paperback edition published in 2013

A CIP catalogue record for this book is available from the British Library.

ISBN: 978-1-4714-0025-4
1

Typeset by Palimpsest Book Production Limited, Falkirk, Stirlingshire
This book is typeset in 11.25 Horley Old Style BT

Printed and bound by Clays Ltd, St Ives Plc

FSC

Hot Key Books supports the Forest Stewardship Council (FSC), the leading
international forest certification organisation, and is committed to printing
only on Greenpeace-approved FSC-certified paper.

www.hotkeybooks.com

Hot Key Books is part of the Bonnier Publishing Group
www.bonnierpublishing.com

For my wife Margaret, with love and thanks for her infinite patience and understanding

One

The Silver Men

JD sat on a tuft of sawgrass and watched the smoke rise over the remains of the old shack. From time to time some piece of grey, bleached wood cracked in the heat as a new, orange fireworm crept over it. JD watched all day 'til there was nothin' left 'cept a pile of hot ash and that small twist of smoke. Then he watched the purple sun sink through the chemical haze and the dark shadows stretch out from the red hills. He watched until the whole Dry Marsh was dark.

When night wrapped around him JD tucked his hands under his armpits, stared at the heap of ash that had once been home and set to figurin' what to do next.

He sighed a deep sigh. He couldn't have known what was going to happen. Why, just that morning, same as every morning when the temperature got too high to stay in bed, he'd dressed in his dungarees and shirt, pulled on his cracked leather boots, tied his leggings up to his knees, put his old cap in his pocket and shuffled into the big room to see if Pa had left anything to eat. Pa was pretty good at getting stuff to eat and JD found two or three twisted roots and some crickets laid out on the box by the stove. He picked up one of the crickets, took its head between his finger and thumb, snapped it off and put the body and legs into his mouth, crunching them into small pieces. JD liked crickets; they tasted good.

When Ma had been around, JD remembered, she'd boil all the grub together in a big pan which made everything taste the same but, while he preferred his crickets raw, it was tough chewing uncooked roots. But now Ma was gone and Pa had no time for cooking. He was out from dawn 'til dusk hunting over the Dry Marsh, scraping and digging for things to eat. He never got back to the shack 'til after dark except once, way back when he'd come in before noon with the biggest insect JD had ever seen. He said he'd found it buried in the wet green. Ma said it was called a crab. JD thought it looked like something from another time. Ma put the crab straight into the pan and boiled it up right then and there without waiting for supper time and when it was done they'd all three sat on the floor and pulled bits off it, cracking the shell with rocks and sucking out the meat. When Pa said it was like Yule in the old

2

times, Ma had winked at him and reached down a glass jar from the top of the dresser. She and Pa swigged from that jar 'til it was all gone and they were laid out flat on the floor. Little JD took the empty jar out of his Ma's hand to see if he could get some of the golden fluid for himself but it was quite dry. All he could do was sniff at the heady fumes. It was just like the smell you got if you found one of the old petrol cars abandoned someplace.

But Ma was gone and now Pa was gone too. When the Silver Men came last they'd found him half-buried out back. Pa always buried up when the vibrations came. He'd scrape out a spot near some sawgrass, lie in it and cover himself with dirt. He had a hollow stem to breathe through, but JD could always tell where he was by the hump in the ground and the different colour dirt where he'd dug it. The Silver Men knew that too. A while back, when two or three of them had done what they came for in the shack, they took Ma out to where Pa was hiding and did it a couple of times more right next to where he was buried, just so's he could hear. Then they put their silver suits back on, replaced their helmets and took off. When they'd gone JD made himself scarce while Ma and Pa fought in the dust.

After dark JD crept back into the shack, crawled into bed and lay with his face in the sacks hoping everything would be OK by morning. But next morning Ma was gone. Pa said she'd gone to the City.

The next time the vibrations came Pa was away digging so JD ran inside, opened up the dresser in the big room and climbed in. He lifted up the loose floorboards and squeezed through the hole underneath, just like Pa had showed him, and lay quiet under the shack.

He heard the Silver Men come in. He heard their heavy boots clumping on the boards above his head. He heard them call and when they saw that Ma wasn't there he heard them cuss and throw things around. They kicked over the stove and it shook the floorboards right over where he lay, making him cower down.

Then they went out back to find Pa. It took them a while but with their jet-packs and all they could cover ground fast. They brought him back to the shack and hit him with things that whistled and cut the air. They hit him a lot but Pa never made a sound. He didn't cry out or nothin' though what they were doing must have hurt like hell. JD guessed that the Silver Men were drinking too because he could smell that smell again just like the time of the crab. He reckoned they must have had a real big jarful too because the fumes that came down through the cracks in the floorboards were so thick and heavy they made him dizzy.

At last the shouting died down and JD heard the Silver Men leave the shack. He hoped they'd start their machines quick so's he could get out and go to Pa; see if he was OK.

4

But JD was having trouble breathing. Sweet, sickly fumes poured like treacle into the narrow space where he lay, filling his lungs and making his eyes sting. But JD kept still, listening, hoping and praying the Silver Men would go quick.

After a while it got real quiet but just when JD thought they might have gone he heard a click. Then one of the Silver Men shouted, there was a big flash and a brilliant orange and blue fireball, swirling and roaring like a dragon, ripped through the cracks in the boards.

JD fell flat to the ground and straight away his back began to burn and his head grew real hot. The hairs on his arms shrivelled into tiny black spirals and his skin began to scorch. He whimpered and tried to crawl away but hot smoke coiled and swirled through that shallow space under the shack, seeking him out, burning his eyes and filling his nose and throat.

He headed for the back of the shack where he knew there was a gap in the boards by the step. Gasping and choking on the hot, grey fog he wriggled and elbowed his way across the dirt. His hair was on fire, his arms were burned and bleeding but he struggled on, digging his fingers into the rough ground, grabbing at it, scratching at it, pulling himself towards that little opening. The flames roared and burned above him, stealing the air, making him keep his mouth close to the dirt, desperate for breath. The

5

heat was so intense it boiled the strength from his limbs, sucking it out until at last he fell flat, spread out, gasping, his chest heaving fit to bust. It was no good, he could go no further. He could only lie still now and wait for the hungry flames to burn him right up where he lay. Lifting one arm, JD tried to push away the blanket of hot smoke that was wrapping itself around him. But his knuckles struck something hard and, raising up his streaming eyes, he saw a patch of light above his head. For a moment the smoke thinned and JD saw he was right under that gap by the back step. With one last frenzied effort he pushed his hands into the hole and, gripping the edge, hauled himself up, forcing his head and shoulders into the air outside. Bit by bit he squeezed through until he fell in a heap by the back step.

JD struggled to his feet and, bent low, he half-scrambled, half-ran to the nearest hollow where he dropped, panting and choking, behind a hump of sawgrass. He pushed his burning face into the dirt and beat at his hair to put out the flames, while all the while the blazing shack roared and crackled and the air vibrated and buzzed from the Silver Men's machines.

JD pressed his thin body against the ground and covered his ears. At any moment those Silver Men would take off and fly right overhead. Then they would surely see him, they must see him. He pushed himself as flat as he could and stuck his head into the sawgrass which cut and stung the raw flesh on his face. The jet-packs revved up and one by one the Silver Men took off. In a matter of moments they would see him stretched out in his shallow hideaway and would swoop down and carry him off for sure.

JD started to sob.

Two

The Old Road

When JD dared take his hands away from his ears all he could hear was the cracking of the burning wood and the whoosh as the old shack fell into the flames. He could still feel the vibrations but they were receding fast, and through the cloud of dust and ash that the jet-packs had kicked up he saw just four little black dots away in the west.

When he was sure the Silver Men had gone, JD sat up and he didn't move from that spot all day nor right through the night. He just sat watching the smoke and thinking.

Next day he set off along the Old Road. All through that night he'd never once thought about the Old Road but somehow when morning came he just stood up, turned his back on the pile of ash that had once been home and walked towards it. When he reached it he hadn't paused neither; he just turned west and strode off. Just like he'd been meant to.

JD knew that in the old times the petrol cars had run on that road but now the concrete slabs were cracked and uneven, lifted to crazy angles by the heat. Sharp yellow grass grew in the gaps and JD had to walk along the dirt path by the edge to save from falling down or having to jump from slab to slab.

He didn't see a single shack all day. From time to time there were square patches of concrete where brick shacks had been, their edges red and yellow like broken teeth. Wires and pipes had been cut off short and shards of white china lay around but everything else was long gone.

He walked all day, even in the hot hours, sucking at his tongue, trying to create spit the way Pa had shown him. His skin, scorched and weeping, hurt bad and he walked bent and twisted like an old man but he knew he had to carry on.

He made sure to stay near the road where the track was as flat and easy as it could be, while all around the scrub stretched away, a mournful desert of red dust, undefined, undulating its way to the horizon. By nightfall he was sore and hungry and began to meander away from the Old Road and into the Scrubland, seeking out the crickets he could hear chirruping in the tussocks. He caught two and ate them quick while they still had some moisture, leaving their heads on. Pa said you could get a lick from the brains.

9

When darkness finally closed in JD lay down where he stopped, put his head on his hands, tucked his knees up to his chest and shut his eyes. With one ear close to the ground he reckoned he'd hear any vibrations if they came.

But sleep did not come easy. JD turned over and put his face into the crook of his arm, trying to shut out the lightning flashes that crackled orange and blue across the sky. All that night he tossed and turned; the heat never let up and he could still taste smoke. Whenever he could shut out his thoughts long enough to drift towards slumber he would hear a cry in the distance or feel a shudder through the dirt and would start, images of Silver Men like livid flames flashing before his eyes.

Well before dawn he gave up trying to sleep and sat up, stretched his neck, straightened his back and looked around. The air was still and dark, the sky a deep angry red except for a faint semicircle of yellow light fading into the west horizon. JD had seen that light before but never so clear. Before sun-up on some days back at the shack he'd seen that same dirty yellow smudge staining the sky. He'd never mentioned it to Pa and Pa had never said anything about it to JD, but when Ma went off and JD had asked Pa where she'd gone, Pa had stared at that yellow light when he said she must have gone to the City. He never said no more but some mornings JD had seen him

10

clenching and unclenching his fists, staring at the yellow glow, anger and hurt etched on his face.

But Pa was gone now and JD knew he had to get on. The Blue Star was fading and soon the sun would rise and sear the ground into another day of furnace heat.

Sitting with his knees drawn up to his chin, JD sucked his swollen tongue and wiggled it behind his teeth but no saliva came. His lips were dry and cracked and under the rim of caked red dust he could feel slivers of skin peeling away. He sucked air in through his teeth, trying to cool his mouth but that was no good neither. Even before sun-up it was just too hot and his arms and hands, scorched and red from the fire, seemed even hotter than the rest of him. He took off his old cap and a cloud of burned hair fell into his lap.

JD looked around. Away to his left, set against the scrub and sand hills, he saw a tree silhouetted against the sky; a wizened, bent thing with broken branches. He'd seen trees before, even standing ones. Way back Pa had taken him to see one. They'd walked north all one morning beyond the Dry Marsh to an old river bed near to where the nuclear power plant had been. They'd found the tree clinging to a high bank, one splintered branch pointing back like a warning. They sat down under that tree, father and son, and Pa had told JD a story about the old times when trees were high and straight and hung with soft green leaves which you could eat. He told JD of a time when small critters flew among the trees and water fell out of the sky. JD loved it when Pa told him those stories even though he knew they were made up. No one could imagine any such thing in real life.

JD sighed out loud, wrapped his arms tight around his knees and studied this new tree while he remembered that time with Pa. Then he snapped out of his memory and sat up straight. His sharp eyes had detected a movement near the tree and his heart began to pound. Someone was there. The trunk looked like it was wide at the bottom and narrow high up, but when JD concentrated he could see there was a figure hunched at the base of the tree, its head leaning forward. That head wore a broad round hat and from time to time that hat would nod. JD touched his own ragged cap with a finger and wondered what it would be like to own a nice, shady hat like that.

He watched carefully. JD was scared of strangers but was getting so desperate for water he set to wondering if the man by the tree might have something to drink. He watched and thought about water until at last he summoned up his courage and began to creep towards the tree. He stayed low, skirting the sand hills and keeping in the hollows, his eyes fixed on the man, ready to freeze or run if he should turn around.

When he was just a few paces away, right up close behind

the tree, he dropped into a shallow dip and waited a while, keeping low and listening. Then he crawled forward and peered over the rim of the hollow. He was right; there was a man by the tree and he was old, older than Pa, and wore a long coat made of some light stuff. It too was old and had tears all over it. The man's legs and feet were wrapped in layers of paper, tied around with strands of plaited grass, criss-crossed up to his knees. His arms were thin and bent, and his elbows rested on his knees, which were drawn up close to his chest. A mane of grey hair poured out from under his hat and hung straight down his back. JD could see he had a grey muzzle too but the rest of his face was hidden in the shadows. JD was so close he could hear the man breathing; he made a kind of whistling sound as he breathed in, followed by a gurgle and a grunt when he breathed out. It sounded like the old guy was sleeping.

Lying quietly in his hole, JD searched for any sign the man might have something to drink. He scanned the hunched figure from the top of his hat to the tips of his toes, hoping to see the bulge of a water bottle in the thin dustcoat. Then he spotted something. Leaning against the tree was a sort of a bag, an old satchel made out of something soft. There was a bulge at one end and a split where it had dried in the sun and through the crack JD could make out something metallic. Something grey, dull and tubular – just the kind of thing a man might keep a drink in.

JD edged closer. He winced at the pain from the burns on his arms but he kept on going, crawling out of his hole, staying flat to the dirt, using his elbows to squirm towards the bag, all the time flicking his eyes between the sleeping man's face and that dull, metal tube. As he crawled a plan formed in his mind. When the time was right he'd dart forward, grab the bag and run as hard as he could, away across the scrub before the old man knew what was happening. JD ran his swollen tongue across his dry lips, tried to swallow and thought about water.

He crept closer and closer until, about midway between the dip and the tree, he began to raise himself up. He needed to be sure nothing would give him away, a dry twig, a stone that might click against another. But it was all clear; just a fine layer of red dust covered the ground between him and that precious tube. JD licked his dry lips again; he could almost taste that cool, sweet water. One more step and he'd be close enough. He gathered himself for the final spring, drew a quiet breath and lifted his hands clear of the dust, ready to catapult himself forward, grab that bag and run. It was now or never.

'You touch that bag, son, and I'll snap you like a twig.' The voice sounded like it came from the sky; like the growl of distant thunder.

Three

Godrum

JD sat back on his haunches, dropped his head and tried to look innocent. He ran his fingers in the dust, pretending not to be interested in the man or his bag, but when he was sure the old guy wasn't looking he shot another glance at that inviting bulge. He was sure there was a drink in that bag and as he conjured up thoughts of cool fresh water his tongue grew bigger and drier in his mouth. Once more he tried to lick his sun-cracked lips but it was no good. What could he do? There was no Pa to give him a bit of spit in his mouth, no Ma to let him put his tongue on the old piece of glass she kept in the dark cupboard, just an old man and a tree. He had to get a drink from someplace and still wondered if it might be worth the chance. Sure, the old guy knew he was there but JD reckoned he could still grab the bag and make off before getting caught. He tensed;

he was young and the man was old, he was sure he could do it.

'You come around here, boy, where I can see you,' the voiced rumbled again. It was as if he'd read JD's mind.

JD stood up and shuffled forward. The old guy's head was down, his face still hidden in the shadow of that hat. As he sidled past JD shot a quick look under the wide brim and saw two sharp, golden eyes trained on him like weapons. Two tiny slits beneath bushy grey brows, focused right on him, daring him to make one false move just so's he could carry out his threat. JD shuddered.

But he's old, JD repeated to himself; he cain't be as quick as me. He knew his chances were slim but he was so thirsty, he'd do anything for a drink, even risk being snapped like a twig. That terrible thirst was putting thoughts in his mind he knew his Ma would have beaten out of him.

But just then JD saw something that made him stop. Something so scary it drove all other thoughts from his mind. Beneath the intense eyes and the big hooked nose, curved and sharp like a raven's beak, the old man's mouth zigzagged across his face in a jagged line. JD stared. The pale lips had been sewn together with strong leather bands, each stitch crossed over the next, straining the skin tight across the bones, drawing down his cheeks and pulling his chin up from his neck. JD was horrified and fascinated at the same time but there was worse to come.

16

Beneath the man's chin where the skin was pulled up and stretched by the stitches, half-hidden by a long piece of cloth tied in a loose knot JD saw something so dreadful it made him feel sick. Beneath the man's grey stubbled chin was a livid, red hole shaped like a cross. It was cut deep, the edges just flaps of loose skin and from it a small white tube ran down and disappeared inside the man's clothes.

'You circle round to where I can see you, boy,' the man said, his chest heaving, his words pushed out from the hole in his neck on a belch of air. 'Don't you try to run. If you do I'll catch you, break off your arms and drink your blood.' The man gave a dry rasping chuckle which rose from someplace deep inside him, making the loose skin flap in and out of the dark, red hole.

How did he say that, JD thought, staring at the stitches which held the man's mouth closed, trying to figure out how you could speak through a hole in your neck. And it wasn't just how he spoke, it was what he said. JD had never heard anybody say such things. Would he really snap him like a twig or pull his arms off? He was almost sure he wouldn't but just in case, JD did as he was told, shuffling around until he was straight in front of the man.

'That's fine. Just fine,' the man croaked. 'Now, you just sit down there where I can see you plain.'

JD sank down, sat in the dust and crossed his legs.

The old man grunted and, raising his head, he looked straight at JD, his bright eyes scanning him from the fire-blackened curls to the pointed tips of the worn old boots that Ma had sewed.

'What's your name, boy?' the man said at last.

JD coughed to clear the dust. 'JD,' he said, but his voice caught in his dry throat so he tried again. 'My name's JD,' he said, louder.

'JD, eh? And what does JD stand for?'

'It don't stand for nothin'. It's just JD.'

'It has to stand for somethin',' the old man belched, his deep burbling voice rising a tone or two. 'What do your Ma and Pa call you?'

JD shrugged. 'They call me JD, or used to. Ma went off and Pa got burned up in the shack.'

The man sniffed. 'So, young JD, why do you want to steal an old man's things? You tell me that.'

'I'm dry,' JD said without shame. 'I ain't had nothin' for more'n a day 'cept a few crickets and I'm real dry.'

'You're dry so you figure it's OK to rob some old guy then leave him to die out here in the scrub. That it?'

JD shrugged his bony shoulders. 'I didn't mean no harm,' he said, looking at his feet. 'I just want a drink.' His thirst was so strong it was overpowering his fear and at last he summoned up enough courage to ask the question he knew he shouldn't.

18

'Have you got a drink in that bag?' he said, pointing to the old satchel.

'Might have,' the man drawled. 'But if I have, you give me one good reason why I should share it with a thieving Boonie kid who ain't worth a spit.'

'I just want a drink, Mister. I ain't had a taste for two days,' JD said, searching the craggy face. 'I don't want to hurt no one. I just need a drink,' he whined, dropping his head again and looking at his feet.

JD heard the man move and tucked his head into his chest. He was sure something bad was going to happen but he was too scared and too tired to run. If the man with the sewed-up face was going to grab him there wasn't much he could do about it now. He just hoped he wasn't going to pull his arms off, but just in case he tucked his elbows close into his sides and crossed his bunched-up hands tight under his chin.

He heard the bones in the man's knees crack as he stood up, and the sound of his feet shuffling through the dust towards him. JD bowed his head real low, making himself as small as he could, hoping for the best but fearing the worst. He began to whimper.

'Here, Boonie. You take this.'

JD looked up, keeping his head low and peeking through his brows.

The man held a grey, metal tube in one hand and a

screw cap in the other. He offered JD the screw cap and cautiously the boy unclasped his hands, reached up and took it from the long, bony fingers. The metal was cool against his fingertips and JD's heart leapt. Gently, he lowered that screw cap until he could see into it; it was full of clear water and in that moment the whole world beyond JD's fingertips disappeared. The only thing that existed was that small container and its glistening circle of water. There was no scrub, no hills and no valleys, no sawgrass, no sun, no old man and no tree. The whole world was in that precious, metal cap.

JD looked at the screw cap for a moment before gently tipping it up and letting the priceless fluid touch his dry, cracked lips. It was heaven. At once JD's lips seemed to shrink back into place and he worked them together until every part was soft and moist. Then he took a tiny sip, the way Pa had taught him, and let it run over his tongue, wetting it, shrinking it before letting the sweet water run down the sides so he could get the full, beautiful flavour. JD looked up at the man and creased his face into a grin and to his surprise the man smiled back, his dry old cheeks rising, his slit eyes sparkling.

'Take it easy, son,' the old man belched quietly. 'Make that last.'

JD wanted to thank the man properly, to explain what it felt like to take a drink after more than two days, but that could wait. Right now the water was all that mattered. In three tiny sips he wetted his tongue, his teeth and gums. He held the water in his mouth and swilled it all around until finally, reluctant to let it go, he swallowed. A cool rivulet washed its way through the dust in his throat.

JD followed this slow, careful ritual another couple of times until the cap was empty. Then he ran his tongue around the inside, seeking out every last, hidden drop until finally he tipped his head back, lifted the metal cap and shook it, hoping that maybe one tiny droplet might be lurking someplace and would fall, cool and refreshing into his open mouth. But it really was all gone and he offered the cap back to the old man, who screwed it onto the tube before shuffling away to his tree where he flopped onto the ground, leaning once more against the twisted trunk.

'Thanks,' JD said once the old guy had settled. 'Thank you, sir. Thank you very much.'

The man's tortured face creased into what passed for his smile once more. 'That's OK, son,' he growled. Then, pausing for a moment, heaving his chest upwards and noisily drawing air in through his big nose, he said: 'You got good manners for a kid. Where you from?'

'I live in the Dry Marsh, back there,' JD said, pointing east.

The old man nodded. 'And your Ma and Pa are gone, you say?'

21

'Yep. Ma's gone anyways. Pa got burned up like I said.'

'So you did. So you did,' the old guy said like he was thinking of something. 'So where are you going? You lookin' for your Ma?'

JD blinked. It was like something inside him had woken up. 'How can I?' he said. 'She's gone off. Pa said.'

'She must have gone someplace. Did your Pa say where she'd gone?'

JD shrugged. 'To the City,' he said.

The old man gave a grunt. 'They all go to the City in the end.' Then after a while he added: 'If your Ma's there you'd better get yourself off there too. No place for a little kid on his own, not out here in the Scrubland.'

'But I don't know where the City is,' JD said quietly. The whole truth was that he didn't even know what a City was but he didn't like to say that.

'And you say your Pa got burned up. How'd that happen?'

JD had to search his thoughts. He'd hidden away what had happened back at the shack but by screwing up his eyes and clenching his fists JD managed to call some of it to mind. He told the man how the Silver Men had come and how they'd beaten Pa and set fire to the shack. He told him of the other times too, when they'd caught Ma and stripped her off and done those things to her, but it all came out in a jumble, a bit of one story mixed in with scraps of others.

He wanted to tell it like a proper story, like Pa could; starting at the beginning and working through to the end, but it just wouldn't come out that way. He told whichever part of the story came to him at the time, squeezing them out of his memory and letting them escape through his lips. The man nodded as JD stumbled on. He seemed to understand.

When at last he'd managed to say all the things that had been holed up in his head JD began to sob quietly. He felt empty. At first, letting the story loose, sharing it with the old man had made losing his Pa and his home a bit easier but now it was gone and weren't his no more, he felt real sad. The nightmares that had haunted his mind, the visions of flames, the heat and the burning, the Silver Men overhead, all those things that JD had somehow hoped were only a dream, had become true in the telling.

The old man didn't speak until JD's sobs had died away.

'How are old are you, son? Do you know?'

JD looked up. 'I'm thirteen,' he said, swallowing away his tears.

The man studied JD intensely from his old sack cap to his home-sewn boots until, after a long while he said, 'Yep. Reckon you would be too. Thirteen for sure.' Then he stared down at JD and raised a bushy eyebrow like he'd had an idea.

'Can you figure up to thirteen?'

'I sure can,' JD announced. 'One, two, three, four . . .'

'OK. OK. I believe you,' the old man said, holding up one hand. 'That's good for a kid,' he said, almost to himself. 'Real good for a Boonie kid. Who learned you that?'

'My Pa. He was real good at figurin'. He could go on figurin' all day if he wanted.'

The old man nodded, but talking about Pa reminded JD of the Silver Men again. 'Have you ever seen those Silver Men?' he asked. 'The ones that came to our shack?'

'Sure. I might not have seen your particular Silver Men but I seen plenty of others. Why, when I was in the City I seen loads of 'em. Even spoke to some of 'em.'

'Why do they come and do those things to Ma and why'd they burn my Pa up?' JD asked, screwing up his face so's he wouldn't start crying again.

'They're just huntin'.'

JD couldn't believe what the man said at first. Pa used to say he was going hunting when he set off in the mornings to find bugs and roots to eat. It was hard to imagine those Silver Men were just looking for something to eat.

'But what are they huntin' for?' JD said, trying to get his thoughts to match the pictures in his head.

'They're just huntin' for a good time,' the man croaked. 'They just do it for fun.'

'But why?' JD asked. 'How is it fun to burn people up in their shacks?'

'Don't ask me,' the old guy belched. 'But that's why

24

they do it. That and because they can. They're Leaders, you're Boonies. They got the right.'

'Why do you say that and what's Boonies?' JD found himself getting angry. 'You even said I was a Boonie kid. I don't know what that means.'

A sort of rumbling cough came from someplace under the old man's chin. It sounded like a laugh and it made JD look up and stare straight back at the man. He didn't like being laughed at. But as he studied the twisted skin which creased and pulled at the ugly stitches across the old guy's face JD's hurt drained away. He could see it wasn't a real laugh, it was just a noise.

'You don't know much, do you, kid?' the old man sighed. 'I call you a Boonie 'cos that's what you are. Everyone who lives out here away from the City is a Boonie. There are even some Boonies inside the City but if they come from out here in the Scrubland they're still Boonies. I'm a Boonie now although I wasn't before, and you're a Boonie for sure. We're all Boonies.'

'I still don't know what you're talkin' about,' JD snapped.

The old man sighed a low gurgling sigh. 'Look, son,' he said, drawing in a great breath and holding it, preparing for another long belch of words. 'I guess your Ma and Pa never told you nothin' so it ain't strictly your fault. But if you're going to make it either out here or in there, you gotta know some things.'

The old man looked hard at JD as if he was trying to make up his mind about something and after what seemed like an awful long time he nodded his great head and grunted. Then he leaned forward, placed his elbows on his knees and propped his chin in his hands.

'OK, son? Now you sit back and listen up and I'll tell you some of the things your Ma and Pa should have told you way back.'

'Wait. Why do you keep callin' me *son*?' JD interrupted before the man could begin. 'My name's JD.'

'OK, OK. Master JD, I promise I won't call you *son* no more. Now, you ready to listen?' The glinting eyes fixed on JD and JD stared back and nodded.

'Good. As you might have gathered, talkin' ain't that easy for me.' The man tapped the stitches on his lips. 'So if I'm going to tell you all this stuff I don't want no more interruptions. OK?'

'No. I ain't ready yet,' JD said. He was eager to hear what this strange old man with the sewed-up mouth had to say but there was one more thing he needed to know. 'I told you my name but you ain't told me yours. That's rude,' he said. JD wanted things right.

The old man stared down at the pale, thin little boy sitting in the dust at his feet and drew in a deep breath, sucking air noisily into his nose and swallowing it.

'OK. You're right again, JD, and that's the truth. My name's Godrum. Now then, if you'll just hold your peace and stop your interruptin', I'll tell you some things about the kinda world you've just walked into.'

Four

The Big War

JD sat back and waited while the old guy settled himself.

'First thing you gotta know,' he began, 'is that there are only two places to be; in the City or out here in the Boonies. Most folks live in the City because that's where they get their water and, as you've already discovered, the most important thing in this whole wide world is water.' Godrum paused and stared at JD for a long time, his bright gold eyes etching that single fact into his mind.

'Used to be,' Godrum went on, 'there was water everywhere. It used to fall from the sky and folks had all they could ever need. They'd drink it, wash in it, lay in it, everything. Water poured along those old dry river beds and collected into lakes so wide you couldn't see across 'em. Why, there was so much water folks would just throw it on the dirt and let it run away without a thought. Hard to believe that, ain't it, JD?'

JD nodded. Water falling out of the sky. Pa used to say that. Could it be true after all?

'Then some places began to run out of water,' Godrum continued, 'and the folks who lived there tried to move to the places that still had some. That's what started the Big War. You heard about the Big War?'

JD shook his head.

'You really don't know nothin' about nothin', do you, son?' Godrum sighed. 'Now I gotta tell you about the Big War too.'

JD wanted to say he'd called him *son* again but he let it pass; he wanted to know about this Big War.

'Like I said, some folks had water and some didn't, and that's what started the Big War. But the war just made it worse, much worse. The stuff in the weapons spoiled the water and when folks saw that, they thought it would be clever to fill their enemies' rivers and lakes with chemicals and all kinds, which they did. That bad water ran into the sea and that's how the sea got bad too. Do you know, young JD, that in the sea there was once more water than anybody could ever need? Folks used to filter the salt out and drink it. But then the sea started to go down because of the war, the pollution and the heat, and once the water was gone, the trees died and because they died no more water fell out of the sky. The rivers and lakes dried up, even them that was so full of chemicals you couldn't drink 'em anyways. The whole planet got hotter and hotter and the sea went down more and more 'til that was all dried up too. That place you used to live, the Dry Marsh? Why, before the Big War that was surrounded by sea and covered in rivers where water ran day and night. It fair poured out into the sea like nobody wanted it. And no matter how much ran away there was always more coming along behind. It came up through the ground and fell out of the sky. That must have been a fine time, don't you reckon, JD?'

JD smiled. Yeah, you must think I'm real stupid, he thought. It's a good story but you've only gotta look around.

'Anyways, that's all gone now and the only water left is what the New Leaders have and they keep a tight hold on it. They're pretty much the only folks left who have enough and that's why they're the leaders. You got that?'

JD nodded.

'Go on then, you tell me that back.'

'The Big War made all the water bad, then the trees died and water stopped fallin' out of the sky. It got hot. The sea dried up and now the only people with enough water are some New Leaders,' JD said, letting the words rush out before he lost his hold on them.

'That's about it.'

'Who won the Big War then?' JD asked.

'Nobody. Everybody lost 'cos the water dried up.'

'How did you get your water then, Mr Godrum? Are you one of them New Leaders?'

'Nope. Not no more, I ain't.'

'How come you got water then?'

'Because I know a secret. It's the biggest secret in the world and I found it.' Godrum's face glowed with a kind of sad satisfaction. 'My secret gets me my water whenever I need it.'

Looking at the old man and seeing the pride in his twisted features, JD wondered if he could ask the question that burned inside him without bringing on those old threats about being snapped like a twig or having his arms pulled off. He studied the man's worn and battered countenance and beneath the hooked nose and the diamond-sharp eyes he reckoned he could see a gentle, caring man there and he wondered.

'Mr Godrum. Please, sir, won't you tell me your secret?' JD asked, his question starting confidently but tailing away towards the end.

'Don't know why I should.'

'Please, Mr Godrum. I can't think of nothin' better than to be able to get a drink whenever I want one.'

'You're right there, young man. There ain't nothin' better. There ain't nothin' better in this whole dry world.'

31

For a long time Godrum studied the little boy with the pleading face sitting there in the dust in front of him until at last he gave a long gurgling sigh and said, 'OK. I guess I ought to tell someone before I die. You're young and you look like a bright kid so I might as well tell you as tell anyone.'

JD grinned from ear to ear. 'Thanks, Mr Godrum,' he almost shouted. He felt like jumping up and hugging the old man but thought it best to stay put.

'OK, young JD. I'll tell you, but first you look around and tell me what you see.'

JD swivelled his head from left to right then back again. 'I see dust, dirt, sawgrass, your tree and some rocks.'

'That it?'

'That's it.'

'You don't see no water?'

'There ain't no water unless you count what's in your tube.'

Godrum chuckled. 'Now that, young JD, is where you're wrong. Like I say, I don't know why I'm tellin' you this but I will. Men would kill for what I'm going to share with you so you gotta promise to keep quiet about it. OK?'

'What am I promisin'?' JD said. 'I don't see no water.'

'I'll show you some water if you promise to keep quiet. You tell no one what I'm goin' to show you. OK?'

'OK,' JD said. 'Honest, Mr Godrum, I won't tell nobody. I promise.'

'That's good. Now then, what was that last thing you said you seen?'

'Cain't remember. Rocks, I think.'

'Good. You see any rocks close by?'

'Yeah, plenty.'

'You see any special rocks, any rocks that look different from any number of other rocks?'

JD looked around again. 'Nope. Some's bigger and some's smaller but they're all pretty much just rocks.'

'Good. That's the first part of the secret. Make your rocks look like all the other rocks. No straight lines and no circles. Remember this: the best place to hide a rock is with lots of other rocks.'

'Why would I want to hide a rock?' JD asked.

'You'll see,' the old man chuckled.

JD furrowed his brow. Forget the rocks, old man, and let's get on to the water, he thought to himself.

'Right, JD,' Godrum said. 'Now, you go to the nearest rock you see.'

JD looked at the ground and sighed inwardly. Not more rocks, he thought, but looked anyway. Between where he sat and Godrum's tree he could see one medium-sized rock and a few smaller ones not much bigger than pebbles so he stood up, walked one pace and put his hand on the medium-sized rock.

'Right,' Godrum said. 'That's what I call the decoy rock.

33

If you want to hide some rocks, you put a bigger one close by so's it catches the eye, 'case folks come lookin'.'

JD had never heard of hiding rocks or of anybody looking for one but he didn't want to be rude so he said nothing.

'Now, you see them other rocks, the little ones?'

JD pointed to the seven or eight pebbles. 'You mean these here?'

'Yep. Now you're gettin' somewhere. Notice anything else? Look close now.'

JD stared at the rocks and saw they were arranged in a kind of a rough circle around a shallow dip and in the centre of that dip was another smaller stone. JD squatted down and reached out his hand to touch it and to his surprise, it moved. He touched it again and it moved again, bobbing under his fingers.

'Careful now, don't disturb nothin',' Godrum said. 'Now brush away the dust in that dip.'

JD swept the ground with his fingers. It felt strangely smooth and once he'd cleared the dirt and dust, he could see that there was no real ground there at all. The circle of stones was holding down a piece of fabric of some kind and the pebble in the centre was causing it to dip down.

Godrum raised himself and came over to where JD was kneeling, crouched down next to him and put his hand on the boy's shoulder.

34

'Now you watch real careful, young JD. I'm goin' to show you the secret of life.'

JD watched as Godrum carefully removed the central stone then some of those around the edge of the circle. Right up close he could hear the old man gulping his breath, drawing it in through his nose and forcing it down his throat. It gurgled and rumbled deep into his body before rushing out through the hole in his neck. JD had to force himself to watch Godrum's hands as he peeled back the fabric to reveal a hole in the ground. In the middle of the hole, right under where the centre stone had been, was a small metal bowl.

JD leaned forward but Godrum held him back. Setting himself down on one knee, the old man reached into the hole, lifted the little flat bowl between his finger and thumb and placed it in the palm of his hand.

'What do you see in there?' he said, showing the bowl to JD.

In the bottom of the dish a small circle of water glistened and shimmered in the morning light. JD was tempted to snatch the bowl and drink the water right up then and there but he contained himself, sensing he was at the edge of learning something special. Godrum had said it was a secret, the secret of life. He didn't rightly understand what that meant but if it involved picking up water from holes in the ground he sure wanted to know more about it.

'Where'd that come from?' JD asked.

'It came right outa the ground, JD. It came out of the ground while you were sleepin' and I caught it in my trap.'

JD looked up into the old man's eyes. Was he joking? How could water come out of the ground?

Godrum smiled, his face twisting about the criss-cross leather stitches. 'It's true, JD. The only good water left on this planet is in the ground. It's there in tiny droplets so small you can't see nor feel 'em but if you know the secret you can catch 'em in a bowl, just like I've done here.'

JD sat back on his heels as Godrum stood up and carried the bowl back to his tree. Opening the satchel, he took out his grey tube and carefully poured the water from the hole into it. JD heard the tantalising tinkle as the droplets dribbled into the metal tube.

'It ain't much,' Godrum said. 'But it's enough to keep a body from death.'

When the old man had settled himself back at his tree, JD shuffled across, squatted in the dust at his feet and waited. He was hoping to get another drink but wanted more than anything to hear how he could catch water out of the ground.

'Now, JD, you seen what I done? That there is the most valuable secret on this planet. What do you think of it?'

JD nodded his head. 'It looks easy but how do you do it?'

'All you gotta do is get yourself a bit of close-weaved

stuff, plastic is best. Dig a hole in the evening and fix the plastic over it. Hold the edge down with stones and put the weight stone in the middle. Durin' the night, the water comes out of the ground and collects on the underside of the sheet. It runs down under the weight stone and drips into your pan. Easy as that. You sleep, it makes water.'

Godrum's eyes sparkled but JD's mind was already racing ahead to a day when he could make his own water. He saw himself sitting under his old tree munching crickets and sipping away from his own cool tube, content and happy.

'How did you ever discover that thing, Mr Godrum?' JD said. 'Did somebody show you way back, like you just showed me?'

'Nobody showed me,' Godrum said quietly. 'I just knew it. I knew where the water was and worked out how to get it. I thought about it and the idea come to me.'

'And did you never show nobody else?' JD asked.

The old man gave a massive sigh and shook his great head. 'I showed everybody, son,' he said with a kind of resigned sadness. 'I showed everybody how to make water. Not just in little stills like I showed you but in great big ones. Bigger than you can imagine. Folks even called 'em Godrum Stills after me and I was a hero. Everybody was goin' to have all the water they needed and they thanked me for it. They put me in a great place and listened to what I had to say. I tried to help everybody lead a happy life but that was the end of me. The beginning and the end. I didn't see. I just didn't see . . .'

'What didn't you see, Mr Godrum?'

'I didn't see that not everybody wanted things to be the way I wanted 'em to be. I didn't see that some just wanted to use my still for their own ends. I was stupid, JD, and I made a stupid mistake. I believed that if I helped people and made 'em happy, they'd be pleased and that's just dumb. People ain't like that, JD, and don't you ever forget it.'

But JD had already begun to think of other things. OK, so don't help nobody. He knew that anyway. Pa said that. Look after yourself, Pa said. Watch out for strangers but look after yourself. Pa may not have been clever like Godrum but he knew about people and he knew where to find grub and little bits of dirty water for Ma to strain. He knew how to keep his family fed. The thought of Pa bringing home the grub made JD think of food.

'Have you got anythin' to eat, Mr Godrum?' JD asked.

Godrum shook his head. 'I don't eat much. Trained myself not to need it. I got my sip of water. That's enough for me but if you want to go off and find somethin' don't let me stop you. Growin' kid like you needs his grub.'

'Can I have some more water please, Mr Godrum?' JD asked. He thought it worth a try.

'When you get back you can have another sip. Then you'd better get on your way.'

'I ain't got nowhere to go, Mr Godrum,' JD said, looking at his feet again and fiddling with the top of his boot. He'd already decided to stay with this guy. He had water, knew how to make more and seemed willing to share it. Where could he go to find anything better than that?

'Yes, you have, young JD. Of course you got someplace to go. Ain't you off to the City to find your Ma?'

JD started like the old man had hit him with one of his rocks. He was right. From the time he'd walked out to the Old Road, something inside him had told JD which way he should go. He knew he was headed someplace but didn't know where. But now it all made sense. Of course, he was going off to find Ma. That's what he'd been doing all along and now that Godrum had put it into words it was plain. He'd go to the City and find Ma.

'Do you know the way to the City, Mr Godrum?' JD asked. 'Is it a way along the Old Road?'

'Sure is. You just keep goin' west and you'll get there. It's the only place left to go, anyways.'

Five

A Strange Gift

Kicking at the sawgrass and searching around for grubs, JD kept looking back, making sure the old man was still there, his back against the tree, his knees up, his head forward and the old grass hat pulled low. It took a while but JD caught his fill of crickets and began making his way back. Walking through the red dust he felt happier than he'd been for a long time. He'd been promised another drink, he was going to find Ma and everything was going to be fine again.

'Well, young JD, did you find somethin' to eat?' Godrum asked when he got back.

'Yes, thank you, Mr Godrum,' JD said, sitting down in front of the old man. 'Can I have my drink now, please?'

The old man smiled his twisted smile and reached into his satchel while JD watched his every movement. He watched him take out the tube, watched as he slowly unscrewed the cap, poured out a dribble of water and handed it over. JD took the cap and licked his lips. This time he reckoned he'd drink it all in one go. He'd hold the water in his mouth, wash it all around then swallow it in one, great, glorious rush. And that's what he did. This is great, he thought. He couldn't remember when he'd drunk so much in such a short time. When he'd finished he handed the cap back to the old man and grinned his thanks.

'Right, JD,' Godrum said. 'Are you ready now? Ready for the City?'

'Mmm. Yes, sir. Will it take long to get there?'

'About half a day. You should get there by dusk but you gotta be sure to be at the gates before sundown. If you ain't they'll be shut and you'll have to wait 'til morning before you can get in.'

JD looked puzzled. 'Gates?' he said. 'What's gates?'

The old man grunted and gave a deep sigh. 'JD. Little JD. I knew when I first saw you that you were goin' to be trouble. Let me tell you, the City is surrounded by a high fence. Inside the fence is a deep, dry gulch and across that there's a long bridge. The only way inside for the likes of you is the Bridge Gate. It opens at sunrise and closes at sunset. Boonies who work in the City get in and out through the Bridge Gate. That's the only way.'

JD blinked and stared at the wizened old face, then his

shoulders dropped. All these things he didn't know. How would he know this Bridge Gate? What would happen to him if he got things wrong? He was scared and felt defeated before he'd even set out. How could he ever find Ma when there was so much to remember?

'Oh, Mr Godrum. How am I ever gonna find Ma? I don't know where the City is and I don't know nothin' about no gates. I know even if I found this City I'd be too scared to go in. Can't you come with me? Show me how to get through these gates?'

'I can't sit here all day and tell you all about things you don't know, JD. You're goin' to have to find some things out for yourself. Other Boonies have gone to the City and got in. Admitted, I don't know about any little kids like you . . . but,' Godrum sighed. 'I'll tell you what I'll do, JD. We'll rest up today. You can help me set up the still tonight and tomorrow morning I'll take you some of the way. I won't be goin' near the City myself, mind, I have too many enemies there, but I'll put you on your way, show you where to get in and then you're on your own. That's as far as I'll go. What do you say?'

'Thanks, Mr Godrum,' JD said quietly, hoping he might push him a bit more when the time came.

That night, in the quiet, humid time before dark JD helped Godrum spread his sheet of material over the hole and weight it down with stones. The old man let him place the centre stone in position and sprinkle a layer of dust across the surface. For JD it brought back happy times when he'd played with Pa in the dust by the shack and while Godrum knelt and explained every move, naming all the parts of his still, JD could almost imagine it was Pa showing him something new and exciting.

When the still was set, Godrum sat back on his heels and JD did the same.

'You reckon you could make your own still, JD?' Godrum said.

JD nodded. 'If I could find stuff to make it with,' he said.

'Well, that's where I might be able to help you some,' Godrum said. 'But first I want you to do somethin' for me.'

'What's that?'

'Tell me about your Pa. What did he look like?'

JD frowned as a picture of Pa's thin face swam into his mind. This was going to be tough.

'Pa was nice. He was pretty tall but thin. He had curly hair like mine.' JD put his hand up to his head and pulled off his cap. Another shower of burned hair fell into his lap. 'Well, like mine used to be anyways. And he talked soft and never got cross like Ma. Pa was great . . .' JD felt a lump rising in his throat. 'He was real nice . . .' was all he could say as the tears burned his eyes.

Godrum watched the kid struggling with his memory and let things rest awhile.

'What about his eyes, JD? Did he have nice eyes?' he said at last. 'Were they like yours, nice shape and glintin' gold in the sun?'

JD looked up at the old man's gentle face. 'How do you mean?'

'You have real nice eyes, JD. Not round and black like folks in the City. Did your Pa have eyes like yours?'

'I guess,' was all JD could say.

A silence fell between the old man and the burned, dusty little boy in front of him and in the quiet, Godrum studied JD carefully. From time to time he smiled, his tangled face twisting about the cruel thongs while JD made unthinking shapes in the dust with his finger, thinking about Pa and letting his sadness cover him.

'Let me hear your figurin' again, JD,' Godrum said as quietly as his belching allowed him.

Puzzled, but happy to indulge the old man, JD took a deep breath and through his dry tears chanted the numbers that Pa had taught him. When he was done he smiled a smile of satisfaction. He knew he'd done it right but to his surprise Godrum was frowning. 'What's the matter?' JD asked.

'Don't you know what comes next?'

JD shook his head.

'You need to know more than thirteen,' Godrum said. 'If you learn the next three numbers I'll give you somethin' special as a prize. What do you say?'

JD nodded and right up until the evening lightning stalked the horizon Godrum taught him the numbers that followed. He made the boy repeat the sequence many times until he was perfect and when he could figure from one to sixteen without any mistakes he made him draw out the numbers in the dust. He made him do it over and again, setting out the figures in four lines of four, one above the other in a neat square pattern.

'Oh, Mr Godrum,' JD said at last. 'Cain't we stop now? I've done all my old figures and your new ones over and over. Cain't we stop now?'

Godrum grunted. 'It's important, JD. Could be the most important thing in your whole life; more important even than making a still. Now you do it one more time and you can have your prize.'

Again JD scratched the figures in the dust, reciting them out loud, pointing to each one as he went. Godrum watched intensely, studying the strokes and curves the boy marked out on the ground.

'Why do you do that?' the old man said, pointing to a little curl, a flourish that JD made at the end of one of his figures. 'It don't need that.'

'That's the way Pa showed me. He done his figurin' that

45

way,' JD said, looking Godrum straight in the face. 'He always done it like that.'

Godrum grunted and JD scratched that single number in the dirt once more, making the same little flick at the end of the five.

At last, Godrum seemed satisfied and told JD he could put his stick down. He studied the figures in the dust, walking between them and peering down. When he'd checked them all he screwed up his face into the best sort of smile a man with his mouth sewed up can manage, went to his tree, picked up the bag and ferreted about inside. From among the papers that crammed the old satchel he drew out a thin, tight-folded square of plastic.

'Here, JD. You keep this safe. No matter what happens, you keep this close and it will serve you well.'

Godrum handed the plastic to JD, who took it, looked at it, turned it over in his hands and tried to see what was so special about it. 'What am I meant to do with this, Mr Godrum?' he asked.

'This will be your membrane, JD. Use it if you need to make a still but like I said, it's special. You'll see when you open it up.'

'How is it special?' JD said. He'd hoped his prize was to be another drink, not a piece of plastic.

'You'll see when you come to use it. You'll see, and if

46

the time is right, you will see it's the most special thing in this whole dry world.'

JD thanked him and tucked the little package into the slim pocket Ma had sewed inside the bib of his dungarees. Aware that Godrum was still watching, he patted his chest and smiled, hiding his disappointment at the strange present.

Godrum heaved himself back to his tree but said no more and as the light faded and the lightning streaked the sky, the boy curled up at his feet, resting his head on his arm and sank towards sleep. Just before he dozed off, JD heard the old man draw in a last tortured breath.

'I've done what I can, now it's up to you, little JD,' he said to himself. 'We'll set off fresh in the morning and then we'll see if I'm right about you.'

And so it was that at first light next day the old man and the little boy stood together with their backs to the rising sun. Then, without a word, they set off.

Six

Danger

By afternoon JD saw that the Old Road was changing. The slabs were flatter, not so damaged, and it became easier to walk. The roadway was still cracked and broken but it was like someone had tried to level it off, tried to get it back the way it must have been when the old petrol cars had run there. JD noticed something else too. As the day wore on he saw stuff along the verges: a single piece of litter, a scrap of metal, an old box, a strip of sun-bleached fabric twisted into the sawgrass tufts, the kind of things Pa would have gathered up, hugged to his chest and taken back to the shack where Ma would have shaped them into something useful: clothes, shelves, tools, something new for the shack. JD wondered why nobody picked up these prizes and carried them off to their shacks, and how strange it was that even Godrum passed them by without a second glance.

48

About noon, they saw a man walking the road up ahead, shambling along, weaving from side to side. JD hung back. He wanted to run away and hide. People spelled danger, Pa always said that, but somehow Godrum seemed unperturbed. Then there were two more strangers, walking together, and as the day wore on there were more still, some up ahead, some coming up behind, all dressed the same in blue tunics and trousers and with peaked caps to shield their faces from the sun. All these strange folks made JD feel real scared inside but looking up at Godrum, he slowly gained an uneasy confidence. As long as the old man walked with him he reckoned he'd be safe. One thing he did notice though was when some stranger drew close, the old man pulled his hat down low over his brow.

One time a solitary young man overtook them, passing so close to JD that his swinging arm almost brushed against him. JD winced and pulled his arm tight to his side but Godrum put a hand onto his shoulder.

'Take it easy, JD,' he whispered. 'Take it easy. Nobody's goin' to harm you.'

JD's heart was pounding in his chest but with Godrum's hand on his shoulder, it soon slowed down and his confidence seeped back.

All day they walked, pacing along the white concrete, veering away only when other travellers came by. By the time the sun began to get low in the sky, the flow of people slowed up and eventually as good as dwindled away altogether.

Godrum stopped and leaned over JD, his eyes pointing ahead. 'See there, JD? Way ahead. D'you see that grey line?'

JD had been able to see it for some time and nodded.

'That's the wire, the high fence that runs right around the City. Once inside that, you're in the City.'

'And that's where Ma is, d'you reckon?' JD said, his eyes fixed on the grey line.

'I reckon.'

JD's heart lifted; all he wanted now was to hurry on and find his Ma. He put his hand up to his shoulder where the old man had laid his, took hold of the long bony fingers and tugged.

'Come on, Mr Godrum. Come on. Let's get there quick.'

JD tried to take off, but the old man's hand was heavy and unyielding. He seemed rooted to the spot. JD turned around and looked up into Godrum's face.

'Come on, Mr Godrum. We're nearly there.'

'Take it easy, young JD,' he said. 'I cain't go to the City. I told you that. I'll take you aways nearer but then you'll have to go on your own.'

'Oh!' Disappointment showed in every part of the boy's body. 'Oh, Mr Godrum. I thought . . .'

Godrum put up his hand. 'I did tell you, son.'

'But why not, Mr Godrum? Why can't you go there?'

50

'It's a long story. It's a very long story but all you need to know is if the guards or your friends the Silver Men ever caught me it'd be the end.' Godrum drew a long bony finger across his throat. 'I'm too well known in the City and hated by too many. My life wouldn't last 'til sundown if I came with you.'

'But, Mr Godrum. How'm I goin' to find Ma? I need you to show me where to go and what to do and I'm real scared of those Silver Men.'

'Yeah, and you just stay that way, son. Stay scared of them Silver Men. It's the only way.'

'But what'll I do? You said yourself I don't know nothin'. How am I goin' to find Ma if you won't come with me?'

Godrum squatted down next to JD, the joints in his knees cracking as he lowered himself down.

'Steady up, son,' he said. Reaching out and turning the boy around, he looked deep into his eyes. 'Now you listen careful, boy. This is what you gotta do. When you get up near them gates, you wait around 'til a crowd of Boonies comes up, then you mix in with 'em. You're small enough not to get noticed. I reckon you can stroll right by those guards real easy as long as you stay in the crowd. Then once you're inside you just stay close and keep your eyes open. You've got to find your way through the streets and out to a place they call the Farm. That's where your Ma will be for sure.'

JD swallowed hard. There were just too many things to know. 'But Mr Godrum, I can't find my way without you.'

'Sure you can. You just go right on through the City and out the other side. If you get lost, you ask another kid. There are lots of kids there; you'll be OK. And here's a thing, you walk around like you know where you're goin' even if you don't. If anybody asks, just tell 'em you are goin' back to the Farm.'

Godrum stood up and took JD's hand. 'Now, come on, JD. Chin up, shoulders back. This is your time. Time for you to go and find your Ma. I'll go aways with you but remember, I can't take you right in.'

They set off again hand in hand, JD's eyes fixed on the grey line, watching it rise ever higher the closer they got to it. And as it rose a strange feeling began to grow inside him. He was excited at the thought of seeing Ma again but scared at the same time. Scared he'd get lost. Scared he'd get caught. Scared he'd be on his own.

At last Godrum stopped again and stared ahead once more. JD followed his gaze and away in the distance he could make out some tall, grey shapes standing in a group. They were like the biggest shacks JD had ever seen, high and square and reaching near up to the sky. A faint wisp of white smoke rose vertically from the tallest one, while all around a dirty yellow haze lay close to the ground. Between where they stood and the tall shacks the wire

52

stretched away on each side as far as he could see and like an arrow the Old Road led straight towards it, broad and white. Where the road met the wire were two high metal gates, one closed, one open, each topped with sharp spikes, and by the gates stood a group of men dressed in grey uniforms, high boots reaching up to their knees. Two of them were questioning a cluster of blue-suited Boonies while others stood and watched. They all had bright silver weapons slung on their shoulders or held in their hands ready for use.

JD shivered, but Godrum squeezed his hand. 'OK, JD. Now it's up to you. Remember what I said, wait for a bunch of Boonies to come along then mix in like you belong. Don't make eye contact, neither with the Boonies nor the guards. They don't stop too many folks so you should be OK. Stay in the bunch right across the bridge and remember, look like you know where you're going.'

'Yes, sir, Mr Godrum,' JD said, his voice shaking. 'But I sure wish you would come with me.'

'No, son, I'm sorry. I cain't. But before you go there's just one more thing. In the City, don't you ever mention my name nor say that you know me. Understand?'

JD nodded. He was too frightened to ask why.

'Now off you go, JD, and good luck. Remember me and what I've told you. Life in the City will be tough and you will need to be on your toes but I reckon you'll be OK.

When you find your Ma, you look after her. Have a good life and who knows, you and me might even meet up again someday.'

JD felt a lump rising in his throat. 'Yes, Mr Godrum,' he croaked. 'I do hope so and thanks for your help and everything.'

'It's been my pleasure,' Godrum said, releasing the boy's hand. 'Now go on and do your best. There are some Boonies comin' up behind now. Dawdle along 'til they catch up then mingle in. Off you go now, think positive and don't forget the old man at the tree and what he taught you.'

JD looked up into Godrum's sewn and battered face. The old man gave him the nearest thing to a tender smile that he could manage and JD took his first steps forward. It felt like he was starting out to cross a chasm on a high wire but he set his jaw and walked off along the Old Road towards the City gates.

Seven

The City

JD didn't turn around. If he had, he knew he would have cut and run. He felt so small out there and he was sure those guards were just waiting for him to come within range of their shiny weapons. But he did as Godrum had told him, walked straight ahead with his eyes down waiting for the band of Boonies to come up to him.

Glancing back, he saw them passing Godrum, a group of ten or so sad-eyed, blue-clad figures, ambling along the cracked concrete. One of them looked at Godrum as he passed and a few paces later he nudged one of the others and whispered something in his ear. Godrum just stood at the side of the road and watched. JD could feel him willing him on.

By the time the Boonies caught up, JD was not far from the gate. He let them get past then slipped into the back of the group like Godrum had said. Nobody seemed to notice him because one of the Boonies was talking excitedly. He seemed riled up about something and was berating the others, who didn't seem to share his enthusiasm.

'It *was* him, I tell you. I'm sure it was. You remember the posters. He looked just like the picture. And the reward! Those bills said a big reward. Let's tell the Pigs before he gets away.'

Frustrated by the lack of interest from his friends, the excited Boonie ran forward, sprinting towards the gate. The guards saw him coming and drew up across the gateway, pointing their weapons, but the approaching Boonie waved his arms at them.

'It's the Evil One,' he yelled. 'I've seen him. He's on the road back there. Quick, quick. I've seen him and I claim the reward.' The man ran towards the gate with one arm pointing behind him.

The guards stared to where the Boonie was pointing, then turned to each other and began talking. They looked confused but then something triggered one of them into action and he took off towards a low concrete shack behind the gates and ducked inside, while three of the others began to jog towards the waving man.

'Oh no!' JD said under his breath. This was all wrong. 'Oh, Mr Godrum,' he said and in a panic turned and started to run back to where he could still see the old man standing by the side of the road, just where he'd left him. When the guards rushed past JD, still the old man didn't move. JD waved at him as hard as he could.

'Get back, get back,' he shouted. 'They know who you are. Get back. Quick. Run, run . . .' JD's voice was cracking with fear but still Godrum didn't move, and it wasn't until the guards were almost right up to him that he seemed to understand the danger and turned, shambling away into the barren scrub.

The guards were weighed down by their uniforms and guns, which JD hoped might give Godrum a chance, but the steady beat of their heavy boots on the road sent fear into his heart. Glancing back to the gate, he saw the Boonie still pointing, first at himself then to where Godrum had stood but by then there was no sign of Godrum, just the three guards jogging away into the Scrubland.

'Oh! Run, Godrum, run,' JD mouthed, watching the uniformed men stagger clumsily over the scrub and sand hills. They looked so awkward away from the road that JD hoped against hope they would tire long before they could reach the old man. You can do it, he urged silently. Go on, Godrum, you can do it.

But then that glimmer of hope that had flared inside him flickered and died. There were vibrations in the air.

'Oh no,' JD moaned under his breath and looking back, he saw the sight he feared most. Climbing up through the yellow haze of the City were four silver shapes. They rose higher and higher, turned towards where he stood, then roared overhead, smoke and flames belching out from their jet-packs.

'Run, Godrum. Run,' JD screamed but he knew it was too late. How could an old man hobbling among the rocks and dust of the Scrubland hide from Silver Men? He watched them zoom away, the hot air from their exhausts shimmering in the sunlight. He watched them bank to the right, then cluster and gather for a moment before two of them broke away and dived towards the ground. JD knew then it was all over for Godrum.

More guards ran past, leaving JD with his fists clenched by his sides, fear for his friend in his every sinew, in every line on his face. One of the guards clattered into him, knocking him to the ground, but he rolled right over, propping himself up, unable to tear his eyes away from the action. All around, the air shook, the guards were running and shouting, the Boonie trailing in their wake, screaming about 'the Evil One' and how he was due some big reward. JD watched him with hatred in his heart. He wanted to jump up and pummel his ugly face to a pulp. But in all the confusion he noticed something else too. There was nobody left between him and the open gate. The other Boonies had gone and so had the guards. JD looked from side to side, then scrambled to his feet and set off, half-walking, half-running, trying not to seem too anxious, and in no time he was at the gate. Way ahead, the Boonies shambled on and just in case anyone was watching JD called out, 'Wait for me,' in a voice he was confident nobody could hear, then he jogged through the gates and onto a wide, concrete bridge.

The bridge spanned a deep ravine and between the once fine balusters that lined the edges JD could see a wasteland of red dust and broken boulders far below. Looking down from such a great height made him dizzy so he veered back towards the middle of the road and hurried after the men in blue. His heart was pounding. He'd made it, he was in the City but through his excitement his heart ached for his friend. He remembered the old man drawing his finger across his throat when he described what would happen to him if he was caught and JD shuddered. But he had to keep going. He knew Godrum had sacrificed himself just so's JD could get away; he couldn't let him down now, could he?

JD caught up with the Boonies then slowed, before falling in at the back where he took to slouching along like they did. He took a deep breath to calm down. There was no sound from behind and though his mind was racing he forced himself not to look back. At the far side of the bridge the Boonies walked straight on into the shadows between the tall buildings. JD followed but soon began to hang back, his eyes searching left and right for some clue as to where he was, and all the while on the lookout for another child; someone he could ask about the Farm.

JD dragged his feet until the Boonies were well ahead and then he stopped. There was no point just trailing along behind, he had no idea where they were going. But no sooner had he stopped than one of the Boonies stopped too and turned to stare at the thin boy in his faded dungarees standing alone among the high, concrete towers. The Boonie called to the others, who stopped too, and pretty soon the whole group were standing, shoulders down, staring back at JD. When the first Boonie started to walk back JD began to feel afraid.

He walked right up to JD and stared down at him. 'Who are you?' he said in a monotone.

JD shrugged. 'Nobody,' he said. 'I ain't nobody.'

'What are you doing here? We've never seen you before.' The Boonie's voice was flat and low, his eyes round and dense black. JD sensed danger and shuffled his feet.

'I'm lost,' he said. 'I've gotta get to the Farm.'

'Why?'

'My Ma's there. I need to go to my Ma.'

One of the other Boonies stepped forward.

'You are too big to be at the Farm and anyways, we saw you on the road. You were with the old man, the Evil One.' He came right up to JD, looked down and blinked his big round eyes.

'There might be a reward for this one too,' he said, reaching down and putting his hand on JD's shoulder. 'What do you think, Comrades?'

The Boonies closed in around JD, shutting out the light, towering over him just like the tall buildings towered over the City.

The man's grip tightened on JD's shoulder. 'Come, Comrades, take his arms. Let us get him back to the guards. We could get extra water for him.'

A forest of arms reached down, grasping fingers spread out like claws. JD looked up at the blank faces, the dull black eyes and the slack lips. He shrunk back, crouching down as low as he could, and tried to think. What would Godrum have done? What would Pa have done? Godrum was too old to do anything which was why he'd been caught, and Pa would have run off and hid in the dirt, but in that instant JD made his decision: he'd run. He ducked and pulled, trying to break the Boonies' grasp, but struggle as he might, he could not get free. Too many hands held him. He was caught in a web of Boonies.

The blue-clad men dragged him back towards the bridge, chattering about the reward they would get. JD was in despair. He'd only just made it to the City and now they were taking him back; they would hand him over to the guards and he'd never get to the Farm, he'd never find Ma. He wanted to cry.

The untidy gaggle of Boonies, their captive in their midst, were only a few steps onto the bridge when JD felt the vibrations come once more and it was not long before the Boonies noticed them too. They stopped and looked up. Flying towards them high above the gates were the four Silver Men, two spread wide and two close together, the sound of their machines all around. JD could see that the two close together were carrying something between them. They flew lower than the others, their machines labouring and sending out trails of thick smoke. The Boonies turned their faces upwards and JD watched too, horrified, as he realised what it was the Silver Men carried between them. He saw the flying coat and paper-bound legs and when a round, grass hat dropped down and drifted into the ravine JD's heart sank to his home-made boots.

Two of the Boonies let go of JD and put their hands over their ears to shut out the noise and despite his sadness it dawned on JD that maybe, just maybe, Godrum might save him yet again. In a single movement JD squirmed free of the inattentive Boonies, ducked between their legs and pushed his way through. The Boonies were slow and seemed unable to grasp what was happening and by the time they tried to grab him they were clutching at nothing. JD was away and running, sprinting as fast as he knew how towards the City. Straight off the bridge a side turning appeared and JD dived into it, running hard along a narrow roadway.

Fear spurred him on. He ducked into another narrow street then turned into another, turning and running, running and turning, gasping in the yellow air, his throat burning with the effort. But it didn't take long, running hard through the yellow smog, before he was completely out of breath and could run no more. He took one last turn into a narrow gap between two tall buildings and threw himself to the ground where he lay gasping on the rough concrete.

Panting to recover his breath, he lay there, his heart pounding in his chest. By the time he'd recovered his wind his confidence was seeping back too. When he felt brave enough he pulled himself onto his feet and peeked back around the corner. The street was empty; there was not a soul in sight. He'd given the Boonies the slip. With a sigh of relief, JD let his back slide down the wall and he sat with a bump on the ground. He was shaking; he felt tired and tearful. A lot had happened since he'd walked away from the burned-out shack and he'd had just about all he could take. His mind was buzzing and his heart ached for his Pa and for the old man from the Scrubland but his limbs felt so heavy. JD closed his eyes, let his head fall back and tried to rest.

Eight

You Will Be Shot

JD sat up with a start and shook his head. He must have been asleep. The light had faded and the small patch of sky above his head had become fiery red, transforming his refuge into a cavern of purple shadow. And there was silence.

Cautiously, JD stood up and looked back into the street, searching for any sign of danger, but it was quite empty. Big round lamps now glowed from the tops of the buildings, sending splashes of orange light down the blank walls and across the ground. JD reckoned this might be a good time to move on, a good time to find the Farm before night came on. Making sure there was nothing to be seen or heard, he crept around the corner, staying close to the wall, flattening his hands against it as he went. At the next corner another identical, grey concrete road lay before him. He padded on and at each turning he stopped and peeked around the edge of the buildings. Each time it was the same, an empty road stretching away between tall towers. Still nobody in sight; no Boonies, no guards and, JD smiled, no Silver Men. After a while a strange feeling of freedom began to wash over him. He stopped and took a step away from the wall into the wide road, his eyes searching right and left. In the gathering gloom the orange lights seemed to glow brighter, and from where he stood JD could see the full length of the highway stretching away, narrowing into the yellow haze. He took another step and then another until he stood right in the centre of the empty road. He was in the City, he had beaten the Silver Men, beaten the guards at the gate and beaten the Boonies who'd tried to capture him. All he had to do now was to find Ma and everything would be fine again. Then, for no reason he could name, he spread out his arms, put his head back and turned around in a circle. He gave a little laugh then turned again and again, spinning slowly, looking up, watching the tops of the tall shacks leaning in over him. He felt intoxicated, somehow free and safe.

But his good mood was shattered in an instant by a sudden wailing sound. It began like the cry of a tortured soul and grew louder and louder, rising from a low, deep murmur to a wild, high-pitched scream in no time. It became so loud that JD had to cover his ears and tuck his

65

head between his knees to stop from going mad. Then, as quickly as it had come, the noise stopped, leaving just a lost echo bouncing between the walls. JD eased his hands away from his head but no sooner had he done that when a loud voice boomed out.

'Curfew. Curfew,' it called. 'Return to your stations. Anyone found outside their allotted space will be shot. Curfew. Curfew.'

JD stared up, searching, trying to work out where the voice had come from. It was as if a giant was shouting down from the top of a high building. But JD could see nobody. Then the awful wailing came again, flooding the street with its wild shriek. JD's head rang and he ran to a wall and pressed his face against it, his hands once more held tight over his ears. When the noise stopped, the voice repeated its warning: 'You will be shot, you will be shot . . .' rang through the empty streets.

JD was scared and he ran, retracing his steps, stumbling back towards the side streets. Something told him if he could find the alleyway where he'd slept, he'd be safe. He ran down the street, searching from side to side but there was no alley; he must have come the wrong way so he turned around and ran back. 'You will be shot. You will be shot,' filled his ears and bored into his brain. He crossed the road and doubled back, desperate to get away from the voice. On and on, panting and searching, while all the time the siren wailed and the voice boomed: 'You will be shot. You will be shot . . .'

JD was desperate. That voice was talking to him, he knew it was. It was seeking him out, taunting him, and why couldn't he find his alley, his narrow, dark, safe little space? On he ran, turning at each corner, panting hard, grazing his arms on the walls and searching, searching for somewhere to hide until, at last, dazed and breathless, he just had to stop. He slumped back against a wall, dry tears of fear burning his eyes, his heart thumping, his dry tongue swollen in his mouth. His last drink had been the one that Godrum had given him. How he wished that wise old man was with him now.

The siren came again but this time in short, staccato bursts. The voice boomed out, right over JD's head.

'Intruder in Sector Four, intruder in Sector Four. Halt, intruder. Stop or you will be shot.'

Now JD was sure the voice was talking to him but he ran on, across a wide junction then turning once more into each and every entrance and alley he came to. But before too long he had to stop again; he was fighting for breath. The siren was still wailing, the voice still warning but he seemed to have left it behind, which made him feel a bit easier. If he could only find some cosy little alley to hide in. He had to keep looking but just as he was about to set off something froze him in his tracks. He felt vibrations in the air.

He looked behind him and there, high above the buildings, he saw them: Silver Men, a cluster of six or seven hovering over a road junction. They hung in a tight circle in the darkening sky, the orange lights reflecting against their suits. They faced inward as if they were talking, then one separated from the bunch and swooped low. A dazzling shaft of light sprang from his jet-pack, lighting up the street beneath him. One by one the other Silver Men switched on their searchlights and their stark white beams speared down, piercing the gloom, banishing the shadows and sweeping the streets.

JD watched as the Silver Men spread out. They formed a long line in the sky before moving away in pairs, their white lights swinging back and forth, searching every road, every street and every alley. JD swallowed hard. How could he possibly stay clear of them? All he could do was run and hope to find some place to hide; some crevice or hole where those cold beams couldn't find him.

He set off again, running hard, but no matter how fast he ran the vibrations grew ever closer. He didn't have to look back to know they were gaining on him. JD's feet became heavier, his heart beat harder and his pace slowed. He turned into one more narrow alley but the walls that bounded its length were as clear and sharp as all the others. There was no escape, no refuge here. JD's shoulders drooped. The Silver Men were so close he knew they'd catch him now. What was the point in running on, when there was nowhere to hide? Why not just stop now, he thought, walk out into the middle of the road and give himself up? Even Godrum hadn't been able to escape the Silver Men so what chance did he have? He was just a kid from the Dry Marsh. With tears in his eyes, JD turned and began to walk back to the open road. He reckoned when he got there he'd sit down quiet and bow his head then maybe they wouldn't hurt him. When they saw he was just a little boy, surely they wouldn't shoot him; not if he gave himself up.

JD took his first step towards captivity. He would soon be in the light that flooded the road just a few short paces ahead. The noise from the machines was loud in his ears; he wouldn't have long to wait. Then something caught at his dungarees. He jumped back and looked down. There was a hand and an arm reaching out from the ground; a tiny hand and a thin white arm snatching at him, grabbing at his clothes. JD pulled away. In the distance the siren wailed and the voice still barked its warning. The jet-packs' hum filled the air but above it all JD heard a hiss.

'Psst. Quick, down here,' a little voice said.

The voice seemed to come from the hand so JD dropped to his knees and put his face close to the ground. He saw a narrow fissure at the bottom of the wall and from deep inside the jagged split, two large, bright eyes shone in the dark. The hand beckoned him.

'Quick, get down,' the voice said. 'Squeeze in here. Quick, they're nearly here.'

JD pressed his face up to the crack and saw that where the concrete had crumbled away, a long, narrow gap had formed between the base of the building and the ground. He lay down along the opening and began to edge his way into it, his face scraping the roadway, his back grazing the top of the fissure, while all the time little hands tugged at his clothes, forcing him deeper and deeper into the tiny space. They pulled at his legs and feet and pretty soon he was almost inside the gap, just his back, shoulders and his head sticking out. The stark, white lights probed the street just a few paces away and JD tried with all his might to squeeze into the crevice. But no matter how hard he tried he couldn't do it, it was just too small, too tight even for his bony frame. Then JD began to panic. He couldn't get in and when he tried to get out the rough concrete held him fast; he was stuck. He was at the mercy of the Silver Men and still the terrible warning boomed out: 'You will be shot. You will be shot.'

Nine

Aqua

Perhaps it was despair or maybe it was because he was so exhausted but JD relaxed and it was this that saved him. The little hands pulling at his clothes seemed to gain extra strength too and without warning JD's head and shoulders scraped into the gap.

But no sooner was JD through than he felt himself falling, rolling off a ledge of some kind into pitch-black, empty space. He went to cry out but before he could he sprawled onto something soft.

'Get off. Get off me, you great lump!' a high-pitched voice squealed.

The soft cushion was fighting back, pushing him away. JD scrambled to his feet and just then the searchlights in the alleyway probed the ground exactly where he had lain a few moments before, their brilliance sweeping across the opening, throwing a shaft of light into the darkness, lighting it up like day.

JD saw he was a in a low room full of pipes which twisted this way and that, joining others in great, bulbous joints before snaking away into the distance. The light flashed across his face, dazzling him for an instant but not before he saw the figure of a thin child, a little girl, smaller than himself, dressed in blue dungarees and a loose-fitting jacket. JD guessed she had to be the owner of the eager hands that had dragged him to safety. In the flash of light he saw a soft, round face with big black eyes set in skin so pale he felt he could almost see right through it.

The bright light moved away, searching deeper into the narrow street, leaving the two children staring at each other in semi-darkness. JD opened his mouth to speak but the girl put her finger to her lips. The hum from the Silver Man outside grew louder as he descended. Light flooded the alley again and the beam worked its way back across the ground towards the fissure. The girl grabbed JD's arm. She pulled him to the floor and dragged him under a tangle of pipes. The searchlight flashed and JD lay still, trying to smother the sound of his breathing. At last the Silver Man turned away, back towards the main road, off to probe the next street in his search for the intruder. The underground room was in darkness again.

JD felt the girl tug on his arm. She slid away and guided

him out from under the pipes and in the grey half-light he could just make her out against the pale glow from the opening.

JD coughed. 'Who are you?' he said.

'One-Seven-Nine-Six-Six. Female.'

'That's just numbers. Don't you have a name?'

'Only Leaders and special people have words for names.'

'I've gotta name,' JD said.

'You can't have. You're just a boy.'

'Maybe I am but I've gotta real name.'

'What is it then?'

'JD.'

'That's not a real name. It's just letters, what's your number?'

'I ain't gotta number.'

'We've all got numbers and anyway, who said you could have a name? Even a silly name that's just letters.'

'My Ma and Pa. They called me JD. Anyhow, you don't need permission to have a name. Anyone can have a name. You can call yourself whatever you like.'

The girl went quiet. In the darkness JD could only just make her out. She seemed to be standing with her head down, thinking about something.

'I always wanted a name,' she said quietly, her voice barely above a whisper. 'I even thought of a really nice one.'

'What is it?' JD asked.

'Aqua,' the girl whispered. 'I thought I'd like to be called Aqua.'

'Then I'll call you Aqua,' JD said firmly. 'If you think of yourself as Aqua, then Aqua is who you are. I will never call you by that silly number.' JD saw the girl raise her head and he could see that her round face was smiling. 'I'm real pleased to meet you, Aqua,' JD said. 'And thank you for savin' me.'

He didn't know what else to say and Aqua seemed unable to say anything either. Eventually she gave a little cough as if clearing her throat.

'That's OK, JD,' she said. 'Any time.'

JD felt embarrassed. He could tell Aqua was on the verge of crying but all of a sudden she coughed again, reached out and pushed him gently on his shoulder.

'Well, JD,' she said brightly. 'What are you doing out after curfew anyway? They nearly caught you. If I hadn't seen you they would be carrying you away to the Grinder right now. Probably eat you for supper.'

JD was shocked. 'Do they do that? Eat people?'

'Some say they do. All I know is if they take you away that's the last anybody ever sees of you. They might eat you. I don't know.'

JD's mind was racing. Godrum hadn't said anything about being eaten; that couldn't be true and, shutting his mind to the thought of being someone's supper, he

74

looked around, forcing himself to concentrate on his surroundings.

'Where are we?' he said.

'Just one of the old buildings. Don't worry, nobody comes here any more. Not unless they get here by mistake, like you. Where did you come from, anyway? '

'Outside the gates; a place called The Dry Marsh.'

'Never heard of it. I didn't know people lived outside the City. I thought if you went out there you died. They say there's no water.'

'You can find water. My Pa used to find water.'

'Where's your Pa now then? Has he got any water?'

JD shook his head. 'Pa's dead. The Silver Men killed him.'

'Silver Men?' Aqua asked from the gloom.

'Yeah. Them folks out there.' JD gestured towards the crack above their heads. 'The ones with the lights. I think they're called Leaders. That's what Godrum called 'em anyhow.'

Aqua gave a little gasp.

'What's the matter?' JD said.

'You said…*Godrum*.' She whispered the name.

'What about it?'

'You're not meant to say that.'

'Why not?'

'You're just not,' the girl said. 'It's illegal.'

JD stared. That's silly, he thought. Why can't you say someone's name?

'What are you doing here anyway?' the girl said before JD could ask any more. 'Running the curfew and nearly getting yourself taken. Where did you think you were going?'

JD was happy to get back onto safer ground. 'I don't know nothin' about no curfew,' he said. 'What is that?'

'When it gets dark we have to stay in our stations. That's curfew.'

'I don't understand that neither,' JD said. 'What's a station?'

'It's where we sleep, stupid. You really are dumb, aren't you? You don't know anything.'

'I never been here before. I told you.' JD said.

'So you did. So why have you come here from your Dry Marsh? Whatever that is.'

'The Dry Marsh is where I lived. We had a shack out there. I came here to find Ma.'

'Where is your Ma then?' Aqua asked.

'Don't rightly know but G—' JD tried again. 'Don't rightly know but someone said she might be at a place called the Farm. That's why I come. I come to find this here Farm but I don't know where it's at.'

Aqua laughed. 'Well, there I can help you. My station's on the Farm. If you like I'll take you there when the search dies down.'

JD's heart leapt, his eyes widened and his mouth fell open. 'Can you really take me there?'

But Aqua put her finger to her lips and tilted her head to one side, listening to the distant drone of the Silver Men's jet-packs. Then she turned away leaving JD with his joy still bottled up inside and climbed onto a pipe which ran along the wall, bringing her face level with the opening. She looked out into the darkness.

'Looks like they've gone,' she said. 'But I don't think it's safe to go out yet. If they don't find anybody they might come back to search again. We'd best stay here awhile.'

She stepped down from the pipe, came back and stood in front of JD. His eyes had become more accustomed to the darkness and he could make out the little girl's big, dark eyes and lively face.

'Seems funny you actually wanting to go to the Farm,' she said. 'I'd do anything to get away from it.'

JD didn't know what to say. He didn't understand much of what Aqua said and sometimes he thought she sounded so bossy. The way she spoke, making each word separate, talking to him as if he was just a kid or something. It made him feel uncomfortable. And whatever he said, she questioned it. If there was some other way of getting to the Farm and finding Ma, JD would have taken it, but deep down he knew that sticking with Aqua was going to be his best hope.

'Is your Ma there too?' JD asked, searching for something to say that would focus the girl's mind back to where he wanted it. 'At the Farm?'

The little girl shrugged. 'Don't know. Suppose she might be.'

'Why don't you know? Don't you live with your Ma?'

Aqua didn't answer straight away. She looked up at JD, studying his face. 'I think your Dry Marsh must be very different from the Farm, JD. We don't live with anybody. We are born on the Farm; they look after us until we are big enough to go to work. We don't have our own Mas and Pas. Nobody does.'

JD was crestfallen. 'No Mas and Pas?'

Aqua sighed. 'I don't really know what you expect to find at the Farm, JD. The only thing I can do is take you there and show you.' She looked back at the opening. It was dark and quiet. 'I reckon we should be OK now,' she said, and reached out for JD's hand. 'Follow me. Do what I do and don't say anything. When we get outside we'll have to be careful. Don't go out into the open, just stay close.'

'OK,' JD said. He was keen to get going and felt a surge of excitement. The trials of the day suddenly seemed a long way off. Now, with the help of his new-found friend he felt he really was going to find his Ma.

Ten

The Farm

Aqua led JD towards the opening. Letting go of his hand, she stepped up onto the pipe, put her hands on the ledge and in a single, lithe movement swung herself up onto it. Once settled she turned onto her back, shuffled about until her little body was parallel with the narrow gap then wriggled into it. A few more wriggles and she slid out of sight and was gone.

Alone in the dark basement JD began to feel a bit scared. He was going to have to squeeze through that narrow crack again and the thought of it filled him with dread. But if he was ever going to get to the Farm he'd knew he'd just have to do it. Shutting his mind to the fear, JD climbed onto the pipe, pulled himself up onto the concrete ledge and, before his courage could desert him, started to ease himself into the gap. But with only one shoulder wedged into the opening he stopped. It was too narrow. Aqua was only half his size; there was no way he could get through. JD steeled himself and thought about Ma, and when he felt he'd gathered up enough courage he tried once more to force himself into the gap, squirming about and pushing with hands and feet. But it was no good, he couldn't possibly fit into the jagged little opening, let alone get through it. With one shoulder and one leg jammed into the fissure, the sound of his own breathing loud in his ears, he began to imagine the wall above with all its great towering, impersonal weight pressing down on him. In a panic he wriggled back, pushing with his hands and knees until he fell with a crash onto the floor of the dark room.

'What's the matter?' Aqua whispered through the gap. 'What are you waiting for?'

JD scrambled to his feet, his head spinning. 'I can't do it,' he whispered. 'That gap's too small. I'll get stuck for sure. I can't do it.' He couldn't shake off the thought of being caught forever between the ledge and the thick concrete above, suffocating to death as the wall slowly crushed him.

'Don't be silly,' Aqua whispered. She sounded cross. 'You came in this way. You must be able to get out. Come on. Climb up onto the ledge and I'll pull you through.'

JD swallowed hard. He'd do anything not to have to crawl through that tiny gap but in his heart he knew there was no choice.

Reluctantly, he climbed back onto the ledge, lay face down, swallowed hard and edged into the crack. He put out his arm and felt Aqua grab it. He pushed himself deeper in, his face grazing the rough ground, the dust filling his eyes and nose. Aqua pulled at his arm and JD had to force away thoughts of falling walls and crushed bones. Deeper and deeper he wriggled, flattening his shoulders to the ground, turning his head to one side, the smell of dry concrete filling his nose. But the further he went the greater his fear became and the more he tensed up, his muscles tightening, jamming him hard into the concrete jaws.

'Come on, JD. Come on,' Aqua grunted. 'You're nearly there,' she said, pulling with all her strength on the boy's arm. 'Push. Push.'

Panic washed over JD in waves; the fear was tying him in knots. 'I can't. I can't,' he whimpered. 'Oh Ma, Ma. Help me. I want my Ma.'

'Shut up, you big baby,' Aqua hissed, pulling with all her might. With her feet against the wall she heaved at JD's arm with both hands. 'If you want your Ma you'd better stop whining and get out here quick. If those Leaders come back and find you you'll never see your Ma or anyone else ever again. Push, you stupid boy, push. Stop lying around feeling sorry for yourself and push!'

Pressing his face onto the dust JD made one last effort,

scraping against the floor of his tiny prison, until suddenly he found himself looking up into Aqua's smiling face.

'Well done. That's your head through. Now wriggle your body. You're nearly there.'

JD pulled his other arm out into the alleyway. He shook himself free of Aqua's grip and pressed his palms onto the ground. Twisting his hips, he heaved and strained until at last his body slid clear of the gap. He collapsed, exhausted, panting for breath.

'I made it. I made it,' he gasped.

'Yes. You made it,' Aqua said. Her voice was so sharp it made JD ashamed at the fuss he'd made. But it really had scared him, being trapped in that tiny gap. It had reminded him of being caught under the shack in the fire.

'Come on, JD. We can't stay here,' Aqua snapped. 'Get up and follow me.'

Before he could protest she was off, trotting along the alleyway, moving like an animal, bent at the waist and peering ahead into the yellow night mist, stopping every few paces and listening.

JD struggled to his feet and loped after her. 'Wait for me,' he whispered. 'Wait for me.'

But already Aqua was way ahead, just a soft grey outline in the gloom, and JD had to sprint to catch up. The girl stopped at the corner and JD almost bumped into her as she peered out, holding her head to one side, looking and listening.

'What's the matter?' JD whispered.

Aqua cupped her ear with her hand and JD did the same. Through the silence he could hear a siren wailing in the distance and could feel the vibration of the Silver Men's jet-packs in the still air.

'They are still looking,' Aqua said, over her shoulder. 'But they are over that way.' She pointed to her right.

'Come on,' she said and set off to the left, crossing the mouth of the alley and turning into a broad empty road. JD couldn't see the far side through the mist but Aqua seemed so confident he hurried after her without a second thought, keeping close, determined not to lose her.

They ran on along the edge of the broad road until at another junction Aqua stopped and peered up into the night as if she was searching for something.

'What're you lookin' for?' JD asked.

'This is a watch point. Follow me closely now and do exactly as I do.'

Before JD could ask what a watch point was, Aqua had run into one of the side roads. Ten paces along she turned, crossed the road and ran to the building on the far side. As soon as JD had joined her she set off back to the junction, sliding around the corner, keeping very close to the wall. JD looked up at the row of lights ranged along the top of the building opposite and by the time he looked back Aqua was gone. He searched right and left until at last he caught a glimpse of her, just a shape in the dark, and set off, closing in on the sound of her bare feet pad-padding along the road. When they were well clear of the junction, Aqua stopped.

'They watch the centre of the junctions,' she whispered. 'If you stay away from the middle when you cross you're OK.' Then, without waiting for JD to answer, she turned and ran off again, hugging the wall, crouching as she went.

Junction after junction, past side roads and alleyways JD followed close until after a while he noticed that there were fewer buildings, more open spaces, little patches of arid scrub at the corners of the streets. As they ran past one of these open spaces something made JD look up and through the dirty yellow air he could see the sky, red and angry with just one or two weak and washed-out stars twinkling through the gloom. Then as the road swung to the left and the horizon opened out, he caught sight of the lovely Blue Star hanging low in the sky, sparkling through the chemical haze. It seemed to be drawing him on and he felt excited, following along behind the tough little girl on his way to find his Ma. Soon, he'd be at the Farm, he'd find Ma and everything would be good again. He ran on, settling close to Aqua's shoulder, matching his stride to hers. She looked up, saw his grinning face and smiled back.

Then the road spread out, the hard surface was gone and the ground became rough and dusty. A few paces further and JD saw a high wire fence stretching away on either side. He remembered the Bridge Gate with its guards and wondered if he'd have to do that all again. But there was no sign of any entrance, just a high fence, strands of grey wire fixed to heavy metal posts.

But Aqua showed no concern, just kept up her pace, running silently through the night. As they got closer, JD saw the fence had big lights over it, piercing the yellow mist which clung to the ground all around. He closed up behind Aqua and touched her shoulder.

'What?' she said without stopping or drawing breath.

'Isn't that the City fence?' JD panted.

'No. It's the Perimeter. That's the Farm. Look.' Aqua pointed ahead.

JD stared hard. Beyond the wire he could just make out some shapes; low, square-ended shacks, long lines of dark shadows disappearing into the murk. His heart skipped a beat. Could Ma be inside one of those shacks?

Without a pause Aqua ran right up to the high fence where JD joined her, panting softly in the night. Up close he saw that the wire was wound with evil-looking spikes, narrow slivers of sharp metal glinting in the light. JD shivered but could not resist touching one of the spikes with his finger. The tiny metal blades were real sharp. If you tried to climb that, he thought, you'd be cut to pieces.

Aqua put her hand on JD's shoulder, shook her head and wagged her finger at him. JD nodded; he knew he shouldn't have touched the fence. Looking down at Aqua, stationary for almost the first time since they'd met, he noticed that she looked real nice. When her features weren't drawn together into a frown of concentration or her lips pursed to scold him for something or other she was quite pretty. She had a soft, heart-shaped face, round eyes, big and black, and a little nose which tilted upwards. But the prettiness was spoiled, JD thought, by her thin lips which were hard and drawn wide, giving her a belligerent look, as if she was laughing at some joke that only she knew. Wisps of brown, close-cropped hair stuck to the perspiration on her brow. JD found himself studying every feature of the girl who had rescued him.

But in a moment she turned away, looking at the ground and shuffling her feet in the dust. Crouching down close to the wire, she looked along its length, muttered something under her breath, beckoned to JD and trotted away. After a few paces she stopped next to a tuft of sawgrass which sat on a pile of dirt. It was growing up against the lowest strand of the sharp wire, most of its spiky leaves pointing away from the fence but a few woven through it.

86

Without hesitation Aqua grasped the tuft with both hands and pulled. The whole thing, the grass and the mound of dirt on which it grew, moved, and she dragged it away from the fence. Where the sawgrass had been there was a shallow hole in the dirt beneath the wire.

'Come on,' Aqua said quietly. 'Through you go. And no fuss this time, please.'

JD looked at the stern little face and sheepishly dropped to his knees. He turned on his back and lay in the dirt then wriggled his head and shoulders into the hole. Quickly he pulled himself through the gap and under the wire, determined not to make a fool of himself this time. He still felt that cold twinge of fear as he scraped through the shallow space but out in the open it all seemed a whole lot easier.

As soon as Aqua had slipped through behind him she turned, reached back and pulled the little mound of sawgrass back into place, threading a few blades of grass through the lower strands of wire, making the clump look just like it had before.

'Right,' she said, standing up again. 'Now follow me. I'll take you to my station.'

Without waiting for him to ask any of the questions that were filling his head, Aqua set off towards the line of shacks disappearing into the mist. JD followed across the flat, hard ground which seemed to have been cleared of rocks and sawgrass. JD had expected more. To come all this way and be faced with just a barren expanse of flat ground with lines of featureless shacks was real disappointing. And it was so quiet. There had to be more than this, he thought as he followed the wiry little girl towards the dark buildings. She ran straight to the second line of shacks and turned into the space between it and the next row. JD hurried after her, looking from side to side, wondering if Ma could be close by.

He saw that each shack stood on supports with a space underneath just like his home back in the Dry Marsh. Above his head were lines of pipes, dull and metallic, running across the roofs of the shacks, dipping into each one before continuing on to the next row.

Just past the pipes Aqua stopped, looked around, grunted to herself and dropped to her knees. She stuck her head under the shack, flattened herself to the ground and disappeared into the space beneath the silent building. JD sighed. It seemed she was determined to lead him into dark, enclosed spaces.

Reluctantly he fell to the ground too, following the girl's blue-clad legs and bare feet into the narrow space beneath the building. He crawled forward, blinking hard, adjusting his eyes to the darkness. A few rays of orange light lit the edges of the shack and JD was relieved that after just a short distance Aqua stopped, turned onto her back and pushed up with her hands. There was a creak and a section of the floor above her lifted. A square of pale light shone onto the rough ground, briefly lighting up Aqua's features before she drew herself up onto her knees, poked her head through the hole and pulled herself inside.

Alone in the narrow space JD forgot his fear as a jumble of happy thoughts rushed into his head. He felt excited. Godrum had said Ma would be at the Farm and here he was at last.

Eleven

A New Dream

'Ow!' JD said as he pulled himself through behind Aqua. Something had hit him on the head. He twisted his neck to see what it could be, only to find a flat ceiling just above him. Aqua was sprawled on the floor next to the hole, grinning back at him.

'Mind your head,' she giggled.

'Thanks,' JD said, crawling out beside her. He was under what seemed like a low bed, just like his old bed back home. When he was little he had sometimes crawled under that too. It had been fun to hide from Ma and hear her looking for him, calling his name and talking to herself. 'Where is that boy?' she would say. Then he would pop his head out from under the bed and Ma would scoop him up and hug him. She'd whirl around with him in her arms and they would laugh. Rubbing the bruise on his head, JD remembered those happy times and felt warm inside. Don't you fret, Ma, he said to himself. I'm a-comin'.

JD crawled to the edge of the bed and peeked out. It was not a bit like he'd expected. Everything was white. The walls, the roof, the floor, all were dazzling white. Looking up, he found himself blinking into a row of narrow, bright lights which lined the roof, flooding every corner of the shack. And he was inside a sort of room, three sides of which were lined with tiers of narrow bunks while the fourth side was a tall wire fence separating the room from the rest of the shack. The whiteness of it all was dazzling; everything was white, even the bunks that stretched from floor to ceiling, four in each stack. On each bunk lay a single, pale child. JD looked at them and they all looked at him, their wide round eyes staring blankly. It seemed to JD that these pale kids were all eyes, so round, so big and black. Their unblinking stares made him feel uncomfortable so he crawled back under the bed.

'Where are we?' he asked, speaking into the underside of the low bed.

'Just where you wanted to be,' he heard Aqua say. 'This is the Farm.'

'OK. But who are all these people?'

'Just kids.'

'I can see that but what are they doin' here?'

'They aren't doing anything. They're just here. This is their station.'

JD squirmed around and looked out into the shack once more. The children hadn't moved – their soft round faces still stared down at him. They made no noise either, they just stared.

JD became bolder. 'Is it all right if I get out from under here?' he asked Aqua.

'If you like. They won't hurt you.'

JD slid out from under the low bed, stood up and looked around the room. There was little to see except for the stacks of beds piled one on top of another. The slots between were shallow, not much higher than the supine body of the child which lay within each one. JD turned around and looked at the tier from which he had emerged. The lowest bunk was empty but the three above each contained a white-faced child. He smiled at them, hoping to appear friendly, but in an instant, the three round faces pulled back and each child flattened itself against the back of its bunk. Two of them whimpered so JD turned away. The four children on the opposite side of the room immediately did the same thing, cowering back, hiding in the deepest recesses of their narrow slots.

JD knelt down. 'What's goin' on?' he asked Aqua, whose face now looked out from the lowest bunk.

'They're scared of you. They've never seen anyone like you before.'

'What's the matter with me then?'

'Nothing. It's just that they've never seen anyone except other farm children.'

'Why not?'

Aqua laughed. 'Because they've never been anywhere else and I've never brought anyone back before.'

'Do you live here then?'

'Yes. Of course. This is my station too,' Aqua said, crawling out to the edge of her bunk and patting it.

JD was confused. A stark white room full of timid children who seem to be scared of everything and a tough little girl who was afraid of nothing. It was all too much.

Aqua swung her legs out, stood up and stretched herself. JD shook his head. She looked so much like the children in the bunks but was so different.

'They're stupid,' she said, sensing JD's confusion. 'They don't understand. They just stay in their stations, wait for their rations and think that's all there is. But not me. Right from the time I became an Intermediate I knew I had to get away.'

'What's an inter—' JD was not sure of the word so let it dribble away.

'An Intermediate. When you are too old to be in the milk pens you are an Intermediate. Now look,' Aqua went on, 'we'd better rest. If we are going to find your Ma we'll have to wait 'til let-out. I'll get into my station and you get back underneath. Get some sleep if you can.'

JD asked no more questions, although plenty buzzed around inside his head. Aqua rolled into the bottom bunk and JD curled up underneath, his back against the wall, as far away from the open room as he could get. Once out of the bright light of the shack JD found he was real tired and sleep came quick, despite his brain spooling through everything that had happened to him that day. But Ma had to be close by now and before long he would find her and they would go back to the Dry Marsh together.

As JD drifted into sleep a picture formed in his mind of Ma standing in the doorway of a new shack in the Dry Marsh, watching him set off on a day's foraging, just the way Pa had done. In his mind's eye he strolled away to search for crickets, roots and water while by his side skipped a round-faced little girl. They were all laughing.

Twelve

Let-out

JD woke with a start. His cosy vision of a happy life in a new shack had gone and he was trapped, held fast under a great concrete wall. He struggled and struck out and his arm hit something solid just above his head. Oh no! He began to whimper but something inside told him to keep quiet so slowly, dreading what he might see, he opened his eyes and looked around. Close above him was a solid board, to one side a wall. But there was light and to his relief he found he could see and move. Slowly he remembered the Farm, the shack, the narrow bunks and the round-eyed children and he relaxed. Then he remembered the best thing. Ma was close by, she might even be in this shack, standing on the same floor he was lying on right now.

JD blinked the sleep from his eyes. Through the gap between the bunk and the floor he could see the stark white room. Under his shoulder he could feel the loose boards through which Aqua had led him the night before. He decided to get out and go to Ma but something told him to stay back. Beyond his hiding place he could see a row of ankles and feet, all lined up against the wire fence. He studied them. They were nearly all the same; white, chubby and soft as if they had never trodden dirt or rough ground. Only one pair differed from the others. They were dusty and scratched. JD smiled to himself. They had to be Aqua's feet for sure.

JD wriggled towards the light and peeked out. The children he'd last seen cowering in their beds were all standing at the wire, staring out, looking to their right. Every now and again one child would jostle the one next to it, who would straight away push back, but JD noticed nobody tried that on Aqua.

JD reached out his hand and touched the hem of Aqua's trousers, tugging lightly on the thin cloth but in an instant Aqua kicked back, shaking herself free.

'Get back,' she hissed. 'Get back.'

JD was confused and a mite hurt but did as she said. No sooner was he back out of sight than a great noise echoed down the shack. A door was being drawn back at one end and immediately all the little feet started to move and shuffle on the floor. Children were pushing each other, forcing themselves closer to the wire. JD eased forward again and could see that all the kids, Aqua included, had put their hands through the wire and were waving them, like they were beckoning to somebody. Some were moaning. Then, from the end of the shack JD heard voices shouting, harsh and threatening, and once more he crawled back out of sight. The children moaned louder; some sounded almost frantic, but as the angry voices came closer their cries began to die away.

A pair of heavy boots came into view; a key rasped and was followed by a harsh metallic scrape as a door in the wire was drawn back. As if a signal had been given the children were all in a heap, a bundle of blue-clad arms pulling at each other and fighting. Then the boots passed out of JD's sight, the fight was over and as if by magic the children were gone. There had been no patter of feet, no sound at all, they were just gone. It seemed they had all been whisked away. JD blinked and looked again. There really was nothing and nobody there but, and here his heart skipped a beat, the door in the fence was wide open. The whole place was quiet, there were no heavy boots, no nothing. This was his chance; his chance to slip away and find Ma.

JD edged forward and risked a glance outside. The cell and, it seemed, the whole shack was empty.

JD stuck his head right out and looked up. In the tier of bunks opposite he was amazed to see that all the round-eyed children were back in their slots, their stations as

97

Aqua had called them. But they were all turned inwards, their backs towards him.

JD waited, listening, not sure if he should come out from under the bunk or not. Then, right above him he heard a movement and guessed Aqua was in her station too. Still he waited, expecting her to say something, to explain what was happening, but all was quiet. When he could wait no longer JD slid out from under the bunk. Like all the others Aqua was turned away, tucked deep into her station, her face and body pressed against the wall. Tentatively, JD reached out and touched her. In an angry movement the girl turned and scowled from the shadows of her narrow bunk, her hands clasped to her chest.

'Get away,' she snapped. 'Get away or I'll call the guard.'

JD drew back, stunned by her anger and frightened by her threat.

'Hey, Aqua, it's me, JD. What's goin' on?' he said timidly.

The girl glared at him, her body hunched, her hands clenched and her eyes bright and fiery. JD dropped his arms to his sides, not knowing what to do. He couldn't figure it out. What had he done? He thought they were friends, she'd been so kind but now there was real hate in her eyes.

'Aqua?' he said. 'What's wrong? What have I done?'

Aqua glared back and JD's heart sank further. Her face was set as hard as the concrete wall behind her. JD felt close to despair but just then and just a little, the girl's face softened. The taut, clamped little mouth began to relax and a glimmer of hope flickered inside JD. But he dared not move in case it brought back the anger. He tried a smile and she, still clasping one hand to her chest, began to reach out towards him. Then she hesitated and drew back again.

'Sorry, JD,' she said with a half-smile. 'Here,' she added, her voice almost back to normal. 'Have a sip.' She unclenched her hand and offered JD a small metal container. He recognised it instantly as a smaller version of the one Godrum had and he took the tube, unscrewed the cap and poured a few drops of water into it. He wetted his lips and swilled the water around his mouth, before swallowing gratefully. Carefully and deliberately he screwed back the cap and returned the tube to Aqua.

'Thanks,' he said. 'Is that what the fuss was about? All the moanin' and groanin'?'

'What else?' Aqua said. 'We need our water or we'd die, wouldn't we?'

JD decided to say nothing. Water was as precious to him as it was to everybody but he hoped it would never make him behave like that. But then he remembered how he'd planned to creep up and steal Godrum's water back in the Scrubland and flushed with guilt. That was just as bad, perhaps worse. Aqua was just guarding her own water; he had planned to steal Godrum's and leave him to die of thirst under a blazing sun. That made him feel real bad. What a wicked thing he'd planned to do. The memory made him feel very small, but through his guilt he remembered that thanks to Godrum he could make water any time he felt like it. Putting his hand inside the bib of his dungarees, he touched the piece of plastic.

But that angry look on Aqua's face had hurt JD. He smiled his thanks and slid back under the bunk to be alone and to think things out. He stayed hidden away for some time, curled up, turning stuff over in his mind.

After a while he felt a movement above his head and sensed that Aqua had come to the edge of her bunk and was looking at him. But he kept his face turned away. He would have loved to share his problems but remembered how Pa had always told him not to trust folks. He'd come to the City to find Ma and chance had thrown him in with Aqua. At first he'd been happy to be with her. She'd been a good, reliable friend, ready to help him, but that look on her face had put real doubts in his mind. No, he decided, he'd find Ma on his own if he had to, but something Godrum had said began buzzing around in his brain. He said it was OK to ask for help from another kid. Was that because Godrum knew that children lived on the Farm or was it that they were the only ones to trust? Perhaps both. The more he thought the more he realised that it would be dumb to fall out with Aqua. She knew the Farm and had enough about her to break out at night and roam the streets of the City. She'd even known how to keep out of the way of the Silver Men, which was more than he did. Without her help he'd have been carried off like Godrum for sure and then where would he be? It was a tough call but after a good long time thinking he decided he'd have to swallow his pride. Aqua seemed to know all the things he needed to know if he was to find Ma and anyways, he couldn't deny that he quite liked the tough little girl.

Just when he'd made up his mind to climb out from his hiding place and talk to Aqua again he heard a hiss.

'Psst, JD!' a voice said from above.

JD turned over. Aqua was looking at him over the edge of her bunk.

'It'll be let-out soon. Wait for the door to open and stay close to me. Don't look at the others. You'll only scare them and they might panic and that would be sure to alert the guards. Stay quiet and keep your eyes down. OK?'

'OK,' JD said.

She disappeared again and JD smiled to himself. She'd spoken as if nothing had happened and from what she'd said she must have been thinking about him like he'd been thinking about her. She'd had that old crooked smile on her face too, just like before. JD relaxed. It seemed they were friends again.

Then Aqua's face reappeared.

'And another thing,' she said. 'Take that stupid hat off. It makes you stand out too much.'

JD pulled a face. He liked his old sack hat and anyways, Ma had made it for him. But before he could argue Aqua grinned again. 'And those stupid boots. Only Pigs wear boots,' she said. 'Stupid.' She grinned and was gone.

He was going to protest, say he wasn't stupid and explain about his hat and boots but somehow her parting insult made him feel sort of warm inside. In a funny way the word bound them together. It was something that only they shared.

JD took off his boots and hid them away in a corner. He took off his old sack hat and tucked it down the front of his dungarees and sighed. He sure did like that girl.

Lying quietly, JD waited, wondering what he would find outside, but before his imagination had properly set to work he heard the door in the end of the shack slide back. In a flash the pen was filled with chattering kids slipping out of their bunks, crowding through the doorway and spilling out into the corridor.

JD crawled out from his hiding place and this time nobody paid him no heed; the kids were all swirling around in their eagerness to get outside. In the corridor JD and Aqua were surrounded by children from other pens, all running towards the open air. Aqua took JD's hand and together they ran too, letting themselves be carried along by the crowd. They smiled at each other and began shouting and laughing just like the others but beneath it all JD was watching for danger. He reckoned he saw trouble right away.

At the door stood two older kids, taller but still with those same wide, dark eyes. They did not laugh with the others; their white faces were fixed and cruel. It seemed to JD that they sneered at the happy throng. Although they were dressed like all the others JD noticed one striking difference. The kids from the pens had their hair cut short but these bigger ones had long hair pulled back to a kind of short bunch at the back of their heads. JD stole a glance at the pair by the door but quickly remembered what Aqua had said and cast his eyes down again. He skipped along with the crowd but he'd seen the grim faces of the big kids by the door, seen them trying to look tough. JD tried not to smile. Sure, they were trying to look hard but their silly hairstyles just made them look dumb. Nevertheless, dumb or not, JD understood the danger.

Aqua ran ahead, tugging at his hand, pulling him towards the doorway, keeping them in the centre of a bunch of laughing kids. JD ducked his head as they got close to the door and in the blink of an eye they were through and outside in a whirling mass of kids squealing and laughing, happy to be free of the shack and out into a wide open yard.

Right, JD thought, now to find Ma.

Thirteen

Ma

JD had never seen so many kids. Back home it had just been Pa and Ma and him. He'd only once ever seen another kid back at the Dry Marsh. He'd come by one day, wandering down the track from the Old Road, looking drawn and sick. JD had been pretty small back then and the sight of another boy had scared him. He'd called out to Ma and she'd come a-running. She chased the little guy back the way he'd come, shouting and lashing out at him. JD remembered the kid whimpering and holding out his hands but Ma had slapped his head and sent him packing. The memory put a pain in JD's stomach. The kid had probably been like him, his Ma and Pa gone somehow. Likely he was only looking for a sip of water or something to eat but Ma beat him and sent him away. That's just the way things are.

Aqua gripped JD's hand and pulled him away from the other children. Some of the little ones were staring at him. In his faded dungarees and threadbare shirt he knew he looked different and he knew that different was dangerous.

Aqua pulled him into the shadow of one of the long shacks, watching the others crowding around each other, jostling or playing at fights.

'Now look, JD,' she said. 'If we're going to find your Ma we'll have to get over to the Brooders.'

'Brooders?' JD asked. 'What's brooders?'

'Just more buildings like these,' she said, pointing at the shack they stood by. 'They're at the other side of the Farm though. They call them Brooders because that's where all the Mas are.'

'I don't understand.' JD said. 'Are there more Mas? I thought . . .'

'Of course there are more Mas. There are lots and lots of Mas. They live in the Brooders with the babies, stupid.'

This time JD didn't find the word quite so endearing. He was puzzled by Aqua's offhand description and it must have shown. Aqua sighed and looked up at him.

'Look, JD, this is the way it works. The Brooders are way over there.' Aqua pointed again. 'Way, way over there. The first three rows of buildings are Brooders. That's where the women are; it's where they have babies.'

JD stared. Lots of Mas? Babies? This was too much.

Aqua sighed again. 'Women have babies, even you must know that. Where do you think we come from? We are all babies to start with. Here on the Farm the babies stay with their Mas for a while then, when they are old enough, they go to the milk pens. Then, when they get to be Juniors they get moved to the Junior stations, that's the next couple of rows. You can sometimes hear them at night. They cry a lot. When they get bigger they get to be Intermediates and move into the Intermediate stations. That's where we are now. My station is Intermediate Two. That's where we've just been.'

'What happens then?' JD asked. 'What happens after you're an Intermediate?'

Aqua looked down. 'Then we go to work.'

'How's that?'

Aqua shrugged. 'Don't rightly know. Some say the boys go to the Pits and the girls go to the City but . . .'

'But what?'

Aqua shrugged again. 'The Pigs tell us terrible things. About how the girls get beaten and . . . well . . . other things and how the boys all die in the Pits. They say there's a horrible man in the Pits who eats boys too but I don't know if that's true.' Aqua's voice had become husky and her self-assurance seemed to have drained away. She turned away and fell silent as if she was thinking about something.

'That's why I've decided to escape,' she said. 'I'm not

going to stick around like all the others to have my life run by Pigs. I heard of a kid who escaped once. He got right away and now he lives outside the City, happy and free.'

JD suddenly had a vision of the boy who'd come to the shack that day when he'd been little. The one Ma had chased away. He might have been the one, the kid that escaped and was happy and free. He'd had on a blue jacket and trousers like all the other kids in the Farm so it really might have been him. He might have been free but he sure didn't look too happy. Then something Aqua had said flashed into his thoughts.

'Hey, Aqua, you said Pigs. You said Pigs told you about what happens and decide what you do. What's Pigs?'

'Oh, JD! Pigs are guards; those men in their big boots. You've seen them.'

'Yes, I have,' JD said quietly. 'But what are they? What do they do?'

'They make sure we don't do anything we aren't meant to. They are put over us by the Leaders to make sure we obey the rules and do as we're told; stop us getting away. They're horrible. They are bullies and try to frighten everyone, particularly the little ones. They get extra water for being Pigs and they taunt us with it, telling us we are all going to die of thirst while they have plenty of water. You have to be very careful, JD. Always look at the hair. If it's long and pulled back, that's a Pig.'

'What about those kids at the door of your, er . . . station? They have long hair.'

'Piglets. Big kids who want to be Pigs when they grow up. They hope that if they're mean to us, when the time comes they won't get sent to the Pits, they'll be sent off to Pig training camp. They're horrible too, sometimes worse than real Pigs. They punch us and are as spiteful as they can be. They try to show the real Pigs how nasty they are. They think it will help them and who knows, it just might. In a way I suppose you can't blame them. If they don't get to be Pigs they'll go to the Pits like all the other boys. And die.'

JD sighed. Aqua spoke so fast and said so many things that were new to him he wondered how he was ever going to remember it all. Leaders, Guards, Pigs, Piglets, Brooders and Stations, there was so much to know. Aqua seemed to sense his confusion and put her hand on his arm.

'Oh, JD, try to understand. You'll never survive here if you don't know these things.'

'I don't want to survive here,' JD said firmly. 'Soon as I find Ma we'll get out and go back to the Dry Marsh. I'll build a new shack and it'll be just like before. We'll be happy and free too, just like the boy who got away.'

Aqua looked up at him, her eyes sad. 'I didn't know him. Don't really know if it was a boy or a girl. It's just a story that people tell. It might not be true. Might be nobody ever gets out.'

'They must do. My Ma and Pa lived in the Dry Marsh and you see other folks out there all over. Some must get away. Anyways, Pa said Ma wanted to go *back* to the City. That means she must have been here in the first place, don't it? Stands to reason.'

Aqua's eyes smiled again. 'What's it like in the Dry Marsh, JD? Tell me.'

'Well . . .' JD said, casting his mind back. 'It's OK, I suppose. It's still hot and there ain't much to eat nor drink but it's a darn sight better than this.' JD waved his arm, taking in the buildings, the children and the compound.

'But where do you live and who brings your water?' Aqua asked.

'We lived in a shack. Sort of like your station, only smaller. Pa built it from things he'd found around and about. We had a big room where Ma had a stove and a window. Then Ma and Pa had a room where they put their bed. They had some boxes for their things and they had a window there too. I had a room the same; bit smaller but the same. I had a bed which Pa built and a box for puttin' things in and my own window which Ma made a curtain for.'

'It sounds wonderful but what about water? How did you get water?'

'I don't rightly know. Pa went out into the Marsh every day and sometimes he'd bring back a bit of water and some

109

crickets or some such. Ma used to cook the crickets and she'd boil the water and put it in a jar. When it was cooled off we'd have a sip or two with our grub. But we could just go out anytime we felt like it, no Pigs had to unlock no doors for us. Why, I used to play outside all day and when Pa came home we'd all sit on the stoop and enjoy the colours when the sun went down. Then we'd watch the Blue Star rise. Yeah . . .' JD's voice trailed away. 'The Dry Marsh is OK.'

'That's where I want to go,' Aqua said excitedly. She made her hands into little fists and held them close to her. 'I'll run away to the Dry Marsh and build a shack just like you said and live there for ever and ever.' Her round eyes sparkled and she danced from foot to foot. 'There will be no Pigs, no Leaders and I'll be free. Free to do just what I want.'

The mention of Leaders cleared the rosy clouds from JD's mind. 'Well,' he said. 'That's all fine and dandy but it ain't all good. The reason I come here to find Ma in the first place is because of your Leaders, what I call Silver Men. They used to fly out to the Dry Marsh and catch Ma. Then they came and killed Pa and burned down our shack so it ain't all good. It ain't all good by a long ways.'

'But if we were both there and with your Ma too we'd be all right, wouldn't we? We'd find someplace where the Silver Men couldn't find us. You and I could find water and food like your Pa did and your Ma could cook it. We could have windows too and your Ma could make some more curtains. Oh, JD, wouldn't it be just great? Do you know such a place, JD? I bet you do. Tell me where we could build our shack. Tell me.'

JD began to catch Aqua's enthusiasm. The three of them in a nice new shack someplace. It sounded just fine. But where? The Silver Men could fly all over with their jet-packs and he was scared of them. They'd surely come back to find Ma and he'd have to hide in the ground like Pa did. JD thought hard, trying to work out some way they could all live in Aqua's dream. In his head he saw all the places he'd ever known or even dreamed about and pictured the three of them, Ma, Aqua and him, all living in a nice smart little shack with plenty of water and grub, sitting out in the evening watching the Blue Star. But it wasn't long before he imagined Silver Men in the sky, circling over the shack then roaring down and him running away into the scrub.

JD shook himself. 'It ain't no good dreamin'. We can't do none of this 'til I've found Ma. Ma will know what to do right enough but we still gotta find her.'

'I know,' Aqua said, her face still shining with ideas. 'But when you and your Ma go back to the Dry Marsh, you will take me with you, won't you? Say you'll take me. Please, JD, say it.' She gripped his arm hard, her nails making marks in his skin.

'It's fine with me, Aqua, but I still gotta ask Ma and I don't even know where she is right now.'

'Come on then. I'll show you. We'll go to the Brooders. We'll find your Ma then you can ask her.' She pulled at JD's arm. 'Come on, JD, let's go. Let's go find your Ma.'

JD let Aqua pull him away, following her to the corner of the long shack. He looked around the end. More wide-eyed children stood in groups, some talking, some playing and some just standing. Some followed JD and Aqua with their eyes as they crossed the end of the long building and strolled as nonchalantly as they could across to the next one.

Children played all around the shacks but the further he and Aqua went JD noticed the kids were smaller and quieter. After five or six shacks they were little more than babies sitting in the red dust looking lost, staring into nowhere.

Aqua pulled JD's arm whenever he slowed, her enthusiasm driving her on. At last she stopped at the end of yet another long, grey, windowless building where a group of tiny children clustered near an open door.

'There,' Aqua said, pointing across a wide, open space. 'That's the Brooders. All the Mas are in the next three stations. If your Ma really is here then she's going to be in one of them.'

JD was gripped with a mixture of joy and fear. The hairs

112

on the back of his neck rose and his heart beat fast in his chest. Was Ma really here, right up close? He studied the first building carefully. It differed in only one way from every other shack he'd seen on the Farm. It had big square windows down the side and each window had some kind of transparent material covering it. JD stared. He thought he could see folks moving about inside, hazy images of heads and shoulders passing by. Maybe one of 'em was Ma, he thought and without another word he set off towards the first Brooder.

Aqua scampered after him and grabbed his arm. 'Where are you going?' she said. 'You can't just stroll in and look around. There will be Pigs everywhere. We aren't allowed inside the Brooders.'

'But I've gotta go. I've gotta find Ma,' JD said, pulling himself free. 'I'm goin' in. You can come if you want but I'm goin' whether you come or not. Nobody's goin' to stop me findin' my Ma.'

'You can't, JD, you can't. If we get caught we will be in real trouble.'

'What can they do?' JD pouted. 'When I find Ma she'll tell 'em it's OK. She'll soon scare those old Pigs away, you'll see if she don't.'

'No, she won't. You don't know what it's like here, JD. If your Ma's in there she's more of a prisoner than we are.'

'What do you mean, *prisoner*? Ma wanted to come here.

113

She told Pa. She said she'd be better off in the City. That's why she left.'

'Then she didn't know much,' Aqua said angrily. 'If your Ma's in the Brooders she'll never get out until she dies or gets too old to have more babies. The best she can hope for then is to be one of the old women that helps out around here. Helps the Mas have their babies. And they are awful too. Worse than Pigs.'

'I don't care,' JD hissed. 'I've come to find Ma and that's just what I'm goin' to do.' He pulled his arm away and ran to the first Brooder, ducking around the end to where he reckoned he could get inside.

The big, sliding door stood open and without a second thought JD slipped into the building.

Inside the door JD stood quite still so's he could figure out what to do. The Brooder was all white just like Aqua's shack but there were no bright lights in the roof; instead sunlight flooded in through windows set down each side. The first thing JD noticed was the strange smell. Sniffing, he looked down the long corridor that stretched the length of the shack, trying to understand where it was coming from. Instead of a wire fence, a low white wall ran right down the shack and JD reckoned the sweet smell came from behind it. He stepped forward and, standing on tiptoe, he looked over the wall. There were no tiers of bunks this time; the pen was divided up by another white wall running from front to back with only a narrow gap to get through. JD peered down into the pen. Below him, on a plain bed, sat a large woman, white-skinned and naked but for an old stained sheet wrapped around her. She was nursing a little baby, which nestled in the crook of her arm, while on the bed three more little ones wrestled each other in a mock fight. The babies were stark white with the familiar wide-set eyes. At the sight of JD they scrambled over the woman and tried to hide themselves, pushing their faces into her rolls of flesh and whimpering. JD only had to glance at the woman to see that this was not Ma. Ma was slim and pretty and much younger than the flabby creature sprawled behind the wall.

'Hello, dearie,' the fat woman said, turning to see what had startled her babies. 'You lost, are you?'

'No,' JD said firmly. 'I ain't lost. I'm lookin' for Ma.'

'That's as maybe,' the woman said. 'But you shouldn't be in here, you know, dear. You're a big boy. You should be over at your station. Now, you run along before the guards catch you. Go on.' She clutched her babies close to her with one great flabby arm and waved JD away with the other. When he didn't move she waved at him again. 'Shoo,' she hissed. 'Go on or –'

JD didn't wait to hear what else she had to say; he was already moving down the pens. The next one was the same. One low bed and one fat woman, younger this time but still white and flabby. She was curled up on the bed with two babies close by. Her eyes were closed but one of the babies saw JD and squealed, then tried to burrow under the twisted bed-sheet.

JD moved on, running from pen to pen, lifting himself onto his toes and searching for a pretty young woman with kind eyes, but each time it was the same. Big, fat women lying motionless on crude, low beds, all nursing babies among a tangle of dirty white sheets. None of these women looked like Ma. They were old and dull-eyed like the children they nursed. There were no tough, wiry women like Ma and anyways, JD knew that Ma didn't have no babies. Aqua must have got it wrong. This couldn't be the right place.

Behind him JD could still hear the voice of the Ma in the first pen, whining out a stream of words. 'That boy shouldn't be in here. He's way too big. He should be at his station.' Another voice joined in from a pen close by, 'If we called the guards, we'd get extra water.'

As if in answer JD heard a shrill little voice calling from the end of the building. 'Come back, JD. Come back, you'll get caught. Come back. It's too dangerous.' He turned to see Aqua framed in the doorway, hopping from foot to foot.

'Oh, JD, be careful' she cried. 'Please be careful.'

JD turned away. The women's voices were rising and he knew that pretty soon one of them would call out. He could almost hear the pounding of heavy boots coming for him but he had to carry on, he had to see into every pen. There were only three more left but he knew he'd have to be quick before the women gave him away so he moved on, deeper into the building.

The next pen was just the same. A pale, stupid-looking woman, wound up in her bedclothes, nursing a single baby. This one was staring at the window but when JD's head popped over the wall she turned and looked at him over the head of the child in her arms.

JD ducked down below the wall and was about to run to the next pen when he froze. Slowly he lifted his head over the wall again and stared.

'Ma?' he said. 'Is that you, Ma?'

The woman was fat and Ma was thin. Ma had a bright, kind face and this woman had a drab, lifeless look but there was something familiar about her. JD stared and then his face broke into a broad grin.

'Oh, Ma, Ma, it's you. I've been lookin' everywhere for you.'

The woman stared back and blinked. There was no sign of recognition on her face. Her dull eyes stared at JD but the more he looked the more he was sure. This woman had narrower eyes than the others and lines in her skin from squinting into the sun. She was fatter than Ma and whiter than Ma but JD was sure. It was Ma.

'Ma,' he said, almost crying with joy, beating his hands on the top of the wall. 'It's me, Ma. It's me, JD. Don't you recognise me? I come to find you. I come all the way from the Dry Marsh. Oh, Ma, it's so good to see you.' He stopped beating the wall and reached out towards her, stretching his arms over the wall, his face screwed up in a frenzy of emotions. At last, he'd found Ma but she was different; she wasn't what he'd expected. And not just because she had a baby in her arms, after what he'd seen he'd almost been expecting that; but it was the way she looked at him. Half-afraid and half-angry, she seemed unable to understand what he was saying.

JD's mind was in a whirl. It was Ma, he was sure it was Ma, yet this woman looked so dumb, and seemed unable to take in what he was saying. But he shouldn't have to make her understand. Ma was strong and clever. This wasn't like Ma, this was a woman with a baby who had once been Ma. JD felt crushed. His dream was falling apart.

Still the woman with the baby stared. She clasped the child to her, using it as a shield against the thin little boy peeking over the wall.

'Ma,' JD said quietly. 'Ma. Look.' He dropped his hands to his sides. 'It's me, JD. I come to get you,' he said, his voice breaking. 'I come to get you, Ma,' he choked. 'I come to get you.' JD felt his eyes begin to burn and a dry sob rose like a huge ball in his throat.

Still the woman stared. Then, at last she spoke. 'JD?' she said. 'What are you doing here? You shouldn't be here.'

Hope flared up again when she said his name. 'Ma, Ma. I come to take you home. Ma, the Silver Men came. They burned the shack and killed Pa but I come to fetch you.' JD choked out the words but his bright new hope was already fading. 'We'll go back to the Dry Marsh, Ma,' he said. 'It'll be just like before.' But there was no urgency, no excitement left in him. He spoke the words like he was telling a story. A story he'd told many times before and was now beginning to tire of.

The woman with the baby, the woman who had once been his Ma, stood up. She draped the old sheet around her but instead of coming towards her son, standing forlornly behind the wall, instead of hugging him to her as he ached for her to do, she turned her back and looked out of the window. She stood perfectly still, then glanced over her shoulder at JD. There was no sign of recognition now. Her face was as blank as the walls around her. Then she reached out towards the corner of the pen and for the first time JD noticed a long wire stretching from the floor to the ceiling. Ma wound her fingers around it and pulled hard.

Straight away a siren sounded, a short sharp bark of ear-splitting noise. The woman pulled the wire again and the siren roared again.

JD knew what she'd done. He didn't need no telling. Ma, his Ma, had called the guards. The chatter of the children playing outside fell silent. He felt, or did he hear, the pounding of boots on the hard ground. In what seemed like just a heartbeat there was a clatter at the end of the building and out of the corner of his eye JD saw two men, tall and heavy, running towards him, their ragged ponytails swishing around behind their heads.

The women in the end pens were shouting again. 'I saw him first. It was me. I saw him first. The extra water is for me . . . It's for me.'

The guards paid them no heed and nor did JD. He didn't turn to run, he just stood with his hands flat by his sides, his chin against the low wall, staring at the woman who'd betrayed him. The men grabbed him roughly, pulling him off his feet and away from the pen. JD didn't fight back, he neither looked up nor cried out. When they threw him to the floor he fell like a rag doll and lay with his eyes screwed tight shut, waiting but not caring what might happen to him now.

Fourteen

The Pits

The men dragged JD's body into the yard, past the build-ings and away to a wire fence where they dumped him on the ground. JD opened his eyes and blinked. He saw a gate and two men talking to each other who stood by the wire. Overwhelmed by tiredness and despair, JD closed his eyes again. Through a daze he heard the click of a lock, the clank of a chain and the creak of hinges. He felt strong arms grab him and drag him through the dust then they let him go again. JD fell to the ground and lay there. They yelled at him to stand up. They kicked him, driving the toes of their heavy boots into his side. JD curled up into a ball but it was automatic, he cared little for his safety. His own Ma had drawn a line through the rest of his life. She'd given him up for a sip of water. JD didn't like the pain of the men kicking him but what did it really matter?

What did anything matter any more? There was nothin' to live for now. Pa was gone and Ma didn't want him. They might as well keep kickin' him 'til he died.

After a while the guards seemed to tire of kicking JD's meagre little body and pulled him to his feet again. JD figured he'd better try to stay upright and despite his lack of energy or will to survive he managed to keep his feet. The men pushed him in the back, making him stumble forward and he staggered across the dusty ground towards a large square metal box on wheels.

By the time they reached the box JD was only just conscious. His head swam and he felt sick. The men lifted him up and shoved him into the box. They slammed the door hard behind him and JD's head rang as the sound echoed through the darkness. It was hot inside the box. JD rolled onto his back and lay still, panting hard, but no sooner had he recovered his breath than he heard a whine from somewhere under the floor, the box juddered and it rolled forward.

As the box gathered speed and began bumping over rough ground JD spread out on the floor. He lay like a star, his arms and legs straight out to stop himself sliding around too much. The box rumbled on, jumping and crashing, climbing and descending, tipping first one way then the other. There was nothing to cling onto so JD's body slid around, banging into the sides of the box until he became exhausted. He didn't know how long he'd been bounced around when the box finally squealed to a halt.

JD lay quite still, listening to the silence, then the door was thrown open and a guard was silhouetted in a square of bright sunlight. JD screwed up his eyes, shielding them with his hand.

'Out,' the guard shouted.

His body aching from the kicking and from being thrown around, JD moved slowly and before he could get to the door the guard had grabbed him by his dungarees, dragged him out of the box and dropped him onto the ground outside.

'What's happenin'?' JD asked, staggering to his feet. 'Where are we?'

The guard gave a grim smile. 'Look around you, kid. Where do you think you are?'

JD looked. He blinked. He'd never seen such a place before. The Dry Marsh and the Scrubland were barren and empty, flat with just a shallow dip here and there so what he saw now was beyond his imagination.

Immediately in front of him was an enormous hole. It was round and covered an area nearly as big as the Farm. The distant edge was so far away it was just a dark line in the red earth and the hole was so deep JD couldn't see the bottom. Beyond it, piles of dirt and rocks spread out in all directions, some rising so high that JD had to look almost straight up to see the tops. All around were more holes and more great heaps of red dirt, while between them a narrow winding track, a worn strip of packed dirt, stretched away into the distance. It was a terrible sight. The whole place was utterly ravaged and the devastation stretched as far as JD could see.

He guessed where he was without being told. Something inside told him that these great holes and dirt piles were the Pits. Aqua had spoken of them in a hushed voice and said that boys who went to the Pits all died. JD swallowed hard.

'Is this the Pits?' he asked the guard.

'Sure is. You never been here before?'

JD shook his head.

'Where did you come from then? Back there they said you'd got away from the Pits and made your way back to the Farm somehow.'

JD shook his head but something inside warned him not to explain. He might have to say how he got to the Farm and then Aqua would be in trouble.

'I just come to find my Ma,' was all he said.

But he needn't have worried. The guard had other things on his mind. 'Show me your arm,' he said.

JD put out his arm. The guard grabbed it, pushed back the sleeve of his ragged shirt and studied the burned skin. 'The other one,' he snapped, letting JD's arm fall back to his side.

JD did as he was told and held out his other arm.

'Hmm,' the man said. 'You ain't got no number.'

JD looked puzzled.

'Your number. You ain't got a number. How am I meant to know who you are?'

'I'm JD,' JD said.

'Yeah,' the man said. 'But that ain't a number. Kids gotta have numbers.'

'I don't,' JD said. 'I just come to find my Ma.'

The guard grunted. 'Whatever,' he said, spitting on the ground and scanning the barren landscape. 'But you're a Pit kid now and all Pit kids got numbers. If you ain't got a number how can I tell which pit you belong to? You'd better get back in the truck and I'll just take you to see the man.'

JD climbed back into the hot metal box and pretty soon they were bumping over the rough ground again. When they stopped JD expected to be hauled outside like before but the door stayed shut. He sat there in the silence, getting hotter and hotter, and by the time the door did open he was gasping for breath and scrambled towards the light without having to be told. Outside, his guard was talking with two other men; one of them had the heavy boots and scragged-back hair of a Pig but the other was a very strange sight indeed. He was covered in red dirt from head to toe; his face and long straggly hair were plastered with it too.

His bare arms were thick and strong but they too were caked in dirt. His clothes were just filthy rags tied loosely around his body, hanging in ribbons right down to the ground.

'Out,' the Pig shouted and hit the side of the box with a short metal rod.

JD dropped onto the dust in front of the men but as soon as he tried to stand the man in rags grabbed him by the neck.

'Heh, heh,' he chuckled in a high squeaky voice. 'Not a lot of meat on this one.'

JD struggled free and took a step back, pressing himself against the truck. 'Get off,' he said, determined not to show how frightened he really was, and glared at the ugly man.

'Oh! I'm terribly sorry if I hurt you,' the man leered. 'I'm really, really very sorry if I bruised your delicate little neck. I really must watch my step. You look so big and strong I really am quite afeared of you.'

The guards seemed to find this real funny and laughed out loud. JD cowered back against the side of the box, looking from one man to another, searching, trying to work out where the main danger might come from. The dirty man in his rags, the Pig with the metal rod and the driver all sneered and snarled together.

The wild man in his filthy rags lunged forward again, grabbed JD by the arm and pulled him close. JD cringed

126

and turned his face away; the man smelled as bad as he looked.

'Enough of your cheek now, tough guy. Let's get you to work and see how tough you really are. Let's see if a few days in a pit will teach you a bit of respect.' He swung JD around in front of him then shoved him hard in the back. 'Now get down below.'

JD stumbled forward, nearly falling headlong to the ground.

'Take it easy,' the Pig laughed. 'Don't kill him before you get a couple of days' work out of him.'

'Don't you worry,' the Ragman cackled. 'I'll see we get good value from this one before he moves on to higher things.'

This set them all off laughing again but although JD felt his heart pounding hard he really didn't care. So he was goin' to have to work in a Pit, how bad could it be? Worse than your Ma turnin' you in? Worse than everythin' you ever wanted bein' snatched away? JD turned away but when he saw what lay before him he found he did care after all.

He was on the edge of another pit, even bigger than the one he'd seen before, and all around its rim great metal poles stood high out of the ground, leaning outwards and anchored by guy-ropes. From the tops of the poles, thick steel wires stretched deep down into the Pit where they

127

were fixed to something big, black and shiny, pulling it tight, stretching it right out to the edges. The black thing, a sort of shimmering shroud, was so vast it covered the whole crater, dipping down sharply in the centre. JD turned to look at his captors and they leered back.

'Pretty, ain't it, boy?' the Ragman laughed. 'But you'll find it ain't half so pretty down below.'

The Ragman shoved JD in the back again, forcing him forward until he was tottering right on the edge of the hole. Beneath where he stood a steep flight of steps was cut into the side of the pit, leading towards a flap in the side of the black shape.

'Don't just stand and stare, Boonie. Get your skinny arse down there pronto.' The Ragman gestured towards the steps and, fearing that another shove might send him tumbling off the edge, JD did as he was told. Putting one foot gingerly onto the top step, and keeping close against the steep side of the Pit, he set off down. Step after careful step he climbed down, the Ragman close behind. When he reached the flap he put out his hand and pulled it aside. A blast of hot, stagnant air hit him and beyond, everything was darkness. JD swallowed, this was getting worse. He turned but the Ragman pushed him again. The only way was down; down into the pitch black. He felt the heavy breath of the Ragman on his neck and wanted to whimper, he wanted to be anywhere other than where he was, but with the horrible shambling man so close behind he had no choice. The flap fell back behind them, shutting out the daylight.

Beneath the black dome, no light at all penetrated the intense, dark world that JD now faced. As he stepped down into the all-consuming darkness he had an awful feeling he might never see daylight ever again.

Fifteen

The Faller

For every downward step JD took the pit grew hotter and more foul-smelling. But down he went, struggling from one deep, dirt step to the next, keeping his back close to the wall for fear of falling into the abyss below.

Bit by bit, JD felt his eyes getting used to the darkness and found it was not as completely black as he'd first imagined. First off, he saw a single light, a tiny, wavering flame close to the step where he stood. Then he noticed another, then two more and soon there were lots of sharp, little lights flickering all around him, small candles set into the sides of the pit. As he climbed lower JD could see that the lights were ranged along narrow galleries, long winding ledges which spiralled down to somewhere far below. He stopped for a moment to catch his breath and to try to understand where he was. Over the sound of his own breathing and the curses from the ragged man a few steps above he thought he could hear scraping, a rhythmic, metal-on-stone sound. Holding his breath, he listened, trying to work out what was making the noise. It seemed like hundreds of tired insects were all calling to each other, some close by and some far away.

JD peered into the darkness. On the nearest gallery not two paces from where he stood he saw a tiny, crouched figure, a dirt-caked child, scraping at the sides of the pit. Beyond him was another, kneeling with his face close to the steep side, his thin, bare arms working up and down. JD began to understand. Throughout the great hole where the lights flickered there were many more narrow ledges each filled with skinny kids all crouched against the walls, all scraping away, each with only his little candle marking his spot. It was eerie to think of all those small people, balanced precariously on narrow, winding galleries, but in a way JD found it kind of comforting to find that he was not alone.

JD stared at the boy working close by. He was caked in grime; his face, his hands, his arms and clothes were all stiff with red dust, and when the thin figure turned towards him, JD was shocked. The child's eyes were sunk so deep into his face that only the occasional glint of candlelight told him that he had eyes at all. JD shuddered. The whole pit must be full of emaciated kids, all crouched on their narrow ledges, all scraping and digging at the hard-packed dirt. Is this how I'm goin' to end up? JD thought. Balanced on a narrow ledge high above a dark, stinkin' void, scrapin' at dirt walls?

He turned his eyes away, scared at the prospect, but now he found himself staring at something worse. A great cone of shining black plastic filled the space in the centre of the Pit, dipping down from high above, hanging like some evil lung in the centre of the great hole.

'You, kid, get moving before I kick you down.'

JD felt a rush of air as a boot swung past his head. Whatever fate had in store for him he didn't want it to begin with a kick in the head and a long fall to the bottom of the Pit, so he started off down once more.

Step after step he descended and soon began to wonder if the Pit had a bottom at all or if the steps just went on and on, never reaching anywhere, just steps after steps. But down he went, the Ragman cursing him from above, past gallery after dim gallery, past rows of silent children scraping away at the Pit face.

Just when JD was on the point of summoning up the courage to ask how much further he had to go, he reached the bottom. He felt flat ground under his bare feet and took a cautious pace away from the wall. He looked up and saw looming above him the shining black cone, extending wider and wider the higher it went. Its towering

132

presence was overwhelming, like something from a terrible dream; a thing that could never exist in real life and yet it did.

Aqua had spoken of the Pits as a place too fearful to describe and now JD knew why. It seemed such a short time back he'd been thinking about a new life of freedom and laughter with his new friend and now he was heavy with despair. It seemed that the mighty cone was bearing down on him, squeezing away any tiny ray of hope that still flickered inside him. JD couldn't stop staring at it, hanging there, so wide high up, narrowing down into a kind of pipe at the bottom which passed through a big metal ring. Close to where he stood heavy ropes spread out from the ring, stretching down to be lashed around great metal stakes driven into the ground.

When the Ragman eased himself down from the last step he lurched towards JD. 'So, you've never been down a Pit before, eh? You look too old to have avoided it. Where have you been?'

JD didn't answer, just shrugged.

The Ragman jabbed him in the shoulder. 'Speak up, boy,' he snapped. 'Answer me. Where have you been?'

JD rode the blow and stood his ground. Something seemed to have clicked inside him and out of his despair, anger began to rear up and he welcomed it like an old friend.

'I ain't been nowhere,' he said. 'I just been at the Farm.'

The Ragman stared hard into JD's face and jabbed him again. 'And I say you ain't. You don't look like a Farm kid. You don't talk like a Farm kid and anyways, I can tell by your eyes you ain't a Farm kid. They ain't big and round like them. I reckon you're from the outside. You're a Boonie, ain't you?'

'What if I am?' JD said belligerently. 'What if I am a Boonie? What's the difference?'

'I don't like Boonies, that's the difference. Boonies think they don't have to work. Boonies think they can do what they like. Boonies is trouble. That's what.'

The filthy man wiped his mouth with the back of his hand, leaving a pale streak across his face. JD saw a hard glint in the narrow, slit eyes and began to wonder if he'd been too smart. Maybe he should have stuck with his first instinct and shut his mouth but it was too late now.

The Ragman studied JD hard but although he still felt scared inside, JD stared back. He met the Ragman's eyes with his and set his face. Sure, inside he was scared, real scared, but he wasn't goin' to show it, not to some filthy old guy who lived down a hole in the ground anyways.

The Ragman sneered, he licked his lips and cleared his throat and JD steeled himself, hoping he could cope with what was coming next. But before the man could begin, a dull thud shook the ground. The Ragman spun around. Behind him, a dark bundle lay in a heap by the wall.

'A faller. A faller,' came a shout from above and soon voices were coming from all around. 'A faller. A faller.'

Ragged boys scrambled about in the candlelight. Some even jumped from the galleries and in no time at all a tight bunch of them were on the Pit floor, pulling at the bundle, fighting each other and tearing at its clothes. JD backed away but the Ragman shambled over to the shape as quickly as his feet could carry him and began beating at the crowd with his fists.

'Get back. Get back, you scum. Get back to work,' he growled. 'Leave him be. Get back to work.'

But the boys took no notice. Despite the blows the old man rained onto their backs, they continued tearing at the bundle and all the while more boys dropped down from above to join the melee.

JD stepped back from the twisting mass of kids as they screamed, scratched and tore at each other. He was shocked at their frenzy, their pulling and tearing at the fallen child.

Then a cry went up: 'He's got it. He's got it. Give it here. I saw him first . . .'

Two or three boys, it was hard to tell how many, rolled on the ground, fighting in the dust, punching and scratching at each other, so entwined that JD could not make out one boy from another. The fighting, spitting bundle of arms and legs rolled in a tangle towards JD who recoiled, stunned by the brutality. He looked around, searching for some way of escaping the dreadful sight, but just then a tall, straight boy stepped out from the shadows from behind him.

He was much taller than JD, less caked in dust than the others. His clothes were smart and well cut, his highly polished black knee-boots gleamed in the candlelight and, JD noticed, even his hands were clean. The boy stood erect and surveyed the scene before him with a kind of haughty indifference and then, without a word, he reached into the scrum that scuffled at his feet, lifted one of the fighters clear off the ground and threw him aside.

'Get away,' he spat.

The boy turned, his round eyes flashing. He pulled back his arm ready to strike out but stopped, frozen in mid-punch. He dropped his fist and lowered his head and shoulders. With an envious glance towards the writhing boys still fighting at the newcomer's feet, he slouched away into the shadows.

The tall boy stepped between the remaining fighters, put a large booted foot on the neck of one and grabbed the other by an ear.

'Give it here,' he said, his voice cold and mean, and in an instant the two boys stopped fighting.

With a flick of his arm the older boy threw one squirming kid aside. He crashed to the ground, rolled over and over then slowly rose to his feet. He crouched, facing the tall boy, hatred in his face. JD thought he was going to fling himself straight back at his assailant; he flexed his hands into fists then spread his fingers wide, breathing heavily all the time. But then his shoulders dropped too and taking one last, long look at his attacker he slunk away.

All the while the tall boy's foot pressed onto the neck of the remaining fighter and he kept it there until the boy lay still.

'Hand it over,' the tall boy said quietly.

'I ain't got nothing –' But the end of the sentence was lost in a choking grunt as the tall boy's shiny boot pressed harder.

'Hand it over,' he spat through clenched teeth.

The kid on the ground, his face twisted in pain, reached into his clothes and pulled out a metal tube.

The tall boy snatched it, lifted his foot from his victim's neck and kicked him aside.

JD watched the victor unscrew the cap and put the tube to his lips. In the darkness hundreds of envious eyes were on him, boys licking their dry lips, enjoying the drink in their imaginations but after a few moments the tall boy shook the tube, muttered something under his breath then threw it across the Pit floor.

'Pah! Empty,' he muttered. 'You'd have thought the little bastard would leave a few drops.' He walked over to the crumpled body of the fallen child and poked it with his toe. 'Bastard,' he said and turned away.

Despite the humid atmosphere JD felt cold. He couldn't believe his eyes. Children tearing at the body of a dead comrade, scavenging for a few drops of water. He knew the pain of thirst but hoped he'd never stoop so low as to ransack a corpse just so's he could wet his lips. He shivered and looked up. Boys were clambering back to the galleries and along the narrow ledges, returning to their work.

'Hey! Boonie. Come here.'

The Ragman and the tall boy were standing together and JD walked towards them.

'Right,' the man said. 'This is Bratby, he's your Senior. You do as he says. Savvy?'

JD looked up into the smirking face of the young man and felt his sharp, black eyes boring into him, seeing right inside, delving into his mind, working out what he was thinking. This was no Farm kid, JD thought. This guy is evil.

'You take the place of that faller,' Bratby said quietly. 'He was on the third tier. Now, go and see if his scraper came down with him,' he added, pointing to the dead boy sprawled on the dirt floor.

JD went over to where the body lay, twisted and half stripped from the attack. He searched half-heartedly, uncomfortable in his task, not knowing what a scraper was but guessing he'd know one if he saw it. He checked all around the body but there was nothing to be found. JD turned around and spread his hands.

138

'Look underneath, stupid. He probably fell on it.'

JD turned back to the body. It lay face down, one arm reaching out, as if for help. JD put out a hand and touched the fallen boy's shoulder then drew back.

'Look underneath him, you fool,' Bratby shouted. 'He won't hurt you. He's dead.'

JD tried again. Steeling himself, he gripped the bony shoulder of the dead boy and pulled. The body flopped over onto JD's feet and two blank round eyes stared up at him. JD's jaw dropped open. The child was even younger than him. Beneath the layer of red dust, the little face was tiny, with a high forehead and button nose. This ain't more than just a baby, he thought, kneeling down beside the limp little body. The soft face with its sunken cheeks seemed to smile at him, its closed lips turned up at the ends. JD thought he looked pleased to be dead.

Reaching across the tiny corpse, JD probed underneath until his fingers touched something hard and cold. Grasping it, he pulled out a broad strip of flat metal.

'Good,' Bratby said. 'Now collect up his tube and keep it safe. Without an empty you won't get your rations this evening. Now get up to where he came from and start work.'

JD picked up the dead boy's water tube, found the cap and screwed the two pieces together. Tucking it into his dungarees, he climbed the steps to the third level and crawled out onto the narrow gallery. He had to ease past several other boys but they paid him no heed, they just scraped mindlessly at the dirt sides of the pit. When he came to a space between two candles JD knelt down like the others and began to work at the Pit face, running the metal blade against the hard-packed dirt.

A few minutes later he risked a look down. Below him, two boys had picked up the dead body and were dragging it along behind them. As they began to carry the dead boy up the steps JD wondered how long it would be before his thin little body would fall from the gallery to be fought over by the others. How long before he was hauled up the steps to be dumped somewhere among the hills of red dirt?

Sixteen

Down Below

As far as JD could tell, only one other boy died that day.

After everything that had happened to him JD was pretty tired, and when a shrill whistle sounded from the Pit floor and all the scraping stopped he was mighty relieved. All the boys began to crawl along the galleries towards the steps and one by one climbed down to the Pit floor where they stood in a long line. JD did not know what was happening but he followed and took a place in the line.

Nobody said a word and all JD could hear were the feet of boys on the high galleries padding down the steps. Then a low call came from somewhere near the top of the Pit and everybody looked up.

'Up here,' came a voice. 'A dead one up here.'

JD peered into the darkness and could just make out two boys edging along one of the galleries. Ahead of them, a figure crouched against the wall. It looked like it was working, arms raised up, hands close together but it was quite still, frozen in position. JD watched as the two boys closed in. When they reached the dead boy they quickly searched his clothes. The candlelight glinted on a metal tube they pulled from his rags.

'Throw that down here,' Bratby commanded.

'No good,' a voice echoed from the high gallery. 'It's empty.'

'Throw it down anyway,' the Senior called.

JD heard, everybody heard, the cap being unscrewed and saw the two boys huddle together. The empty tube was quickly thrown down, bouncing with a hollow sound onto the dirt floor, but everybody knew that those two boys had shared the last sip of the dead one's water.

The boy next to JD sucked his dry lips noisily. 'Bratby won't like that,' he whispered. 'That's his by right.'

A short while later the whistle blew again. Long and piercing, it was followed by a rumble from high above. JD looked up to see long ropes tumbling down the sides of the Pit, their ends thudding onto the dirt floor.

'What's going on?' JD asked the boy who had spoken to him.

The boy just stared back, his face blank. Then the whistle blew again and all the boys ran to the ropes, taking up the ends. JD was swept along with them and pretty soon found himself in a line of kids all holding onto a rope at the edge of the Pit.

The Ragman appeared and stood in the centre of the floor, right under the big shiny cone. Next to him stood Bratby and spaced around the point of the cone two more older boys worked at the ropes, tying them to something on the ground. When they were finished they too came and stood near the Ragman, nodding to him as they arrived. The Ragman took a deep breath; his cheeks puffed out and he blew a long, piercing whistle which echoed around the pit. This seemed to be a sign for all the boys to pull on their ropes and JD joined in, hauling hand over hand. He felt a strain come onto the rope, heard a rustle from the centre of the pit and over his shoulder saw a large curtain of shiny black material rising up around the cone. The boys pulled and the curtain rose higher, spreading out towards the walls of the pit, forming a wider flatter cone around the base of the big one.

Another whistle and the pulling stopped. The boys nearest the wall tied their ropes into metal rings in the side of the pit. Around the bottom of the great cone now hung a spout, a kind of tube dangling just above the pit floor and some boys dragged a deep trough to put underneath it.

The next time the Ragman whistled all the boys turned around, filed to the steps and began to climb. JD mingled in. Nobody spoke; the long, straggling line of boys just tramped up the dirt steps, each keeping a pace or two behind the one in front, each with their heads bowed, all climbing wearily upwards. Halfway up, JD paused and looked back at the tall, shiny cone hanging in the centre of the pit and its wide skirt way below right around its base. It reminded him of something but the next boy in the line closed up behind him before he could work it out, so JD turned and trudged up the steps just like all the others, another anonymous kid at the end of his first day's work in the Pits.

At the surface the sun was just dipping below the horizon. The air was cooler and JD breathed in gratefully. The line of kids tramped away from the Pit and JD followed, his head down, his eyes on the boy in front. They filed away in a long winding stream, weaving their way between great pyramids of dirt. Pretty soon they passed other Pits from which more long lines of boys traipsed around the guy-ropes and off between the spoil heaps. JD's column joined onto another and soon hundreds of boys were shuffling through the dust, around yet more Pits, past yet more endless mountains of red dirt.

They trudged along until it was nearly dark, joining and being joined by other streams of weary kids, and then finally they drew clear of the scarred landscape and onto a flat, featureless plain. When he saw rows of shacks ahead, low and dark against the skyline, JD thought they were heading back to the Farm and the thought of seeing Aqua cheered him for a moment, but it didn't take long for him to work out that they'd been walking in the wrong direction.

JD's column shuffled up to one of the buildings where two Seniors stood at the door. One held a clipboard and there was a big flat tank between them. As each boy arrived he handed over his water tube and mumbled something. The tube was dipped into the tank and given back. JD strained to hear what the boys were saying and it was not until the one in front said: 'Three-Seven-Seven' that he understood. They were giving their numbers. He remembered the guard saying he should ask for one or he'd get no water. JD began to panic. He looked up at the Senior with the clipboard and he just knew he was waiting for him to make a mistake. But he wasn't, he was looking at the ceiling, completely uninterested and bored.

'Nine-Six-Six,' JD mumbled. Aqua's number had sprung into his head. He handed over the tube; the other Senior dipped it into the tank and handed it back. JD shuffled inside.

The shack was bare. No wire fences or pens this time, no tiers of bunks; there was nothing, just a vast empty space. As the boys filed in, each sank to the floor and propped his tired back against a wall. They groaned like old men as they settled themselves down along each side.

JD chose a spot and lowered himself to the floor. Others passed him and flopped down until two long rows of silent, exhausted boys faced each other across the hard, empty floor. The only sound was of screw caps being turned and a quiet sip-sipping as day-long thirsts were quenched.

JD smiled at one of his neighbours but the boy didn't return his smile so JD drank a mouthful of water from his tube, closed his eyes and sank into his thoughts. Row upon row of blank-faced slaves floated before him, scraping at walls while dead children tumbled all around. JD snapped his eyes open and tried to blink away the nightmare. When he rested again he forced himself to think of something else and in his mind's eye he strayed back to the Farm, but before he knew it he was creeping into a Brooder and peeking over a high wall. He screwed his eyes up tight and grunted, forcing the memory away. The only thing that gave him any peace was the vision of Aqua, her fists bunched under her chin, chattering away about running off to the Dry Marsh. He clung to that thought, embellishing it, drawing it out into a stream of happy days among the sawgrass back home, laughing and playing far away from Cities, Farms, Brooders and Pits. He imagined himself and Aqua, living in a shack just like Ma and Pa back when life had been good, back when Pa was alive and his Ma still loved him.

146

JD awoke with a start. His dreams were gone and all around him boys were standing up, moving to the centre of the shack and forming into a line facing the door. JD rubbed the sleep from his eyes, struggled to his feet and joined them. They all stood in silence.

'What's happening?' JD asked the boy behind him.

The boy drew back, almost stepping on the child behind him, but didn't answer.

JD was getting pretty fed up with all the silence and blank stares. He wanted to shout out and ask if anybody could say something, anything. The only emotion he'd seen from any of these miserable wretches was when some of them chose to fight each other over an empty water tube. Aside from that they were like zombies, but just as he was thinking about confronting them the door in the end of the shack slid back, the line closed up and JD felt the boy behind pressing into his back. The line shuffled forward, pushing and shoving, everybody keen to get out. Surely, JD thought, they can't be this eager to get back to the pit.

At the doorway Bratby counted under his breath, touching each boy on the head as he passed. JD slouched forward, Bratby touched his head and he stepped out into the early morning light. Could he have slept right through? It seemed only moments before he'd closed his eyes.

Up in front the line had broken and all the boys had

started to run towards another long shack so JD set off after them.

The door of the shack stood open and the boys streamed in, all holding out their water tubes. JD guessed that they were to be given a new ration and quickly swallowed what was left in his own tube. At the end of the shack each boy offered up his tube to one of the Seniors who stood by the familiar metal tank. JD followed suit and had a full tube of water put into his hand. He couldn't believe his luck. Never before in his short life had water been so easy to come by. He took a tiny sip before screwing back the cap and hiding the tube in his dungarees.

When another queue began forming, JD joined it and once more he found himself shuffling forward. When his turn came he was given a large chunk of something soft, white and porous. He looked at it, felt it and sniffed it. It was squashy, elastic and smelled of nothing. JD looked around. His fellow slaves were all munching and it was only then that he realised that what he held in his hand was some kind of food. He took a bite, chewed a mouthful into a soggy ball which stuck to the roof of his mouth. He swallowed and the glutinous mass travelled down his throat in a lump. No sooner had the ball of stodge reached his stomach than he felt a great need for more and began to chew hungrily, biting off pieces of the soft white stuff . The more he ate the hungrier he seemed to get and he didn't pause until every scrap had gone. OK, he thought, but he yearned for a couple of fresh crickets.

Pretty soon the line formed up again and JD wondered what was coming next. One of the Seniors took up position at the head and led the boys out of the shack. Outside they turned and set off towards the line of dirt pyramids on the horizon. The hand-outs were over and it was back to work.

Back among the spoil heaps, boys peeled off the line and climbed down steps at each Pit to begin their next, perhaps their last, day's toil underground.

JD found himself towards the front of his line when it stopped. The Senior at the head climbed down below the rim, pulled back the flap and called the boys forward. JD was in the first group, fifth boy from the front, but just as he went to step down the boy behind slipped past and almost dived through the flap. JD was puzzled but let him go. Why, he thought, why would someone rush to get into that awful place? He backed off and stood with the others until they too were called forward and filed through the flap.

In the darkness the tramp of footsteps echoed around the Pit. Only one candle burned at each level, the flickering light reflecting on the shiny cone hanging in the centre of the pit. At the bottom, the Ragman stood just where he'd been the night before and JD wondered if he stayed underground all night. There was no sign of the five boys who had been so keen to get to work and JD wondered what had happened to them.

The Senior waved JD and some others down to where the Ragman stood, while the rest made their way along the galleries. Three boys were detailed off to carry fresh candles and soon tiny lights flickered all around the pit. JD stayed on the Pit floor with the others and as the light intensified he saw that the black cone had a kind of sheen that had not been there the night before. Thousands of tiny droplets sparkled in the candlelight. There's water on it, JD thought. He licked his lips and touched the cool tube hidden in his clothes. The sight of so much water was making him thirsty and he wondered if he could risk taking a drink but decided against it. Instead he watched as the droplets combined, running down the cone in rivulets until they plopped and splashed into the skirt hauled up around the base and dribbled into the tank below.

In his daydream of water JD didn't notice the other kids clustering around the Ragman until the sound of their voices made him look up. The Ragman was holding coils of rope and handing them out until teams of three boys each held a rope's end, each rope leading away to the side of the pit where it passed through a pulley block and stretched upwards. JD followed a rope with his eyes, up and up to where it passed through another block just below the rim of the pit and where a single child stood balanced on a high ledge, fastened into a sort of harness which was attached to the rope. Around the high ledge five boys stood, all harnessed up and waiting for something to happen.

'Take the weight,' the Ragman called and the boys on the Pit floor pulled on their ropes and as they pulled the tiny figures on the high gallery were lifted up and swung into the air. The ground crew heaved and soon the harnessed boys were right up into the roof of the pit, hard against the top of the cone. At the word from the Ragman the ropes were eased and the harnessed boys came slowly down, swinging from side to side against the shiny black material, scraping the water drops with their hands, shepherding them down into the funnel. Water cascaded into the tank below and JD watched the lucky high riders pressing themselves against the wet surface, licking their hands and laughing. Now he understood why the boy behind him had been so keen to be among the first five into the pit. He must be one of the lucky ones bouncing off the cone right now, soaked in water, grinning and yelping with pleasure. It was the first time JD had seen anyone actually smiling since he'd arrived and by the time the harnessed boys were back on the ground they were grinning from ear to ear, licking their arms and hands for all they were worth. JD reckoned he'd have a try for that job just as soon as he could.

The next task was lowering the skirt and it was then that

JD noticed the pipe. A fat hose was attached to the container under the spout and led away to the side of the Pit, where it disappeared into the wall. The three Senior boys disconnected the pipe and drained it into a shallow container before it was capped and tidied away. When the skirt came down it was again the three Seniors who folded it away, draining a few more drops of water into the small container. This, JD figured, was their own private supply.

He was finally piecing everything together. A great pit had been dug and a sheet of some shiny material hung over it, pulled down in the centre, and in his mind JD could hear Godrum telling him how water could be harvested from the ground; the secret of life, he'd called it. They even called 'em Godrum Stills, he remembered the old man saying. I showed 'em, he'd said, and now they hate me for it.

Deep underground, looking up at the great shining cone, JD finally understood. The only thing he didn't understand was why hundreds of boys had to work themselves to death scraping the sides.

Seventeen

The Plan

All through that day and through those that followed JD
worked away at the Pit walls. He scraped at the dry, packed
surface until fresh, dark soil showed through. Each evening
he joined in the ritual of rigging the spout, dragging out
the collection tray and attaching the hosepipe, and each
morning five lucky ones cleaned down the cone, gathering
their few drops of extra water as a reward.

At evening drink ration and at night JD joined the rest
of the slaves and at dawn each day he lined up just like
them for his morning slab of food. Each day they worked
and each day some died. Fresh faces appeared, brought
from the Farm to replace those who had gone, and so the
days passed by. The three Senior boys grew bigger and
stronger, taking food and water from the bodies of the
fallers, while the rest toiled and grew weaker. But there was

no complaint; all the poor wretches accepted their lot, working until they got too weak and it was their turn to topple from the ledge and crash, lifeless, onto the floor below. All except one.

JD had a plan. He made it seem like he was working but in fact he scraped very little. He moved his hands in time with the others but he saved his energy by barely touching the sides. It took a while for him to conquer the lethargy that had eaten him up since Ma's rejection but he did it. Despite his tiredness, after a while he felt the old JD growing back inside him; the tough JD from the Dry Marsh, the kid who wouldn't quit. It was then that the plan started to grow and he began to think about how he could escape the drudgery and certain death of the Pit. Carefully, he watched what went on around him, working out the routines and noticing when the system fell down. Like how he noticed nobody paid no heed to numbers. He'd play games by making up a different number for himself each day and mumbling it to the Senior with the clipboard. Stupid kid never noticed.

At night he tried to stay awake as long as he could, thinking of everything that had happened that day, searching for some way he could slip away. When tiredness finally got the better of him and he could think no more he conjured up his memories of the old days on the Dry Marsh with Pa. Somehow the days with Ma had gone.

Late one night, sitting in the darkness and going over everything he'd learned, JD began to feel uneasy. Something told him he was being watched. He looked towards the door at the end of the shack, expecting to see one of the Seniors or even a Pig, but nothing moved. He looked at the boys opposite, searching from one crumpled figure to the next, but they were all slumped down, their heads on their knees, their arms over their faces. He turned from side to side and still saw nothing, but the uneasy feeling just wouldn't go away.

He scolded himself for having such a vivid imagination and settled back, resting his head on the wall. Just then he saw a movement out of the corner of his eye and turned his head quickly. But there was nothing, just a row of sleeping kids, the sound of their breathing filling the humid air.

JD put his head back once more, stretched out his legs and closed his eyes, then, without warning, he quickly turned to his left and this time he did see something. The boy next to him was watching him, his big round eyes staring, but as JD turned he screwed them up and feigned sleep. It was too late though. He knew he'd been caught and opened his eyes again, blinked and focused them on JD.

JD looked back. 'Hello,' he whispered.

At first the boy looked confused, but after a while his lips opened and formed a silent word in response.

'My name's JD,' JD said. 'What's yours?'

The boy said something so quietly that JD couldn't understand him. He turned on one elbow and leaned closer but the boy pulled back.

'I ain't gonna hurt you,' JD whispered. 'I just want to know your name.'

The boy blinked. 'Three-Seven-Seven,' he said at last.

'Hello, Three-Seven-Seven,' JD said. 'Why're you watchin' me?'

Three-Seven-Seven said nothing. The simple exchange of names seemed about all he could cope with. He looked down and picked at his knees with his index finger and when JD tried to ask more questions, Three-Seven-Seven just gave a gentle smile and closed his eyes.

Next night JD tried again but apart from the simple greeting, the boy would not talk. Then, just as JD closed his own eyes and returned to his thoughts, a tiny voice from the darkness said:

'I wish I was back on the Farm.'

Aware that eye contact seemed to frighten Three-Seven-Seven, JD whispered without turning. 'Why?' he said. 'Did you like it there?'

'Mmmm.'

'What did you like about it?' JD asked.

'Friends. Playtime and not having to go down the Pit,' Three-Seven-Seven said, sighing deeply.

'Don't you have any friends here?' JD said.

'No. Not any more. My friend Three-Six-One died. Then you came.'

JD thought about this. Three-Six-One must have been the boy who fell on that first day and in whose place he now worked. He wondered how to respond, afraid that he might be accused of taking his friend's place, but he needn't have worried, Three-Seven-Seven had something else on his mind.

'Why aren't you like us?' he whispered. 'What's wrong with your eyes?'

'Ain't nothin' wrong with my eyes. I just don't look like you Farm boys, that's all.'

If JD had hoped for more he was disappointed because nothing but silence followed this brief exchange and moments later his neighbour's regular breathing told him he'd gone to sleep. But sleep did not come for JD. The brief conversation had set his mind working, thinking about everything as he slouched in the darkness of the sleep shack.

Some nights he'd heard boys mumble in their sleep, once or twice there had been a cry in the night but mainly there was just the low regular sound of breathing. Once, one of the tiny bodies had not risen in the morning. Slumped against the wall, it looked like it was still asleep, eyes closed and head down. Other boys walked past, stepping over the thin, lifeless legs and joining the line down the centre of the shack. By nightfall the corpse had gone.

The first faller had shocked JD but soon he, just like all

the other Pit boys, became hardened to the sight of death. But he always remembered the smile on the face of the first faller, the boy he now knew to be Three-Six-One, and in the night JD thought about him being led away hand in hand with death to a place where he could play, free from the Pits. Then it didn't seem too bad.

Thinking about the other kids set JD to wondering who would be next and something made him glance across at Three-Seven-Seven. When JD had first come to the Pit, Three-Seven-Seven had been strong and climbed easily, springing from step to step without effort. But he worked hard, scraping noisily all day, sometimes grunting with the effort, stopping only rarely to drink from his tube, making his water last all day. But after a while Three-Seven-Seven had begun to look weaker. Even through the layers of red dust JD could tell he was beginning to suffer. His eyes sank more deeply into his head and the bones of his eye sockets became sharp and dark. He gave up any attempt to conserve his water, often drinking it all down as soon as it was handed out, then panting as he scraped, his breath rasping against the dry walls of his throat.

Three-Seven-Seven saved his courage for the darkness, and the routine of short conversations between the two boys grew as time went by. Once, Three-Seven-Seven asked what JD had meant by saying he hadn't come from the Farm. JD explained about the Dry Marsh but this seemed to confuse and upset his little friend, who fell silent and turned away. Nevertheless, Three-Seven-Seven regularly asked the same things.

'Where do you come from? Why aren't you like the rest of us?'

Over the course of many nights JD tried to explain how he'd lived far away with his Pa where he'd played in the dust and sawgrass and watched the stars in the evening before going to his own bed in his own room in his own shack.

Three-Seven-Seven drank in JD's stories like they were a fresh, cool tube of water until, when he could stay awake no longer, he fell asleep with a tiny smile playing at the corners of his dust-caked mouth.

But after a while Three-Seven-Seven stopped asking questions. He was so tired and worn out he just fell against the wall as soon as the sleep shack door rolled shut. If he woke in the darkness and sensed that JD was awake too, instead of asking questions he'd just say, 'Tell me about the Dry Marsh, JD,' and would lie with his eyes closed, listening to stories about catching crickets and going with Pa to see a tree.

The night Three-Seven-Seven stopped asking about the Dry Marsh was when JD decided he really had to do something about getting away. He knew he couldn't just run, he'd soon get caught. He'd also figured he'd need help to get back through the City and that made him think of Aqua. She knew her way and had said she wanted to break out too. JD reckoned that if he could just get back to the Farm and find Aqua, together they'd stand a pretty good chance. He smiled to himself; his idea was taking shape. Yes, Aqua would show him the way through the City and how to avoid the sirens and the Silver Men. They could lie low until the time was right then mingle in with some Boonies to get across the bridge and out through the Gate. Then, all they had to do was follow the Old Road and in a day or so they'd be at the Dry Marsh.

At first the idea had come to him in snatches, disjointed visions of the two of them running hand in hand through empty streets or along the Old Road, but as the nights passed JD's mind joined them up until he could see it all in his imagination. The night it all came together he felt himself filled with a new calm. It wasn't just a dream no more, it was a plan.

Next day, scraping lightly at the Pit wall, JD's head was buzzing. He ignored the shouts from the Pit floor, the growls of the Seniors urging them to work harder, and when a boy fell from one of the high galleries he gave a grim smile. Too soon, he thought, too early in the day; the time has got to be right. Shuffling back to the sleep shack that night he told himself to be patient. His time would come.

Eighteen

Escape

It was a day like any other day. JD worked away in the hot, airless Pit. Two boys fell and a group of new kids, small, round-faced and scared, huddled together on the Pit floor. JD watched out of the corner of his eye as Bratby lectured them like he'd lectured him on his first day. He pulled a face. He'd seen so many clean little boys arrive at the Pit, watched them become haggard and thick with dirt, moving on through their short lives so quickly. JD shook his head and looked down at his hands, gripping the metal scraper. Sharp bones showed through his skin and try as he had to conserve his strength, he knew he didn't climb the steps with anything like the old zip he'd had before. He had to get away while he still had his strength and it had to be soon. If he waited too long he'd soon be like all the others, a worked-out skeleton drained of energy, no hope, just waiting for death and that last crashing fall.

When it happened it was just before the signal for raising the skirt. The Ragman had gathered the Seniors to him and was looking up when JD heard Three-Seven-Seven slump down. His scraper fell out of his hands and JD saw him fumble in his clothes, searching for his water tube. JD shuffled along to where his friend lay gasping on the narrow ledge and leaning down, he gathered the little boy up and propped him on his arm. Three-Seven-Seven opened his eyes and smiled as JD reached into the bundle of rags and bony limbs, found the water tube and gave it to him. But Three-Seven-Seven didn't have the strength to unscrew the cap and when JD tried to help, the boy found some extra strength from somewhere and clutched the precious tube close to him, the bones of his thin fingers showing white in the candlelight.

JD smiled to show he wasn't trying to steal the water and at last the little boy's fingers relaxed. JD took the water tube, unscrewed the cap and held it to his friend's mouth. The boy breathed out noisily and let JD touch his cracked lips with the water. He gasped as it trickled down his throat and, looking up at JD, he gave a little cough.

'Tell me about the Dry Marsh, JD,' he croaked.

JD looked around. He knew that many eyes were on him but when Three-Seven-Seven's bony little fingers closed on his he cleared his throat and began his friend's favourite story: the day Pa found the crab. He'd done no more than whisper the first familiar words of the tale when Three-Seven-Seven slumped back, his eyes closed. Quietly, JD spun out the yarn.

Just when he reached the part where Ma put the crab into the pot, Three-Seven-Seven gave a deep sigh and held out his tube. JD unscrewed the cap ready to wet the boy's lips when his breath caught in his throat. A hollow rattle came from somewhere deep inside the tiny, dried-out little body, it twitched and Three-Seven-Seven's head fell back. Looking down into his dull black eyes, JD knew that no amount of water would help the boy now.

Carefully, he laid the body onto the ground and, with only a passing pang of guilt, poured the remains of the dead boy's ration into his own tube, screwed on the cap and tucked the empty tube inside Three-Seven-Seven's clothes.

At the end of the day when a shrill whistle rent the dusty air, JD waved a hand at Bratby, who was watching from below. The Senior strode up the steps, pushing his way through the stream of boys leaving the gallery, and came to where JD knelt next to Three-Seven-Seven.

The tall Senior looked down dispassionately. 'Is he dead?'

JD nodded.

'Give me his tube,' Bratby snapped.

JD put his hand into Three-Seven-Seven's clothing and pulled out the empty container.

'I think it's empty,' JD said quietly. 'He's been at it all day.'

Bratby shook the tube. 'Bastard,' he said but tucked it into his pocket anyhow. 'What's his number?' he snapped.

'Three-Seven-Seven,' JD said.

'OK. Get one of the others and take him out. Dump him in an empty Pit then get back here pronto. I don't want stragglers and if you're late you'll get no water. Savvy?'

JD nodded and when Bratby turned away he allowed himself a grim smile. He had a full tube inside his dungarees and his plan was starting to work out. Yeah, he thought, I savvy.

The boys on the gallery skirted around JD and stepped over Three-Seven-Seven's crumpled body without paying either any heed but JD caught hold of the last one.

'Bratby said for you to help me get this one out.'

The boy stared first at JD then at the retreating backs of the others. He pulled his hand away and tried to brush past but JD grabbed him again.

'Help me or I'll call Bratby.'

The boy stood, looking beyond JD, uncertain what to do.

'Help me get him up the steps and I'll take him away

on my own,' JD said, but still the boy stood, his eyes darting between JD and the steps. 'If you don't help I'll tell Bratby you disobeyed him and you'll get no water, you know that.'

The boy's shoulders dropped; he gave one last look down, turned to JD and blinked. The plan was still alive.

'Catch hold that end and we'll slide him along,' JD ordered, surprised at how assured his voice sounded when his heart was beating so fast. 'Come on,' he urged. He was impatient to get going.

The boy was still reluctant to help but when JD put his hands under Three-Seven-Seven's shoulders he lifted the dead boy's knees, and the two set off. The steps were steep and the body was awkward so it took some time to get to the surface but at last they pushed through the flap and out into the fading light.

'Right,' JD said after they'd struggled up the last few steps and laid the body down. 'You get back down below.'

But the round-eyed boy didn't move. He seemed confused and looked first one way then the other. JD shook his head. These Farm kids are so dumb, he thought. Unless they've got a line to follow they don't know what to do.

'Go on. Shoo! Get back down there. Go join the others.' JD pointed to the flap but still the boy didn't seem to want to go.

'Get out,' JD shouted, glaring at the boy. 'Get away. Get back down the Pit.'

He stepped right up to him, raised a fist and drew back his arm. Only then did the boy turn and flee, dropping quickly out of sight beneath the black cover. JD heard the scuffle of his feet as he scurried down the steps, back to the security of the line.

Alone again, JD stared at the bundle of rags at his feet. A shaft of pale light fell across the little body while high above, the evening sky glowed livid red. JD shook himself. He had to get on and Three-Seven-Seven had left him a legacy of hope. If there was ever a time for his scheme to work, this was it. This was his chance. It was now or never.

JD rubbed his hands together, braced himself, lifted up the emaciated little body and set off towards the spoil heaps. He needed to get someplace out of sight as quick as he could before the sorry lines of slaves emerged from underground ready to wind their way towards the sleep shacks.

As soon as he was clear of the working Pits with their high stakes and taut wires JD paused to take stock. The angry sun was setting and long shadows grew all around. Putting Three-Seven-Seven's body down, JD climbed a spoil heap and from the top he could see the outline of the City away on the horizon and the tall, light towers and fences of the Farm. Focusing on the third shack from the end, he felt a surge of excitement.

'I said I'd take you to the Dry Marsh, Aqua,' he said

under his breath. 'So you'd better be ready, girl, 'cos I'm a-comin' to do just that.'

Sure of his bearings and keen to get on, JD slid down the heap. Casting around, he saw a hollow in the ground close by where an old Pit had caved in, and picking up Three-Seven-Seven, he walked over to the hole and laid the body in it. He scraped up armfuls of dirt, poured them over his dead friend and when he was finally hidden he smoothed the ground and stepped back. Touching the full drinking tube inside his dungarees, JD looked down.

'Thanks for the water, friend,' he muttered under his breath. 'Sorry you didn't make it.'

With a last glance at the hump of dirt, JD turned away. Trotting along between the old spoil heaps he steadily put distance between himself and his Pit. As the daylight began to fade he climbed one of the dusty pyramids and sat down at the top. Lights were coming on over the Farm and looking back, he saw lines of Pit slaves winding their weary way back to the sleep shacks. There was no sign of anybody following him. JD smiled. He'd made it.

Sliding down the spoil heap with hope high in his heart and the layout of the Farm stored in his brain, he strode away. It felt so good to be doing something. He'd soon find his way back, slip under the wire and collect Aqua. The memory of Ma's betrayal still lurked at the back of his mind but he'd shaken off his despair and lethargy; he was back in control. There was to be no more troopin' along with those no-hope kids, no more scrapin' his life away down the Pit; from here on in it was going to be the way he wanted it to be.

He waited until it was dark before clearing the spoil heaps but when the sun had gone and the lightning walked, he scrambled over the last pile of rocks dividing the Pit workings from the plain and set off across the wide open space towards the Farm. Loping along, keeping his eyes ahead but watching out for stray rocks and dangerous hollows, he planned to run as far as he could then creep up to the wire once he got close. For the first time in he didn't know when, things were finally going his way. Then:

'Halt. Stay exactly where you are,' a voice boomed out and blinding white light enveloped him.

JD's blood froze in his veins. He put his hand up to shield his eyes but the light was so bright he could see nothing. The Farm lights were gone and the sky was all blotted out. He couldn't even see his own feet shaking in the dust.

Wheels scrunched over the ground towards him and when he heard the low hum of a motor he recognised it straight away. It was the box. The sound grew louder, the wheels squeaked and the box drew to a halt. JD squinted into the light, trying to see, but it was no good. All he could do was stand still and wait.

And he didn't have to wait long. He heard a metal door swing open and boots hitting the ground. Heavy footsteps crunched towards him and a large hand gripped his shoulder.

'Where do you think you're going?' a deep voice said.

JD thought fast. 'I'm lost,' he said, making his voice crack as if he was about to cry. 'I had to take a body away and bury it,' he added, warming to his story. 'By the time I'd finished it was dark and I couldn't find my way back.'

The man grunted.

'Please, sir,' JD whined. 'Where am I? How can I get back? I must get to my night station or I won't get no water.'

'Come with me,' the man growled and led JD towards the box, pushed him inside and slammed the door shut. The motor whined and the box moved off, leaving JD wedged in a corner, angry and upset all at the same time. If he'd just waited a bit longer, looked around more. How could he have been so stupid? Too much dreamin' and not enough plannin', he thought, but before he could beat himself up any more the box screeched to a halt and he heard the driver's door open. The sound of a scuffle came from outside and before long the back doors opened up and a small body was thrown in. The doors clanged shut and the box was still and dark once more.

JD heard the newcomer shuffle along the floor.

'Hello,' he whispered and the scuffling stopped.

JD listened but all he could hear was breathing. 'Hello,' he said into the darkness. 'Who are you?'

Still no answer, just more shuffling as his fellow captive tried to put as much distance between himself and JD as he could. JD tried again but still there was no response so he sighed and shut up. These people are so stupid, he thought. But I'm sittin' in the box like he is, so what does that make me?

They set off again. The truck swung around in a long circle and speeded up. JD guessed they were patrolling the scrub, on the lookout for more runaways. Several times the box swerved around, came to a halt and another small person was dumped into the back. Each time JD tried to greet the latest captive but always with the same result. Nevertheless he was cheered by the thought that at least some of the kids had the courage to try to get away. Up until then he'd thought he was the only one to have such ambitions.

The truck patrolled for a long time, gathering up kids all the while, until at last it drove straight and steady for a good way before stopping. The back of the truck opened again and this time the box was flooded with light. They had stopped under some yellow lights by a high wire fence, where the latest runaway was pushed inside.

'Let go,' a little voice yelled. 'Let go of me, you stupid

Pig. I wasn't trying to get out –' but the door slammed shut, cutting the tirade short.

'Humph,' was the last word JD heard from the darkness, followed by the sound of somebody sitting down hard. He smiled to himself. From the depths of his despair he'd found new hope.

'Aqua?' he said. 'Aqua, is that you? It's me, JD.'

Nineteen

Fun for Bratby

In the short time it took to get where they were going all
JD was able to learn from Aqua was that she'd been caught
going under the wire. She said it was the second time they'd
caught her so the guard had called the Ratcatcher.

'What's the Ratcatcher?' JD asked.

'This is,' Aqua said.

'What?'

'This truck. It's called the Ratcatcher. It drives around
all night catching kids who try to get away.' There was a
long pause. 'That's why you're here, isn't it?' Aqua said.
Then she said: 'Stupid,' and JD knew she was smiling.

But JD did not have time to enjoy the moment because
the truck jerked to a halt. Inside, in the darkness it seemed
that all the children were holding their breath. Somehow
they all knew this was not just another pick-up. Even Aqua

stopped complaining and the box was ominously silent.

The bar across the back of the truck grated down and the doors swung open. A flashlight speared inside and JD saw Aqua, blinking into the light, her jaw set as defiant as ever. But the others, all very small boys, were clustered together, whimpering in unison. Startled eyes peered from the tangle of arms as they clung to each other.

JD shuffled in front of the little ones and stared into the light. Aqua came to his side.

Despite the light, JD began to make out some shapes outside. He saw the driver who had picked him up, his silly hairstyle silhouetted against the sky, but beside him was a tall familiar shape which made JD's heart drop.

'Oh, there you are, Boonie,' Bratby sneered. 'How nice of you to come back to us.' The tall Senior paused for a moment. 'Now, out you get. I'd like you to meet a friend of mine,' he said, slapping a thin metal wand against his leg. JD stayed put.

'Out, Boonie. Now!' Bratby barked, smashing the steel rod onto the floor of the truck.

Still JD did not move, so the guard reached in and grabbed him by the ankle. Aqua caught hold of his arm and tried to hold him back but she was no match for the guard and JD was dragged along the floor of the box until he fell out at Bratby's feet. The Senior gave him a welcoming kick. JD staggered to his feet and for the first time saw where he was. The sleep shacks sat a short distance away.

'Do you want any of these others?' the guard asked Bratby, nodding towards the frightened bundle of children in the truck.

Bratby sniffed. 'No. They're only Farm kids. Take them to the old man. He'll probably have the lot for breakfast.'

The guard laughed and slammed the door of the truck. JD thought he heard Aqua cry out and her small feet kicking at the door. Then a muffled voice called to him from inside the Ratcatcher.

'JD! JD! Don't forget the Dry Marsh.'

JD turned towards the truck and opened his mouth to shout back but Bratby grabbed him by the shoulder, swung him around and threw him back to the ground.

'Aqua,' JD shouted, stretching out his hand towards the steel box, but as he did so the motor whined, the wheels bit into the dust and the truck pulled away.

Out of the corner of his eye JD saw Bratby raise the metal rod and scrambled away, searching for somewhere to hide but still following the truck with his eyes. In his heart he wanted to chase after it, to call out to Aqua that he would find her but right now he had other things on his mind.

Bratby brought down the rod. It swished towards JD's head but he ducked and the weapon cut the air close to his shoulder. He backed away, scuffling along the ground and keeping his eyes focused on Bratby's sneering face.

All thoughts of Aqua and the truck had to go. This was survival time. JD kept his eyes locked onto Bratby's, trying to work out what he would do next. The Senior was enjoying himself. He was going to have such fun. A stupid Boonie and no one around to stop him. This was what he dreamed about. He licked his lips, took a deliberate pace towards JD's crouching figure and once more raised the metal rod above his head. JD saw the outline against the lights, saw how tightly Bratby's hand gripped the bar, his knuckles white and sharp.

JD knew he couldn't duck all the blows; Bratby was bound to get him some time. He needed to get away, so, trying not to take his eyes from his assailant's face, he searched all around for someplace to run. The only place was the sleep shack and Bratby stood directly in his way. Somehow he had to get inside into the darkness and it had to be soon. Bratby was advancing again, the steel rod high above his head. JD tensed, lowered his head and charged straight at the Senior. He hoped to knock the bully off-balance but Bratby saw him coming and stepped to one side. JD ducked down as low as he could and kept on running. He heard the rod swish through the air and put up his arm. A sharp pain shot through his shoulder but he was moving fast and the blow only clipped him. He stumbled for a few paces but managed to stay upright. A short spurt and he dived through the door of the sleep shack.

Inside, he didn't slacken his pace and sped up the centre of the building. But before he had gone more than a few paces he tripped, catching his feet on some kid's outstretched legs, and sprawled full length on the floor. Behind him a flashlight pierced the darkness but by the time it had focused JD was gone. He'd slipped to the side of the shed and thrown himself against the wall, pulled up his knees in front of his face, tucked his head down and closed his eyes. The flashlight played along the rows of sleeping boys; some blinked awake in the beam. The light searched up and down the shack but JD kept low, huddling down among the mass of boys, fighting to stifle his breathing.

When at last the light clicked off JD relaxed and risked a quick peep towards the open door. Bratby's shape was outlined against the night.

'You may have got away with it this time, Boonie,' the senior hissed. 'But don't worry, my turn will come. I'll be watching for you and you won't get away twice.'

The door rattled on its runners and crashed shut.

The hut was so quiet it was as if every one of the boys was holding his breath. JD stared into the darkness. He'd done it now. His adventure, his escape, Aqua's rescue and his dream of a new life had gone forever and on top of all that he'd made a powerful enemy. It was the Pits for him from now on in and it was unlikely he'd ever get another chance to escape. Bratby would be waiting for sure.

Twenty

Strike

When daylight began to creep around the door of the sleep shack JD felt the knot inside his stomach tighten up. Bratby would be waiting for him, ready with his steel rod. There was no way JD could avoid what was coming to him. There was no place to run, no place to hide, no one to help him. But when the door slid back, JD was amazed to find another senior was on duty and he filed out with the others.

In some strange way he felt cheated. He almost wanted the fight; he felt in some way it might set him free from his disappointment. He'd lost his dream of a perfect life; his plan had been doomed right from the get-go. He was angry and the more he turned everything over in his mind the angrier he became and the more he needed someone to blame. Everything had gone wrong since that awful day in the Brooder, and it was since then JD realised that he actually expected things to go wrong. He somehow knew he could never succeed and his dream was just that, a dream. He was kidding himself. There'd be no shack in the Dry Marsh, no happy times with Aqua. He was beaten. He was just one more kid down the Pit and pretty soon death would come to him, just like it had to all the others. And what was worse, his death wouldn't even cause a ripple of interest unless the other kids thought he had a drop of water left in his tube. JD sighed. His black thoughts covered him like a blanket and he felt overwhelmed, drowning in a deep pool of his own despair. His mind felt woolly, his limbs heavy and his senses dull. He could feel himself becoming just like the others, mindlessly scraping away day after day, and wondered if he could ever again summon up the will to fight.

But then, for no reason he could figure, a voice, a gruff voice forced out of a jagged hole in an old man's neck, seemed to penetrate his cloud of self-pity.

'Hey! Come on, JD,' it said. 'This ain't like you. Don't you give up now. Don't let 'em beat you.'

And through his hurt his anger swelled up inside him again. And all that day, kneeling in the dirt, moving his scraper up and down, that anger grew and grew. But it wasn't just anger at his failure that stirred him; he seethed at the way everybody around him just gave in so easily. Looking around at all the little, bent figures working themselves to death he wondered: Why ain't they bitter? Why ain't they screwed up like me? Can't they see that unless they do somethin' their misery will carry on day in, day out 'til they become just the next bundle of rags falling off some high-up ledge? They might just as well fling themselves off the galleries right now and have done with it. And for a moment JD wondered whether he should do just that. But he dismissed the idea as quickly as it had come. Suicide was no answer. He'd seen too many kids lose their grip on life to the almost total indifference of the others. No, he'd fight and maybe if he did it right, some of the others might fight with him.

All that day JD's bitterness grew. Twisted thoughts raged inside his head and as time wore on his frustration burned deeper. He felt he would burst if he didn't do something, but each time he tried to work out what to do the awful lethargy gripped him again.

Once, he stopped work and stared at the boy next to him, daring him to look back just so's he could start some kind of argument or better, a fight. That would untie the knots inside him, the screwed-up feeling that was winding him up like a metal spring.

Finally, he could stand it no more and when he threw down his scraper he got what he wanted, but it didn't come from the boys around him. They seemed to have sensed his black mood and scraped harder, keeping their eyes turned away, studying the dirt wall in front of them. One of the Seniors noticed, the one they called Dagger. He'd been lounging against the funnel in the centre of the Pit, idly scanning the galleries, when he heard the dull clang of JD's scraper falling onto the gallery ledge.

'Pick that up,' he called. 'Pick it up and get back to work.'

Slowly, JD turned his head and stared at the older boy.

'Get on with it,' the Senior called, pointing at JD. 'Get working or it'll be the worse for you.'

JD's answer was to sit down and swing his legs over the edge of the gallery. He rested his chin in his hands and studied Dagger as if he was something strange, something he'd never seen before.

'If I have to come up there you'll be sorry, Boonie,' Dagger shouted, baring his teeth and trying to snarl.

JD sneered back, mimicking the silly look on Dagger's face, and began to beat his heels against the dirt wall below the gallery.

'Right,' the Senior said, glaring hard at JD. 'You've asked for it, Boonie. If you're not back at work by the time I get up there you'll be sorry.'

Dagger strode towards the Pit side and began to climb, leaping up the steps two at a time, but JD just sat and stared at him and continued to beat his heels on the wall.

The Pit went quiet. Boys stopped scraping and hundreds of eyes turned to where JD sat, his legs swinging, never for one moment taking his eyes off the approaching Senior.

A low murmur filled the air. Children clustered together,

eager to see what was going to happen, afraid to say anything, but their hearts going out to JD.

When Dagger arrived at the third level, puffing with anger and frustration, he shuffled along the narrow ledge towards where the rebel sat, calmly doing nothing.

'Pick that up and get scraping,' he shouted when he arrived, pointing at JD's discarded scraper, but still JD did nothing.

'I said, pick up that scraper and get to work,' Dagger said through clenched teeth. He poked JD's shoulder but JD just shrugged him away and with all his pent-up hurt and anger welling up inside him, he slowly turned his head.

'Why?' he said.

'Because, you useless twit, I'm telling you to. Now pick up that scraper and get going.'

JD stared up into Dagger's twisted face. The Senior was almost hopping up and down but his anger was having no effect on JD. He was surprised at how very calm he felt. He'd been waiting for something to happen to rid him of his fury and here it was.

'What's the point?' he said quietly. 'Just suppose we all,' he waved his arm around the Pit, 'suppose we all decided not to scrape the walls today? What difference would it make? Would there be any less water in the tank tomorrow? Of course not. So why don't we all just take the day off? You too. You and Mort and Bratby, let's all have the day off,' JD cried, his voice echoing around the Pit.

Wide-eyed faces clustered together and watched in silence. Then one or two turned to each other and whispered. Pretty soon a low buzz began to grow and spread along the galleries.

Dagger began to feel uncomfortable. His dull brain told him that something dangerous was happening but he couldn't think what to do about it. He did understand though that if he did nothing, it would overwhelm him.

'Now, look here, you stupid Boonie, just stop talking nonsense and get working.'

'No,' JD said. 'I don't rightly think I will. I think I'm gonna take the day off. What do you say, kids?' he called out across the Pit. 'Shall we have a day off today?'

Excited whispers came from all around and grew louder and louder until they welled up into laughter. Here and there excited squeals rang out. Then the squeals became a roar, which reached every ledge and every level of the workings. Some kids put down their scrapers and began to jostle their neighbours, urging them towards the stairways.

JD felt his skin tingle and the short hairs on his neck stand up. It was as if a shaft of pure energy had speared into him, driving away his depression and giving him overwhelming strength. He had stirred the soul of every child in the Pit and just looking around at their grubby faces wreathed in smiles lifted him.

Dagger couldn't believe what was going on. 'Get back to work. Get back,' he shouted, trying to look angry, but the Pit slaves only had to look at JD and see him sitting on the edge of his gallery, smiling and kicking his heels against the wall and they knew there was nothing the Senior could do to stop them. JD's insolent confidence filled the whole place with hope. If he could sit there defiantly and Dagger was unable to do anything about it, then what chance did the Senior stand against a hundred excited children? JD watched the liberated mass of kids begin crawling along the galleries, laughing and chatting to each other, revelling in their new-found freedom.

And if they drew their nerve from JD, their smiling faces and happy laughter poured fresh strength back into him. He felt strong and confident.

Dagger stood over him, confused and frustrated. He wanted to kick out at JD, punish him for his idleness and force him back to work. He wanted to see him on his knees. He wanted to see fear in his face; he wanted fear in all their faces. It made him feel so good, so big and strong. It made him forget the days when he'd been one of them, before he'd been picked as one of Bratby's crew.

Dagger drew in his breath. 'You've done it now, Boonie. You've really done it. You wait 'til I tell Bratby. You've stopped the work, do you realise that? You've stopped production. My God, Boonie, you're in it now. Do you realise what you've done? Do you know what will happen if these walls don't get scraped today?'

'No,' JD said calmly. 'What?'

'There will be no water, that's what, you stupid, know-nothing Boonie.'

'Oh, really,' JD said, a cynical smile playing on his lips. It amused him to see Dagger so agitated. 'Why's that then?'

Dagger was almost jumping up and down on the spot, his head whizzing to and fro in a blur as he tried to watch JD and glare at the departing boys all at the same time. His tiny brain was in a whirl. A look of near panic was written across his thin, horse face as the gleeful children filed along the galleries and up the steps. He knew he should rush over and bar their way but he was glued to where JD sat.

'You wouldn't understand even if I told you,' he spat. 'You, you –'

'Try me,' JD said, smiling angelically.

Dagger stepped up and stood right over JD, and for a moment JD thought he was going to push him off the gallery. He wanted to press back against the dirt wall but he steeled himself and sat firm. It was no time to show fear.

'Because, you idiot, if you don't work the still won't make water. Your job, all our jobs is to keep this still working and to do that the sides have to be scraped every day. You know that. Everybody knows that. I don't suppose for a moment that a scruffy, know-nothing Boonie like you can understand such things so just get scraping. Now!'

Convinced that JD would now resume work, Dagger turned to intercept the escaping workforce.

'Rubbish,' JD said quietly.

Dagger spun around and put his hands on his hips.

'Oh, I see. Rubbish, is it?' he shouted, a red flush rising up his face. 'And what exactly is this rubbish?'

'There's no need to scrape the sides of this Pit nor any other pit. If the sun shines on the membrane, water will condense onto it when the air cools down whether we scrape or not.'

Dagger's face became contorted. 'Membrane? Condense? You don't know what you're talking about. Get to work, I tell you. Get scraping.'

The Senior suddenly realised that his voice was now the only sound in the whole Pit. He spun around and saw that the exodus had stopped. Lines of boys stood on the steps and at the ends of the galleries, all looking at Dagger and JD. Hundreds of eyes watched the confrontation between the two boys, waiting to find out what they should do next.

'Get back to work, all of you,' Dagger shouted, waving his arms. 'Get back. Now.'

'Yes,' JD shouted after him, irritated that they had stopped. 'Get back to your stupid, pointless work. Scrape

185

your lives away 'til you fall dead into the Pit. Go on. Be like Three-Seven-Seven and all the other poor kids. Scrape, go on, scrape. It will save you havin' to think.' JD was trying to sound ironic but as he spoke he found his anger welling up again.

'It's all a waste of time,' he continued, spitting the words out. There was no longer any humour in his face, the bitterness that had consumed him all day was back. 'This guy,' he shouted, pointing at Dagger. 'This guy and his friends are even more stupid than you are. They don't know how a Godrum Still works no more than you do and —'

JD stopped in mid-sentence. There had been a universal intake of breath and the boys, who a few moments before had been smiling, willing JD on in his battle with Dagger, now shuffled close together and began whispering to each other. Then, as if the humid air had been cut with a knife, the whole place fell silent.

JD looked along the galleries and up the steps, searching the sea of faces, trying to understand what had changed. The Pit slaves had closed up as if guarding against some kind of attack. Moments before, if he had just said the word they would all have streamed out of the Pit, laughing and jostling each other, but in an instant they had become quiet lines of boys bunched up on the galleries; empty steps above them.

'You've done it now, Boonie,' Dagger said in a hoarse

whisper. 'Come on,' he said and, fired with some kind of renewed energy, he grabbed JD by his collar and began dragging him along the gallery.

'You stupid twerp,' he said, panting with the exertion. 'Let's see you smart-talk your way out of this one.'

The slave boys shrank back against the walls, pressing their hands and faces against the dark soil as Dagger pulled JD towards the steps. JD was so shocked at the instantaneous change that he put up no resistance and allowed himself to be dragged away like an old sack. Frightened, dirty faces watched Dagger haul JD down to the Pit floor.

Bratby and Mort had appeared by the funnel and watched in silence as Dagger threw JD to the ground at their feet.

'Where is he?' Dagger said. 'Where's the Boss?'

'What's going on?' Bratby asked. 'Why do we need the old man? It's just a Boonie slacking. It's what Boonies do. Forget the old fool, we'll just take him up top and teach him a lesson. We can deal with this ourselves; we don't need any help.'

'No, we can't,' Dagger panted. 'You didn't hear what he said.'

'What? Did he call you names or something?' Bratby sneered. 'You'll get over it. Come on, let's get him up top and give him a good kicking. I've got some unfinished business with this one anyway.'

JD's heart sank. Now he was for it.

187

Twenty-one

The Dome

From where he lay JD had an excellent view of the bulging toe-caps on the Seniors' boots. Bratby's shone, the black leather burnished to a high gloss, the criss-crossed laces climbing up his legs. Neither Dagger nor Mort bothered with such niceties. Their boots were scuffed and dirt-caked, the laces broken and knotted, but muddy or shiny, tight-laced or sloppy, JD knew that if he didn't think fast they would soon be inflicting some serious damage on him.

'No,' he heard Dagger say. 'We can't keep him to ourselves. He's got to go. If he'd just been slacking I'd have given him a good kicking myself but it's a lot more serious than that. He said . . .' Dagger suddenly seemed to have difficulty telling his story. He swallowed and his face twisted and he tried to find the right words. At last he walked up to Bratby and, shielding his face behind his hand, whispered something.

Bratby's cruel smile left his lips and he stared down at JD, sprawled on the floor in front of him.

'Are you sure?' he said.

'Yep. That's what he said.'

Bratby glared at JD. 'You're right, Dagger. Much as it would have been good to teach him a lesson ourselves, there's only one penalty for that. He'll have to go to the Old Man. You two get everybody back to work. I'll take him.'

'But I caught him.' Dagger whined. 'It ought to be me taking him.'

'You do as you're told,' Bratby snapped. '*I'll* take him.'

Dagger's shoulders dropped and he kicked the dirt. 'OK,' he said. 'But don't forget to tell the boss that it was me what caught him.'

'I'll tell him,' Bratby said. 'You, Boonie,' he added, nudging JD with the toe of his boot, 'on your feet. You two, get this lot back to work. Don't let them slack off just because I'm not here. Come on, you,' he said, poking JD harder. 'Get up.'

JD got to his feet and Bratby shoved him towards the steps where he started to climb. Up he went, passing gallery after gallery where the poor wretches whom he had so nearly freed watched his progress, their mouths making tiny Os.

JD shook his head. For the first and probably the only time in their short lives these kids had had a glimpse of freedom and now, in a blink of their big round eyes, they'd forgotten all about it. All they could do was stare blankly as he was led away. He'd hoped for some support. At best he'd thought they might protest and come to his aid. At the least he'd hoped they might stop work for a moment and shout some encouragement. But there was nothing. Just stupid kids watching the only person who'd ever tried to ease their pitiful lives being taken away. That's the last time I ever try to help anybody, JD vowed to himself.

When he reached the surface he wondered whether to take a chance and run, but Bratby was too close behind and anyway, where would he run to? As if he'd read his thoughts, the older boy closed up and shoved JD along the worn path, around the soil heaps and across the open ground towards the sleep shacks. JD stumbled along, constantly pushed in the back by Bratby, who strode in silence, his jaw set. They went right past the shacks and down a long track which led away across more arid scrub and red rocks. This was unknown territory and when JD glanced up he saw a small hump in the ground away in the distance. It was towards this that they seemed to be heading.

As they drew closer, JD saw that the hump was a kind of round shack set like the top of a bald head into a shallow hole. Bratby pushed him onwards and between stumbles, JD tried to make out what it was, hoping all the while that the sinking feeling in his stomach would go away.

Up close the thing looked enormous. Set in the shallow dip of an abandoned Pit, it curved high up against the yellow sky. From the edge of the hole, it seemed to JD that the massive dome was the only thing in the world. It was so dark and forbidding that he feared the worst.

From a distance the dome had blended in with its surroundings; dirty red dust covered everything. But up close JD could see that it was not as smooth as he'd first thought. From the ground to the peak the great mound was a tangle of all kinds of rubbish. Strips of plastic, torn fabric, pieces of discarded wood and metal had been woven, intertwined or just dumped over the whole surface and where the dome was set into the ground, drifts of red dirt were piled up against it, making it seem that the whole thing had erupted from the soil and stopped suddenly. It didn't take JD long to figure out that this had to be the Ragman's house.

Bratby gripped JD's neck and pushed him towards the ragged hump. There seemed to be no way in to the dome but, without releasing his grip, Bratby pushed aside a clump of plastic trash to reveal a door. It was not much of a door, just a sheet of metal with nails and bolts driven into it. Down one side were three heavy hinges, the top one a long, curled iron strap half-eaten away by age and wear. In the centre was a square of thick leather, punched and riveted into the face of the door while the bottom hinge was new, bright and shiny, small and neat but fixed alternately with screws and rusty nails. On the opposite side of the door hung a large round handle. Bratby banged on the door with his fist and right away a voice called out from within.

'Who's there?' it growled.

'It's Bratby,' the Senior shouted. 'I've got the Boonie here. I've got to see you.'

JD heard heavy stuff being moved and a low grumbling from inside. He heard the rasp of bolts being drawn. The door opened and the Ragman peered out into the bright light. He was still dressed in his rags but had taken off his boots. Broad feet with long gnarled toes spread out onto a bare dirt floor.

'What do you want?' the Ragman growled. 'What are you doing here? Who's this?' he said, glaring at JD from under his bushy brows.

'You'd better let me in,' Bratby said. 'I've got something pretty important to tell you.' He drew out the words with his familiar sneer and pushed JD past the ragged man into the dark beyond.

Inside the dome JD was surprised at how cold it felt. The heat outside was at its peak but in the darkness of the

Ragman's shack the air was cool and soft. But it was very dark; the only light came from a solitary candle guttering in a metal dish by the door.

'Well. What do you want?' the Ragman demanded as Bratby pushed past. 'Why ain't you down the Pit keeping them kids at it? We can't afford to stop scraping, you know.'

'Yes,' Bratby said, oozing self-importance. 'I know that and you know that but the Boonie doesn't. But don't you fret, old man; Dagger and Mort are keeping them hard at it.'

'OK. They'd better be. But why have you brought this skinny specimen up here?'

'He said the word. Said it right out loud. Everybody heard it and all the kids stopped work. Then he said it again and after that he refused to work. He tried to get all the others to stop too. If I hadn't stepped in the whole Pit would have ground to a halt. There'd have been a riot.'

The Ragman looked at JD and JD stared back. On the way from the Pit he'd been pretty scared but somehow, here with the Ragman, his fear had gone. He knew he should be afraid but from the moment he'd entered the dome he'd felt OK. It was something he couldn't explain even to himself.

The three odd characters stood in the semi-darkness. JD straight and defiant, Bratby somehow less confident and the Ragman shuffling his feet, irritation hanging over him like a cloak.

'So. He said the forbidden word, did he?' the Ragman said at last. 'What'd he do? Did he just blurt it out or did he say anything else?'

'Does it matter? It means death. We all know that. I've brought him here just for the sake of procedure. It's in the Convention. Section One, Paragraph Thirteen, Subsection Three. He has to be put to death and put to death now. I –'

'Oh, shut up and don't quote the Convention to me, sonny. I've forgotten more about the Convention than you'll ever know. You're not a Leader yet, young Bratby, just remember that, and if you don't get a decent report from me you might never be. Just keep that in your evil little mind before going on about Conventions and what must and must not happen. That's for me to decide.'

'You can't do that. I'll tell my father. He'll soon–'

The Ragman spun around, his coat of junk swirling out in a jangling arc around him. 'You forget. I know your old man,' he said, pointing a long finger into Bratby's face. 'He's a pompous know-nothing too. Now, just you get back to your job and leave me to take care of mine. Go on. Get out.' The Ragman waved his arms, shooing Bratby towards the door.

'That's not fair. The Convention says that whoever reports the crime has the privilege of carrying out the punishment and I demand my rights. It's in the Convention. Section Three, Paragraph –'

'Just shut up,' the Ragman shouted, his eyes blazing. 'If you know your Convention so well you'll know he can call for a trial if he chooses. He can bring witnesses. Who else saw all this going on? Who will support your side of the story and who will stand against you? If I'm any judge it wasn't you who got his hands dirty anyway, so just get off back to the Pit and do your job.'

Bratby's eyes flashed but his shoulders drooped as he made his way back to the door.

'You wait, old man,' he hissed. 'I'll tell my father about you and then we'll see who comes out on top.'

'Just get back to the Pit, Bratby, or I'll call the guards. Go on. Get your cocky little backside out of here. Right now!'

'I'll go,' Bratby spat. 'But just you remember, old man. I'll be a Leader soon and when I am I'll come for you. I'll run you into the Scrubland so fast your dirty old feet won't touch the ground.' Bratby pointed a quivering finger at the Ragman's bare toes. 'Then I'll hunt you down and when I catch you I'll sew your mouth up so you'll die a horrible dry death, just like the other old traitor. I don't know why they let you off last time. By rights your bones should be out there now, drying in the sun. If I do nothing else I'll see that you don't get away with pushing me around.'

One instant Bratby was there and the next he was gone and except for an almost imperceptible grunt, the Ragman appeared unmoved. He shuffled to the door and banged it shut. The candle flame wavered, sending up a spiral of smoke before it settled back to a steady light. Bratby was gone but now JD understood something about why he felt so calm. The Ragman hated Bratby more than he did.

JD stood in the silence, staring at the candle, Bratby's words ringing in his head. *'Put to death and put to death now,'* he'd said. It reminded him of the loudspeakers in the City.

'Well, boy, you've made yourself a bad enemy there,' the Ragman said, breaking JD's train of thought. 'He's evil, that boy. Like his father before him; evil and vindictive.'

'Seems he don't like you much neither,' JD said.

The Ragman chuckled. 'You're right there and no mistake. Ever since they sent him down the Pit for punishment he hasn't liked me one bit. But he's right though. He will be a Leader one day and then he'll carry out his threats, no question. Provided I live long enough, he'll be the end of me.'

The old man walked out of the candlelight and into the shadows.

'Come here, boy.'

JD could hardly see a thing, but walked towards the Ragman's voice. After a couple of steps he was beyond the circle of light and in complete darkness. He put his hands out in front of him but quickly came up against a pile of rubbish. Confused, he took a step to his right, still reaching out, his fingers sliding over the surface of the trash. He felt bits of plastic, frayed rope, splinters of wood and metal all tangled together in the darkness.

'Come on, boy. Where have you got to?'

The Ragman seemed to be laughing at JD. This is a game, JD thought and took another pace to the right. The pitch black made him uneasy and he looked back towards the candle for comfort. The steady yellow glow calmed his nerves so he turned back towards the wall of junk. Then he noticed a pale puddle of light on the dirt floor and shuffled towards it. His hand found something solid which he explored with his fingers. It felt like a door frame and beyond it was an opening. Hoping there was nothing to fall over, JD stepped through.

Wow, JD thought. Before him lay a large room lit by a twinkling mass of tiny candles, all floating in water-filled bowls. In the centre of the room the Ragman sprawled in a richly upholstered chair, while next to him was a low table with a jug of water on it, a drinking glass and a shiny bell. JD looked up. High above his head a network of shining wooden staves met in a complex pattern, criss-crossed the walls and arched down on all sides. The floor, which in the entrance had been just hard-packed dirt, was covered in rugs, deep-piled with red and green swirling patterns. Some even had yellow tassels around the edge.

The walls too were hung with richly coloured rugs woven in and out between the wooden struts. But the single most fabulous feature of the wonderful room was something beyond JD's young imagination; a sight that never in his whole life could he ever have imagined.

Behind where the old man sprawled in his chair was a large pool of clear water and in its centre a jet rose a hand's span above the surface, turned over and splashed with a delicious tinkle. The fountain was made from shiny stone that glistened with hundreds of sparkling water droplets and, if this wasn't enough, JD noticed that the air inside this wondrous shack was moving; a cool draught caressed his face. He closed his eyes and tilted his head back, letting the refreshing breeze brush his neck. When he opened his eyes again he saw before him a large oblong of brightly decorated material just like one of the rugs on the floor, only this one was suspended from the roof, wafting to and fro over the pool. JD's mouth fell open in awe; he had never dreamed of such luxury.

'So,' the Ragman said, breaking the spell. 'What was this terrible thing you said, boy?'

JD was surprised that the man who had been so cruel to him before spoke so quietly and without anger. The Ragman had become a different person here in his own home, almost the complete opposite to the ogre in the Pit.

'I said lots of things,' JD said, trying to remember

everything that had happened. 'But mainly I said it was a waste of time scrapin' the walls. I think that was what upset everybody.'

'What made you say that, boy?'

JD shrugged. 'I don't know. I was thinkin' about my friend who died yesterday and it made me sad. I guess bein' sad set me to wonderin' about what I was doin' and why? It just seemed stupid, scrapin' away all day when the water will come anyways.'

The Ragman wriggled his way upright and studied JD.

'Why do you say that? Everybody knows you have to scrape the walls to get water to come in the night.'

'I don't. I know how a still works. There's no need to scrape nothin'. You just dig a hole, cover it with plastic and water condenses when the air cools. It's simple.'

'So, you're an expert on stills, eh? A Boonie kid who don't look, what, twelve or thirteen, and you know all about making water?'

JD shrugged. 'I know you don't have to scrape no walls.'

'Do you, now? So, what should we tell all those fine folk in the City who say that we do? Men who have built hundreds of Pits, all of which work that way? Shall I tell them there's a kid out of nowhere says we're wasting our time? A kid who tells everybody to stop scraping and go play in the sunshine because the water'll come anyway?'

'Why not?' JD said. 'When Godrum showed me how

his still worked he didn't say nothin' about scrapin' walls. He said that as long as you put the membrane in properly and weight it down in the centre the water will come in the night and drip down into your pan. I know the Pits are a lot bigger but it's the same thing. Godrum said nothin' to me about scrapin' walls.'

The Ragman sat straight up in his chair. 'Do you know what you are saying, young man? Forget scraping walls for a moment; do you not understand why Bratby brought you to me and talked about having you put to death?'

JD shrugged.

The Ragman blew out through his lips, slumped back in his chair and shook his great shaggy head from side to side. He lifted the glass of water from the table and took a sip. JD licked his lips and watched him. Up 'til then he'd thought of the Ragman as nothing but an old tramp covered in trash, his hair caked in dirt, wild-eyed and snarling. But sitting there with an enigmatic smile across his features, JD saw a different guy. Now that the angry face was relaxed, it looked different, the face of a man you might ask questions.

'What did I do that was so terrible?' JD asked.

'You heard what Bratby said. You violated the Convention. Section One, Paragraph Thirteen, Subsection Three. Mean anything?'

'Nope,' JD said. He didn't even know what a convention was, let alone what it was for.

'Then let me tell you. It is written as one of our foremost laws that there should be no mention of the individual whom the Leaders proclaim is the cause of all our misery. Our lack of water, the dry unproductive ground, our whole miserable life and our inevitable dust-choked death are all his fault. He is, to quote the book, responsible for our *perilous and parlous situation*. I'm not sure how mentioning his name could make things any worse but our Leaders say that anyone who does so should be punished as set down in the Convention. That's the one that Bratby quoted. Understand?'

JD shrugged again. 'Nope,' he said quietly.

'Then let me explain in words that even a Boonie can understand. Did you say the name of the Evil One?'

'I don't know. Who is this Evil One?'

The Ragman looked towards the door then back at JD. 'Who did you say told you about making water?'

'Godrum,' JD said.

'Well, there we have it. Guilty as charged.'

'Godrum's not evil,' JD said. 'He was very kind to me.'

'And there's another thing. I don't know why you say Go— the Evil One told you these things. He's been dead for years.'

'No he ain't. He ain't evil and he ain't dead,' JD said. 'Or at least he wasn't when I last saw him.'

The Ragman stared straight into JD's eyes. His

expression had not changed but JD noticed a coldness had come into his face.

'He ain't,' JD said weakly. 'I know he ain't.'

'Of course he's dead, everybody knows he's dead. Why, I was there when he was cast out into the Scrubland, his mouth sewn up and stripped of everything except a simple robe. He could neither eat nor drink; he had no home, no shelter from the sun all day or the cold at night. Of course he's dead.'

JD looked at his feet again. He put one foot over the other and balanced unsteadily. In his heart he wanted to say that whatever they did to poor Godrum it was plain he was cleverer than they were. Despite all those terrible things they did, he was still alive.

'Well, boy? Speak up. Why do you say he's alive?'

JD swallowed hard and continued to look at his feet. Most of the time the Ragman spoke casually, as if nothing mattered very much but now, when talking about Godrum, the mask had slipped.

'Speak up, boy,' the Ragman snapped. 'What makes you say Godrum is alive?'

JD opened his eyes wide. The Ragman had said it now. The very thing he was about to be punished for.

'You said *Godrum*,' JD said. 'Ain't that bad? Doesn't that mean you'll have to be killed too?'

The man waved his hand in irritation. 'Never mind all that, tell me why you say he's alive.'

'I met him out in the Scrubland. He gave me water and showed me how to make my own. Then he took me to the City gate.'

'Yes, yes. But how do you know that the person that did all these things was Godrum?'

'He said he was Godrum and he called his water-makin' thing a Godrum Still.'

'Any old fool could *say* that, although I can't think of anyone being stupid enough to want to. Your old man could have been just some tramp pretending to be Godrum. Come on, boy. If you can't convince me you're telling the truth it'll be the worse for you. Do you know what they say I do to little boys like you?'

The Ragman leaned back in his chair and his coat rustled as he crossed one leg over the other. He narrowed his eyes and waved a hand in the air. 'Well,' he said. 'Do you?'

JD looked at his feet again. He could hear Aqua's whisper when she'd told him about the awful man in the Pits and what he was supposed to do.

'Eat 'em?' JD whispered, afraid that if he spoke louder the Ragman would leap from his chair and gobble him up there and then.

But instead he grinned. 'That's right, they say I eat little boys. And do you believe them?'

JD didn't know what to say but reckoned there was the tiniest vestige of a smile playing at the corners of the

Ragman's lips. He tried a weak smile himself in return and shook his head.

The grin faded from the Ragman's face. 'Well, you'd better start believing it. A great many boys have been brought to me for punishment. A few I've handed back to the likes of Bratby to be hunted down but none of the others have ever been seen again. And look at me. Don't I look well fed?' The Ragman patted his stomach. 'Where do you think that came from?'

JD didn't know what to believe. His mind was in a whirl.

'Please, sir,' he whined. 'He said he was Godrum. He had his mouth sewn up and talked through a hole in his neck. When we got to the City gates the Silver Men came and took him off. They flew right over my head. He said he was Godrum, that's all I know.'

The Ragman's interest came back with a bang. He jumped up from his chair, put his hands on JD's shoulders and pushed his face close.

'Where did they take him? Quick, boy. Tell me where they took him.'

JD stared into the grimy face. The eyes were wide and fierce, the grip on his shoulders so hard, so insistent that JD was suddenly very scared.

'I don't know. They just flew over me towards the tall shacks.'

The Ragman shook JD so hard he felt his teeth rattle.

'Think, boy. Think. Where were you when they flew over you?'

'I'd just crossed a long bridge. A long bridge over a dry gulch.'

The Ragman let go of JD and began to pace the carpets. He strode a few paces one way then turned, came back and loomed over JD.

'But which way did they turn? Which building did they head for?'

'They didn't turn. They just went higher. Up and up, over the little buildings towards the centre.'

The Ragman spun on his heel, turned away from JD and punched one hand into the other. He began mumbling, speaking low and fast under his breath. Then, slowly he turned back to JD.

'Did you see where they landed? Think, boy, think.'

'I don't know,' JD almost cried. 'Someplace . . . why? Is it important?'

'Important enough for your life to depend upon it,' the Ragman hissed through clenched teeth.

Twenty-two

An Old Friend

The Ragman paced up and down, punching his hands together. At times he paused, rubbed his chin, furrowed his brow and turned towards the door, but each time he stopped as if he'd thought of something new and resumed his pacing. Then all at once he turned and peered at JD.

'Boy. If I took you back to the City, do you think you could point out where they took him?'

'I don't know,' JD said but the question triggered something in his mind. Back in the City he might be able to slip away, get across the bridge and make off back to the Dry Marsh.

'Yes, sir, I think I could if you would take me,' he said. 'I was near a bridge . . .' he added, trying to appear thoughtful while all the time his brain buzzed with excitement.

The Ragman smiled broadly and JD could see that he

was excited too. He hurried across to his table, picked up the bell and shook it hard. Before the sound had died away an apparition rose from the ground beyond the fountain. A tall, grey-faced, grey-haired woman stood with her hands folded in front of her. She turned her head towards JD, examined him coldly and sniffed through her long, beak-like nose before turning back towards the Ragman.

'Ah, Chatelaine,' he said 'Take this young man below and find him a comfortable room.'

The Ragman smiled but JD thought the woman looked like she had a nasty smell under her pointy nose.

'Go with Chatelaine, young man. She'll give you some-thing to eat and a drink and I'll talk to you later.'

JD was real dry and needed no second telling. He walked across to the woman, who turned away and began gliding down a flight of steps. JD followed but took one last look at the Ragman. He was back to his pacing, walking three steps one way, then three steps the other. He walked fast, his head down, and even through the gloom JD could see the muscles in his face working. Suddenly, he punched one hand into the other and turned, spinning on his heel.

'Yes,' he hissed and threw himself into his chair, but before JD could see any more he felt a tug at his ankle.

'Boy,' the woman snapped and he had to go.

The steep stairway spiralled down, its rickety stairs a mass of old wooden poles and metal bars lashed together with frayed ropes leading down into the depths of what must have once been a Pit. JD trod carefully and looked around. The workings were quiet and there was no black funnel but the galleries were still there, extended out at each level onto a cranky old balcony which hung perilously over the abyss on a criss-cross web of poles and sticks. The galleries themselves had been dug back into the walls of the old Pit and divided into rooms, each dimly lit with a grille across the front.

The grey woman led JD down past two levels before stepping off onto one of the fragile balconies. She waited for him to catch up, sniffed at him, turned and walked away. The floor beneath her feet creaked as she went and JD had visions of the whole thing giving way and him cartwheeling through the darkness to the Pit floor, but when he thought about it he reckoned that if the balcony supported the grey woman it must be strong enough to take him.

He hurried on after her, looking forward to his comfortable room, but began to feel uneasy when he glanced through the grille into one of the spaces behind. A tiny figure sat on a low bed, staring at the bare floor. In the next room another single Farm kid sat motionless. He looked up at JD as he passed with a forlorn stare.

'In here, boy,' the woman said, holding open the door to the next room. JD hesitated but before he could remind her of the Ragman's promise she grabbed his collar, pushed him into the little cell and slammed the door. From the folds of her grey skirt she produced a long chain with a great jumble of keys attached to it, selected one and pushed it into the lock, closing it with a heavy clunk.

'Hey!' JD yelled at her retreating back. 'Where's my water? And my grub? He told you I was to have water.'

Chatelaine stopped. She did not turn nor did she acknowledge JD's shout but her rigid back and the folds of the severe grey dress shook with barely controlled anger. She paused for only a moment, then lifted her chin and strode to the end of the balcony, up the spiral stairs and out of sight without a backward glance.

JD threw himself down onto the narrow bed and seethed. He'd been tricked again. The Ragman's friendship had been an act. He felt cheated. Not just cheated out of a drink but out of his chance to get out, to get away and back to the Dry Marsh. He searched his tormented brain for something to release the frustration that boiled inside him but nothing came.

'Bah!' he almost shouted, turned onto his face and bit the rough bedcover. He put his clenched fists on his ears and held his head tight between them. His whole body was stiff with frustration.

JD did not know how long he lay there but when he heard a footstep on the gallery he sat up with a jerk. He glared at the door, still full of anger and ready to tell the woman what he thought of her, but as the steps drew nearer he began to think more clearly. No, he thought. That would be stupid. He'd sit still, wait 'til she unlocked the door then he'd charge past her and away up those stairs before she knew what was happening.

The steps came closer and JD kept his head low, just like the other kids. Nobody would know he was wound up like a spring.

But something was wrong. The steps were light; the fragile gallery did not creak and groan under their weight. There was no heavy tread from the likes of the Ragman nor the rattle of Chatelaine's keys, and by the time a pair of child's feet came into view JD's plan had dissolved.

At the grille was a young girl, her eyes cast down. She held a drinking tube and a square of food on a board. She knelt to push them through the bars.

'She said to bring this to you,' the girl mumbled. 'If you're the boy they just brought in?'

The girl was dressed in a long blue tabard which reached from her neck to her knees. Her arms were bare, as were her feet and legs. She had short hair and a round face and although most Farm children looked alike, JD knew this face well.

'Aqua,' he said. 'Aqua. It's me, JD. What are you doin' here?'

Until that moment the girl had kept her eyes down but

at the sound of his voice she looked up for a moment and smiled. But it was not her real smile, not the carefree grin that JD remembered so well.

JD took the food, unscrewed the top of the drinking tube, took a swig then held it out to Aqua. 'D'you want some?'

The girl shook her head and turned away. 'I've got to get back.'

JD shot his hand out through the bars and grabbed her arm. 'Don't go, Aqua.'

'I can't stay, JD,' she said, shaking his hand away. 'I have to go or Chatelaine will beat me.'

Aqua looked awful; her eyes had sunk in her head and were surrounded by black circles. Her old belligerent mouth was turned down and her shoulders drooped.

'Aqua. What's wrong. What's the matter with you?' JD said softly, reaching out again.

'Please, JD, don't,' she said, drawing back to evade his hand. 'It's no use. I haven't long to go. I've been here a while and there aren't many girls left . . .'

'Left? What do you mean?'

'Come on, JD. You know what happens here. I told you before.'

'Oh, Aqua. Don't be silly. I know what everybody says but that's just to frighten us. Nobody would really –'

'Eat us? Don't fool yourself, JD. Since I've been here five girls have gone and every day Chatelaine threatens us with the Grinder. They take them away and they just don't come back. We all know what happens to them.'

'I don't, but I'm sure they don't *eat* us. Anyways,' he said, setting his face angrily, 'even if they do they're not goin' to eat me, nor you. We'll get free. We'll go to the Dry Marsh. Remember? C'mon, Aqua. Cheer up. We'll get there somehow.'

'You're fooling yourself, JD. There's no escape from this place. Look around you.' She waved her arm to take in the galleries, the cells and the whole quiet Pit. 'We are all going to the Grinder. They wait until there are enough of us then they take us away. We all know where we're going.'

'Well, I don't,' JD said. 'And the Ragman is goin' to take me to the City. I said I'd show him where they took Godrum but I plan to get away. I'll make him bring you too, Aqua. I will, I promise. Then we'll give him the slip and run away to the Dry Marsh just like we said.'

Aqua looked deep into JD's eyes. 'What are you talking about, JD? The Evil One died long ago and if your Ragman is going to take you to the City it's for only one reason. And it isn't so that you can spin him another of your stories.'

'Oh, not you too, Aqua, and don't call him the Evil One. His name is Godrum, he's a wise old man and he was very kind to me. I told the Ragman I know where they took him and he's goin' to take me to the City so's I can show him.' JD's eyes shone bright in the gloom. 'I'll tell

212

him you were with me and you might remember more than me. Then he'll have to take you too, we'll give him the slip and we'll get away together.'

'Stop it, JD. Stop it.' Aqua stamped her foot, clasped her hands together and screwed up her face. 'Don't be silly. When we were little it was all right to have daydreams but that's all they were: dreams. This is what happens. This is what life is. You locked up in a cell being fed and watered until there's enough of you to make a decent meal and me working for Chatelaine until she decides it's my turn.' Aqua looked back at JD and he saw tears in her eyes.

'Aqua,' he said. 'Don't give up. There must be a chance. There's always a chance.'

Aqua bowed her head but just as JD was going to reach out to her, another hand, a thin, bony hand, appeared and clamped itself around the back of her neck, gripping it like a stick. Aqua squealed and JD jumped back into his cell.

'I told you not to talk, girl. I told you to give him his food and come straight back. I'll teach you to disobey me,' Chatelaine spat. She forced Aqua's head down until she was almost bent double. JD could see the thin, pointed nails digging into the pale skin on the little girl's neck. Aqua cried out but the more she squealed, the deeper the woman dug her talons in.

'And you, miserable wretch,' she said, turning to JD. 'I heard what you said. The only escape you'll have is the one you all have. When I've finished with this one I'll be going straight to him up top. Then you'll have a reason to shout. The last little whelp that caused trouble here he threw off the ledge. He had all the candles lit so's everyone could see. It's time we had another show like that; give you all something to think about.'

As the grey woman dragged Aqua towards the stairway, JD ran to the bars and pushed his head against them, straining to see. He heard the stairs creak and saw the grey shape climb the stairway, pulling the little girl behind her like a rag doll.

When the creaking stopped JD slouched back to the bed and threw himself onto it. Poor Aqua, he thought. What could have happened to her? Ever since he'd known the tough girl with her mischievous smile he'd thought of her as somebody who would survive no matter what happened. She was so strong. She'd only been caught because of her adventurous spirit. He remembered the times he'd lost hope and how it was only because of her that he'd got through. If she hadn't rescued him the Silver Men would have killed him just like they killed Pa. She got him to the Farm and it wasn't her fault about Ma. He owed her so much. He had to find a way to help her. It didn't matter that she was scared and seemed to have lost hope now. If he could get her away she'd soon be the old Aqua. He knew she would.

'I'll get you out, Aqua,' JD said under his breath. 'I'll get you away from here. I promise.'

Twenty-three

Back in the Dome

JD felt better. His silent promise had buoyed him up but before he could help anyone, he knew that first he had to get himself out of there.

He looked around his cell and saw it was dug into the Pit side with just the metal door at the front. He went to the bars and shook them. They rattled but they were fixed good. Dropping to his knees, he wondered if he could get underneath. He scratched at the floor with his fingernails but the ground was packed hard and he soon gave up the idea of digging his way out. He inspected the walls around the edges of the grille. He spent a long time searching his cell, peering and poking at things, scratching at the walls and floor. He examined every part of the little room then sat on the bed once more, lay back and cradled his head in his hands. There was no way he could break out; he'd

215

have to wait 'til he was let out and take his chances from there. If he could get the Ragman to take him to the City like he'd said, then all JD had to figure out was some way to get the old guy to take Aqua too.

JD began to wonder why the Ragman wanted to find Godrum. He hadn't known why the Silver Men wanted him neither but it was plain they did. Perhaps the Ragman's reason was the same but JD couldn't figure it out. If it was because of somethin' he'd done, surely sewin' his mouth up and banishin' him to the Scrubland was punishment enough? Or if they just wanted to kill him they could have done that easier than takin' him away. Thinking about Godrum, JD remembered all the things he'd told him and how it seemed that he had the answer to everythin'. Perhaps that was it. Perhaps they wanted Godrum for somethin' he knew, somethin' real special.

When JD felt a hand on his shoulder he realised he must have drifted off to sleep.

'Get up, boy.' Chatelaine was bending over him, sneering into his face.

JD jumped to his feet. His cell door was open and he was going to dive towards it and take his chance, but before the thought had properly formed he saw the outline of a figure in the doorway. It was a Senior boy, tall and rangy with hard boots, and he held a rope loosely coiled in his hands. Chatelaine called him into the cell and he bound

JD's hands behind his back, made a noose in the other end of the rope and put it around JD's neck. Taking the slack in one hand he tugged it, jerking JD's head back. He smiled, then looked at the grey woman. She nodded and JD was pushed out onto the balcony and shoved towards the spiral staircase.

'Get going, Boonie,' the Senior grunted and poked JD in the back.

There was lots of activity outside. On each gallery girls in blue tabards were hurrying to and fro with trays of food and drinking tubes. JD searched their faces, hoping to find Aqua, but she was not among them. The sight of the drinking tubes made him thirsty and his heart sank when he remembered he'd left his in the cell.

The Senior shoved him up the rickety stairs, through the trapdoor and into the dome where the Ragman was waiting for him, towering over the stairway. Once more, JD found he was not actually frightened but pretty soon he certainly became less confident. The old man was not alone. At first JD did not notice anything, but a movement and a short gasp made him peer into the shadows beyond the fountain. In the gloom a child cowered against the frames of the dome, and when a flicker of candlelight caught her face, red-hot anger erupted through JD's body. Aqua was crouching on her knees and like JD she had a rope around her neck, but what angered JD most were the terrible bruises on her face. One eye was almost closed, the skin around it dark and puffy.

JD started to rush towards where the little girl lay but before he had taken a single step the rope around his neck jerked tight and he fell backwards onto the ground. But he would not give up. He struggled to his feet.

'What have you done?' he cried, turning towards the Ragman. 'Who did that?'

The Ragman smiled back. 'My, ain't we the young gentleman?' But his smile faded quickly. 'She misbehaved and was punished for it.'

'You bully,' JD spat, all caution forced away by his flaming anger. 'She's just a little girl. What did you do that for?' He glared at the old man but he turned away.

'I don't administer the punishment,' he said. 'I leave that to those who enjoy it.'

JD turned and saw the cruel smile on the acid features of the grey woman. Frustration and anger mixed together in his throat and he struggled to free his hands. He wanted to lash out at the evil apparition but the Senior held him fast.

The Ragman turned to the Senior. 'Tie this one up and leave me,' he said quietly.

JD was led close to where Aqua lay and his rope was lashed to one of the frames of the dome. Chatelaine came to check that the tether was fast. She tugged at the knot

218

and grunted her satisfaction but could not resist tweaking the rope and snapping JD's head back. He fell onto his heels and, while trying to struggle upright, he toppled over, trapping the grey woman's hand against the side of the dome. He'd not planned it but if he had, it couldn't have turned out better. In a flash he saw his chance, twisted his head round as far as it would go and sank his teeth deep into the woman's wrist.

'Aaargh!' Chatelaine yelled, shaking her wrist, desperate to pull it free of JD's sharp young teeth, but the more she struggled the more he hung on. He bit deeper until he felt warm blood on his lips. He shook his head, wrenching and tearing at the woman's bony arm.

'Get him off. Get him off,' she screamed. 'Help me.'

But JD gripped on hard, clenching his jaw for all he was worth, and it was not until the Senior grabbed the rope and pulled it tight around his neck that he was forced to release his hold.

The grey woman held her wrist to her chest and JD saw with satisfaction that a steady stream of blood began to stain her dress.

'You swine,' she hissed. 'I'll kill you.' Turning to the Ragman, she screeched, 'Look what he's done. Kill him. Fling him into the Pit. Kill him, kill him. Look what he's done to me.' She held up her arm. Shreds of skin hung from her wrist and blood dripped onto the floor. JD was certain he caught the white flash of exposed bone in the candlelight.

The Ragman walked over to JD and poked him with his bare toes. 'What did you do that for?' he asked.

'She deserved it.' JD said defiantly.

'Kill him,' the woman screamed again. 'He can't do this to me. To me!' she repeated. 'I'll chuck him in myself. Let me have him. I'll hurl him from the highest level. Let me do it. Please, let me do it. It will show those filthy children what happens if –'

The Ragman held up his hand and the grey woman reluctantly closed her mouth.

'You really are a troublemaker, young man. Every time I see you, you are up to some mischief or other. Perhaps Chatelaine is right, perhaps it's time to be rid of you once and for all. Why? Not a day has passed since Bratby was demanding you be put to death and now dear, kind Chatelaine is pleading for the same thing. You have an unhappy habit of upsetting people, young Boonie. I fear you are not destined for a long life.'

Chatelaine smiled and licked her lips. Had her wrist not hurt so much JD was sure she'd have rubbed her hands together.

Twenty-four

The Big Drop

Without another word the Ragman untied JD from the frame, yanked him to his feet and turned him towards the trapdoor. Chatelaine, still holding her injured wrist but with her eyes shining in triumph, stood aside while the boy was dragged towards the rickety stairs. The Ragman shoved JD into the trapdoor and down he went, his mind numb, not quite believing what was happening. It seemed that every time he saw the Ragman his mood changed.

JD was confused but before his head sank beneath the floor he shot a quick glance towards Aqua. Through the legs of his captors he saw she was watching him, her battered face a picture of sadness. She tried a weak grin and JD smiled back but they both knew that this could well be the last time they would ever see each other.

By the time he reached the first gallery JD had begun

to regain his wits. He had to think fast but the constant change in the Ragman bothered him. He'd accepted Chatelaine's demands so easily it was as if he'd lost all interest in finding Godrum. If he had, JD reckoned it was all up for him.

The Ragman tweaked the rope and JD stopped. He stepped off the stairway with his captor close behind and soon the grey woman joined them. Below, the Pit lay like a black pool.

'Let me have them light the candles,' the grey woman cried. 'Let's show them what happens to brats like this.'

'Very well,' the Ragman said. 'Call your girls.'

Chatelaine walked along the upper gallery and through an archway. Moments later, she reappeared at the head of a line of little girls all dressed in the familiar blue tabards. She handed each girl a candle, lighted it and one by one they descended into the Pit.

JD watched them troop off onto the galleries, two girls to each level, and soon candles flickered all around and the whole Pit glowed in a warm yellow light. Had his mind not been spinning he might have thought it quite pretty.

JD peeped over the rail and swallowed hard. Even the rocky floor far below was bathed in candlelight. Was the old man really going to throw him down there? He looked into the Ragman's face, hoping to see a twinkle in his eye, hoping to catch some sign that this was just a threat, a warning to make him mend his ways. But the craggy face was set hard.

The grey woman fussed. Scurrying from one gallery to another, her bloody wrist against her breast, calling to the girls, hurrying them along until she was satisfied that every candle was in place and burning brightly. At last she seemed content and turned her sharp face towards the Ragman.

'Call the brats to their bars,' she said, a note of triumph in her voice. 'I want them all to see what happens to disrespectful children.'

'Very well,' the Ragman said. 'Call them forward.'

The grey woman stepped up to the railing, put her hands to her mouth and drew a deep breath but before she could begin JD spoke.

'It's a pity,' he said with a deep sigh. 'I was so lookin' forward to seein' Godrum again.'

The woman almost choked. She spun around. 'Did you hear that?' she spluttered. 'He spoke the name of the Evil One.'

JD was sure the Ragman groaned. 'Let's not go into that, Chatelaine. We can only kill him once. Anyway, the boy is talking nonsense. The Evil One's dead. Now, get the wretches to the bars if you want them to watch.'

The grey woman took a last look at JD, smiled her cruel smile and descended the spiral stairs.

As soon as she was gone JD said, 'But I know that Godrum isn't dead and I think you do too. I can even show you where he is.'

'You said you weren't sure,' the Ragman said. 'You said he's in the City and I've been thinking. I can search the City without you.'

'Maybe,' JD said. 'But I've been thinkin' too and I reckon I know how we can locate him for sure. Someone else saw him, same as me, and between us I reckon we could pinpoint the exact spot.'

The Ragman looked into JD's eyes. He seemed to be searching for some way of telling if he was speaking the truth.

'You didn't mention anybody else.'

'Like I said, I've been thinkin' and I remember talkin' to another kid who was in the City back then and they told me what they saw. I reckon between us we could fix it exact.'

The Ragman looked around furtively. He peered over the rail and watched the grey woman banging the bars of the cells with her good hand and calling the boys forward. The Ragman rubbed his chin and looked from side to side. JD hoped he hadn't left it too late.

'I don't know,' the Ragman whispered. 'You've cut it too fine. Even I can't get you out of this now. You'll be over this parapet and dropping like a stone in a moment or two.' He pointed down into the bowels of the Pit.

The hairs on the back of JD's neck tingled. He was

playing a dangerous game and knew it. One false move, one word out of place and it would be all over. Had he misjudged it? Was the Ragman really desperate to find Godrum?

The steps creaked as Chatelaine climbed towards them. JD knew his time would be up when she reached the top and shivered. In his mind he saw himself spinning through the air, could hear the crump and crack as his body broke on the rocks far below. JD, the boy from the Dry Marsh, took a deep breath and launched into what might be his last few sentences. If he got it wrong this time, it was all over.

'If you take me away now,' he said in a hoarse whisper. 'If you tell the woman you have to charge me for shoutin' Godrum's name or somethin', I promise I'll take you to him. I promise. I'll tell you who the other kid is and we'll both go with you to the City and show you exactly where they took him.'

The Ragman's eyes darted between JD and the hard-faced woman climbing towards them. JD's heart was beating fast. Come on, come on, he said to himself. She's nearly here.

Just as the woman put her foot on the final tread of the stairway the Ragman stepped forward.

'Stay there, Chatelaine,' he said. 'Stay and keep these boys quiet. I have to ask this kid a few more questions.'

The grey woman's face contorted and she squinted up at the old man. 'Questions? What questions? He's going off the top. You said –'

'Yes, yes. Just give me a few moments. There's something I need to know. You wait here. We'll be back in no time. Then you can have your fun.'

JD could tell that Chatelaine was not convinced so, before the Ragman could change his mind, he turned and without bidding, almost ran towards the steps. At any moment he expected to feel a twitch on the rope, a tightening around his neck and to be pulled back. If the grey woman argued now JD wasn't sure if the Ragman could resist. But no tug came and he began to climb the stairs as quick as he could, the rope trailing loosely behind him. He had to get to Aqua, he had to tell her what he'd said so's she could play her part and not give him away.

As soon as his head poked through the hole in the floor he called her name. 'Aqua,' he said in a hoarse whisper. 'Aqua. Quick, I've got somethin' to tell you.'

But she sat in the same disconsolate pose as when he'd left her.

'Aqua. I've thought of a way to get out of here. You and me.' He scuttled across the floor and squatted down beside her. 'Come on, Aqua, listen.' JD shook the girl's shoulder and she looked up. She had tears in her eyes.

'JD? I thought you would be dead by now,' she said.

'Not me. Look. I haven't got time to tell you the whole story but I've had an idea.'

Aqua opened her mouth to speak but JD ploughed on. He told her what he'd said and how the Ragman seemed to have believed him enough to put off throwing him down the pit. All the while he could hear the tread of heavy feet and the creaking of the stairway as the Ragman climbed nearer.

'You see,' JD said at last. 'If you just say you saw the Silver Men carryin' Godrum overhead and reckon you could remember which building they went to, I think we stand a chance. Insist that you have to stand where you stood that day to be sure.'

'When was I meant to have seen this?'

'The day you pulled me into that crack; the first time we met.'

'But –'

'No buts. It's our only chance. Think of the Dry Marsh. Remember the plan.'

A grunt came from the direction of the trapdoor. Quickly, JD slid across the floor and by the time the Ragman's head emerged he was standing by the stairway, his hands behind him, looking down at the old man.

The Ragman climbed out of the hole, staggered to his chair and slumped down. He picked up his glass of water and drained it.

'Ah,' he said, blowing out with the effort. 'Come here, boy.'

JD walked across the fine carpet and stood in front of him.

'Right,' the Ragman said once he'd recovered his breath. 'Now. Tell me every detail about that day and you'd better make it good. It's your last chance.'

JD licked his lips. 'Can I have a drink, sir?' he said. 'I'm real dry.' He spoke in a whine, like a small child.

'Scoop up a mouthful from the fountain then get on with your story. And don't take too long about it. Chatelaine will be up here any moment insisting I chuck you down the Pit. And,' he added, narrowing his eyes and looking hard at JD, 'if I even think you're pulling my leg you'll wish you had been chucked off the balcony, so let's have none of your nonsense.'

JD stepped over to the fountain and put his face to the water. He sucked up a little water into his mouth and swallowed. It was wonderful, so cool and fresh, quite unlike the tepid stuff he'd become used to from the drinking tubes. Dipping his head again he lapped at the water with his tongue and when he'd drunk two good gulps he turned his head to one side and looked to where Aqua sat in the darkness. He gave a long, exaggerated wink and smiled. He could not see her clearly but he was sure she smiled back.

228

By the time JD stood before the Ragman once more, the old man had recovered his breath.

'Now then,' he said. 'Tell me the whole thing from the start and remember, if just for one moment I don't believe your story it's only a couple of steps to those stairs. Understand?'

'Yes, sir.' JD looked towards the open trapdoor and shivered. He decided to start with the truth and explained how he'd met Godrum by the Old Road, what he looked like, what he'd said and what he'd shown him. He told the Ragman about the journey to the gates of the City and how the Boonie had recognised Godrum, told the guards and how he'd slipped through the gates in the confusion.

'Why were you coming to the City in the first place?' the Ragman asked when JD paused in his story.

'To find my Ma,' JD said flatly.

'And have you found her?'

'No,' JD said. He knew this was his first lie but consoled himself with the thought that the horrible woman in the Brooder could not really have been Ma. Not the Ma he knew anyhow.

'Then,' JD said quickly in case the story of Ma was to be pursued, 'when I was on the other side of the bridge the Silver Men flew over. Two of 'em were carryin' Godrum and they went right on into the City.'

'Hmm,' the Ragman said, narrowing his eyes and

studying JD hard. But JD just smiled back. He had told his story without a break, without hesitation. He reckoned he'd done OK.

'And you reckon you know which building they went to?'

'Ye . . . es,' JD said. 'They flew towards a bunch of towers and I reckon I know where they were headed, but there were a lot of tall buildings in the way, blockin' my view.'

'So you don't know,' the Ragman snapped.

'Yes, I do,' JD said. 'At least, I could say which one of 'em I thought they went to.'

JD worked his brain hard, trying to visualise the buildings he'd seen. He had to make the story sound good but he really hadn't taken too much notice of things back then. They all looked pretty much the same. Some were taller and some shorter, some wider and some narrower. Most had been grey but one or two had a red tinge while another looked a bit yellow but perhaps that was just the light. He decided on tall, narrow and red and described a mythical building to the old man.

The Ragman rubbed his chin and raised his eyes as if he was trying to picture the scene for himself. 'And you're sure you could find it again?'

'I reckon, though they did fly between two buildings before they disappeared. They went behind the red tower

230

so I guessed that's where they'd gone. They might have gone into the one behind it, I suppose.'

The Ragman sat up straight. 'That's no good,' he shouted. He shot a glance at the trapdoor then lowered his voice and spoke again: 'I can't go around every building in the City asking if they know where Godrum is. I have to know. Think, boy, think.'

JD gave the appearance of thinking but this was the opportunity he'd been waiting for. The Ragman was now speaking as if they were both on the same side, both in equal danger of being overheard. Deep inside JD felt his plan was working but he took his time before springing the trap.

'There's only one way I could be real sure,' he said, drawing out his words. 'I reckon I could point out the building if I was standin' in the same place. If we start from the bridge and if I could get back to where I was when they flew over and you did the same for my friend, then we'd have it.'

'Why don't I just take your friend? Then I could leave you with Chatelaine, she could chuck you into the Pit and we'd all be happy.' The Ragman leaned back in his chair and smiled a sickly smile. 'Except you perhaps.'

JD knew he'd pushed his luck too far but he couldn't backtrack now. He had to risk everything.

'Look, sir,' JD said in his best and clearest voice. 'You

need to find Godrum, we both know that. I don't know why and I don't really care but I do know I don't want to be thrown down no Pit. I can help you but you've gotta help me. You take me and my friend to the City, we'll show you where the Silver Men took Godrum, then you let us go. That's the deal.'

The Ragman shook his head and JD's heart sank. 'I'll take you and your friend to the City. You help me find Godrum and when I've found him, when I'm face to face with him, then I'll let you go. Not before. I'm not going to take nobody nowhere to point out any old building and then run off. No, sir, if we don't find Godrum, a living breathing Godrum, then you and your friend, whoever he is, will be handed over to Chatelaine double-quick and I'll stand and cheer with her as you both drop onto those hard, spiky rocks at the bottom of the Pit. *That's* the deal. Take it or leave it.'

'When do we go?' JD smiled.

'As soon as I see your friend. He's working down some Pit, I suppose?'

'No, sir. He, or rather she, is right here in this room.'

The Ragman raised his eyebrows. 'You mean that girl over there?' He waved his arm towards where Aqua crouched. 'But you'd never seen her before you came here.'

'Yes, I had.' JD wondered how much to give away but decided he'd have to come clean. 'We met in the City the day they captured Godrum We hid there 'til nightfall and then she showed me how to get into the Farm.'

The stubble on the Ragman's chin rasped as he stroked it. 'Did she now?' he said. 'Girl,' he called. 'Come here.'

'She can't,' JD said. 'She's tied up.'

'So she is,' the Ragman laughed. JD didn't know if he had really forgotten or whether he was just being cruel, but the Ragman eased himself out of his chair, walked over to Aqua, untied her rope and led her back to where JD stood.

JD smiled down at her and his heart soared when she smiled back. She'd been listening. This was more like Aqua. Her tears were gone and she looked more like the girl he'd shared his dreams with.

Twenty-five

The City Again

The Ratcatcher's truck whined into life and once again JD found himself being bounced about in the back. But despite his discomfort he congratulated himself because his plan seemed to be working out. And the screams and shouts from Chatelaine when the Ragman had told her he was taking her victim away really made him smile. He only hoped he wasn't smiling too soon. He'd have to watch his step. If he got anything wrong again he'd be right back there and going off the top for sure.

He'd hoped, he'd expected, Aqua to be in the back with him; he had so much he wanted to say to her. But the Ragman had separated them, putting her in the front next to him. He'd been suspicious ever since JD had first mentioned Aqua.

It wasn't long before the bouncing stopped and the truck

purred over smoother terrain. JD guessed they'd picked up the road to the City and when the truck began turning right and left he figured it wouldn't be long before they reached the centre. When they stopped and the door scraped open and sunlight flooded into the box, JD focused hard on what he had to do.

'Come on, boy. Out.'

The Ragman was standing outside on a grey concrete road that ran away between tall buildings. JD slid to the edge of the box and looked out. He recognised nothing, just streets, towers and a group of Boonies who stood and stared.

JD dropped onto the road, trying to appear cool while all the time his brain rushed between joy and fear.

The Ragman picked up the loop of his tether and drew JD away from the truck. The hot road burned his bare feet, making JD hop from one foot to the other as he searched for something familiar.

The Ragman shooed the Boonies away, which gave JD time to look around, and to his relief he recognised the crossroads above the bridge a short way down the road.

'Is that the bridge down there?' he asked.

'Sure is,' the Ragman said.

'Can we go there? If I can stand where I was when the Silver Men flew over I reckon I can work out where they went pretty quick.'

235

The Ragman squinted down at JD. 'OK,' he said, 'but no tricks. You know what's coming if you lie to me.'

'I'm not lying, sir. I'm just tryin' to help,' JD whined, pulling his face into what he thought was a good-little-boy look. He gazed up at the old man, blinking in the sunlight.

The Ragman grunted.

JD wanted so much to ask where Aqua was but didn't want to make the old guy suspicious so soon.

'Do you need me any more?' the Ratcatcher asked, leaning out of his cab.

'I guess not,' the Ragman said.

The driver looked away; JD heard a click and the motor fired up. 'When do you want me to come to get you?' the driver said.

The Ragman thought for a moment. 'Don't bother,' he said. 'We'll find our own way back.'

JD was trying to stay calm, but inside he was starting to panic. Where was Aqua? He was sure she'd been in the truck when they'd left. He stood on tiptoe and tried to look into the cab but it was too high for him. The truck's motor hummed and as the volume rose so JD's panic grew into anger. Had the Ragman had tricked him? He didn't know how he'd done it but it was plain he'd left Aqua behind.

When the truck began to pull away JD spun around and glared at the ragged old man.

'Where's Aqua?' he shouted. 'Where's my friend? What have you done with her?' Poor JD was beside himself. 'You promised. You said you'd bring her. You said . . .'

All his planning, all his fast thinking and fast talking and here he was, just short of the bridge across which he and Aqua could run to freedom and she wasn't there. The miserable, smelly old Ragman had tricked him. JD's eyes blazed; if his hands had not been bound behind his back he would have leapt at the old man's throat.

And when the Ragman smiled it was all JD could do to stop himself from kicking out. He wanted to pummel that ugly old face to a pulp.

'Turn around, boy,' the Ragman said quietly.

JD spun around and there was Aqua, the rope around her neck, staring at him with her wide, Farm child's eyes. She must have been on the far side of the truck all the time.

'Come here, child,' the Ragman said and Aqua walked towards him. 'Give me your rope,' he said and Aqua handed him the end of her tether. 'Now, you boy, turn around.' JD did as he was told. He felt stupid for making such a fuss but it had served to remind him how clever the Ragman was. He'd set him up and JD had fallen for it. He'd betrayed himself and hoped he hadn't made it too plain that his objective was not to help the Ragman but to run away with Aqua.

With both ropes in his hands and the two children standing before him, the Ragman said, 'Now then, you two, let's get this clear. Between you, you two reckon you can work out where they took the Evil One. Is that right?'

'Yes,' JD said quickly.

'But,' the Ragman said, glaring down at JD, 'if this is some kind of a trick, I'll take you straight back and personally throw you *both* into the Pit. Is that absolutely clear?'

JD nodded again but Aqua sucked her teeth and screwed up her eyes.

'Right,' the Ragman went on. 'As long as you understand, boy, that you ain't just playing with your own life now, you're playing with your girlfriend's life too, we'll get on.'

JD gulped. He hadn't quite thought of it that way but whatever, he was determined to keep to his plan.

'We'll go down to the bridge and start from there,' the Ragman said and shook the ropes.

Despite his tether and the threats the old man had made, JD tried to stand tall. He threw his head back and strode away confidently but Aqua followed with her head bowed.

'Come on, Aqua,' JD whispered. 'We've gotta get as far in front of him as we can.'

He paced away until the rope that held him was almost stretched out straight. Aqua pattered close behind.

When they were as far away as their ropes allowed, JD

glanced down. 'We've gotta be ready,' he said to Aqua out of the corner of his mouth. 'We're bound to get a chance. Come on, Aqua. Think of the Dry Marsh.'

Aqua gave a weak smile. 'It's no use, JD. We've had it. How can we get away now?'

'Don't say that. We've just gotta keep him believin' that we know where Godrum is. That will give us time.'

'Time for what?'

'Time for somethin' to turn up,' JD said, but Aqua just shook her head.

They made a strange sight. A group of Boonies in their drab blue walked past and stared, but when the Ragman glared at them they hurried on. A smartly dressed man in a tailored jacket of shining silver with gold trim looked at them quizzically, but he too got the full blast of the old man's fierce stare. The man sniffed and continued his stroll. A young couple sitting in an air-conditioned bubble passed noiselessly by, a hand's breadth above the highway. The woman pointed and said something to her partner, but he paid no heed and they wafted away towards the City centre.

When they reached the crossroads at the end of the street, JD saw the bridge, hard and somehow hostile in the bright sunlight, stretching across the dry canal. Seeing the broken supports, the crumbling concrete and cracked surface again, JD remembered that first day he'd come to the City. It seemed such a long time ago.

They stopped at the head of the bridge and JD pretended to study the area carefully.

'Is this it?' the Ragman asked.

'Ye . . . es,' JD said, turning his head from side to side. 'I think so. It's hard to tell exactly.'

'What's so difficult?' the Ragman snapped. 'Is it or isn't it?'

JD tried to look like he was thinking. He studied the ground and looked at the sky. He shuffled his feet and shot surreptitious glances across the bridge, trying to see if there were guards at the gate. This was exactly where he'd been when the Silver Men flew over but that was far from his mind. He was trying to work out how he and Aqua could get across that bridge and away.

'I'm tryin' to remember,' he said. 'They came over, one pair of Silver Men high up, another pair low down carryin' Godrum,' he said, turning his head to one side as if focusing on the scene in his imagination.

'Yes, yes, I know that. You've already told me that,' the Ragman snapped. 'Where did they take the old fool?'

JD turned around, pursed his lips and squinted at the buildings high up against the yellow sky. In his mind's eye he could see the Silver Men with Godrum dangling between them heading towards the tallest tower, the one with the thin grey spiral of smoke rising vertically from its summit. But he wouldn't tell the Ragman yet. He needed time; time to gain his trust, time for him and Aqua to be ready. Then he had an idea.

'They went over there,' he said, nodding his head towards a cluster of tall buildings.

The Ragman turned to follow his gaze. 'Where?'

'Over there,' JD said, nodding at a dozen or so near identical concrete towers.

'Which one?' The Ragman growled. 'Be more specific, boy. It's no good you just nodding into the City. Which building did they go to?'

JD smiled to himself. 'That one,' he said as vaguely as before. 'The tall red one. They flew in behind it and didn't come out the other side. Isn't that right, Aqua?' he said, turning towards her and winking broadly.

When JD turned back the old man was studying the buildings. His hands were clenched; frustration was written all over his wizened features.

'That's no good,' the Ragman said. 'I can't tell which tower you're talking about. There are a lot of red ones and a lot of grey ones. Be more precise.'

JD nodded and when again he said: 'That one,' he could feel the Ragman's irritation and thought he'd pushed him far enough. It was time to move forward.

'I can't show you like this,' he said, turning his back towards his captor and raising his hands. 'If you untie me I'll point out the one I'm talkin' about.'

241

With his back turned he hissed at Aqua, 'Get ready. 'He'll have to drop your rope to untie me; the moment he does, go for it. Make for the bridge and run as hard as you can.'

'What about you?' Aqua whispered back.

'Don't worry about me. You just run and leave the rest to me.'

JD felt the Ragman's rough hands set to work on the rope behind his back. His heart was beating fast but he waited and waited. When he felt the knots loosening he jerked his hands away and shouted, 'Go, Aqua! Run. Run now!'

Aqua took off sprinting down the slope, her loose tether snaking out behind her.

'Hey,' the Ragman shouted and when JD felt his rope go slack, he wrenched his hands free and in a single movement spun around and set off after her. But he had not taken two paces before the noose around his neck snapped tight, his head jerked back and he sprawled full length on the hot road.

'Come back here, you,' the Ragman growled.

Looking back, JD saw the loop of rope trapped under the Ragman's foot.

JD let his head drop onto the hard surface. He closed his eyes. He'd done it wrong. All his planning, all his dreams and here he was stretched on a hot road, tied by the neck. It had been his last chance and he'd blown it. His only consolation was that Aqua had got away. He might be doomed but at least he'd saved her.

'Are you OK?' a little voice said from above. JD's eyes flicked open and there was Aqua squatting down next to him. She put out a hand and touched his shoulder.

'What?' JD spluttered. 'I thought–'

'I couldn't go without you,' she said and shrugged her shoulders. 'So I came back.'

'Oh, Aqua! Why did you do that? You could have got away.'

'Maybe,' she said. 'But what would have been the point? I want to go to the Dry Marsh with you, JD. We were going together. That was the idea, wasn't it?'

Her gentle voice made JD's heart swell. She'd given up her freedom for him. What a girl, he thought. And the despair had gone from her voice; it was soft and clear just like before. Despite their predicament, despite the fact that the Ragman would now cart them back to the dome he felt no fear. As long as they were together they'd be OK. When you have a friend, JD thought, a friend who would give up her own freedom for you, anythin's possible.

'Come on, JD,' Aqua whispered. 'You can't lounge around in the sunshine all day. Get up now.' Aqua took JD's hands in hers and pulled him to his feet. Then she smiled her old cheeky smile. 'Stupid,' she said.

243

Twenty-six

Second Chance

The Ragman crouched over JD, retied the knots and when he was satisfied that both children were properly secure, he shook their ropes and drove them up the slope towards the City. With an occasional prod in the back, a twitch on the rope or an angry grunt he herded them into the forest of concrete towers and along hot, featureless streets that burned their feet.

They passed a crossroads which JD thought he recognised, but he soon realised that each one looked much like all the others. JD hoped they'd stop someplace and the Ragman would interrogate him some more about Godrum but nothing came, they just marched on in silence.

The silence suited JD as he was thinking, but all too soon they began to leave the tall buildings behind. JD looked at Aqua and she gave a grimace. They had passed through the City without a pause and both knew that before long they would be back at the Scrubland; by nightfall they would be at the dome where the grey woman waited. JD shivered.

They turned into a broad road where just a few old buildings stood, sun-bleached and crumbling into jagged shapes; ahead lay the Scrubland. On one side of the road a long, low wall threw a meagre shadow on the ground. The Ragman prodded his captives towards it and he sat down.

'Wait here,' he growled, taking out a cloth from his coat and wiping the sweat from his brow. It was the first time he'd spoken since the escape attempt and JD wondered if this might be a good time to ask the question, the only thing that had come to him as he'd tried to figure out some way of avoiding the fate that awaited them. He began tentatively.

'Is it all right for us to sit down too, sir?' he asked.

The Ragman grunted and the children sank to the ground. JD longed to mop his brow too but with his hands tied behind him he could do nothing to stop the sweat trickling down his face. He shook his head in a vain attempt to relieve the stinging in his eyes. Aqua wiped her forehead on JD's shoulder and hunched up one of hers for him to do the same.

'Are we goin' to have to walk all the way back?' JD asked after a while.

The Ragman glared at him. 'Why?' he said. 'You in a hurry to die?'

JD shrugged and looked down. It was not the answer he'd hoped for. 'I just wondered,' he said.

'Unless you have your own personal jet-pack then, yes, you are going to have to walk all the way back and so am I,' the Ragman growled.

'Oh,' JD said to the ground. 'We ain't goin' to look for Godrum no more then?'

'There is no Godrum,' the old man hissed. 'You made all that up just to trick me into taking you to the City so's you and your little friend could make a break for it. I ain't that stupid.'

JD shrugged. 'It's true. I did want to escape but I really did see Godrum and I reckon I do know where the Silver Men took him.'

'So you say, but how can I believe a Boonie? All Boonies lie. It's a well-known fact.'

'I wasn't lying,' JD said softly. 'I'm sorry we tried to get away but you can't blame us. We don't know if you actually will let us go when we find Godrum so we had to try.'

The Ragman grunted again and JD thought he recognised a tiny hint of understanding in that grunt.

JD waited and waited. He needed his words to dwell in the Ragman's mind for a while. There had been no reprimand, no mention of Evil Ones when he'd said Godrum's

246

name, he'd noticed. The Ragman just sat on the low wall, his eyes glazed.

'I could still show you if you like,' JD said, looking up into the old guy's lined face. He caught his narrow eyes with his own and thought he could almost see the Ragman's brain working.

'Honest, sir. We'd show you. Wouldn't we, Aqua?'

'Yes,' the girl whispered. She wasn't sure what JD was up to but they had nothing to lose now.

The Ragman remained silent for what seemed like a very long time, staring at the yellow haze that hung over the Scrubland. When he turned his head towards the towers of the City, JD hoped he was considering his options. He held his breath and waited.

At last the Ragman looked down at the children and let out a deep sigh. 'OK,' he said. 'You take me there.'

'And will you let us go if we do?' JD said.

'We'll see,' the old man replied, fixing JD with his narrow eyes. 'That deal's off. I'm making no promises except this one. If you or the girl try anything, anything at all, you'll both be dead by nightfall.'

JD nodded. 'OK.'

By the time they were back among the high buildings JD knew what to do. It would be no use trying to escape again; his best chance was to show the Ragman someplace the Silver Men might have taken Godrum, then tag along, hoping for a break of some kind. At least he knew the Silver Men really had flown into the City so there was a chance they might find him. What would happen then he could only guess.

JD strode on, getting as far ahead as his lead allowed. Aqua kept pace with him, leaving the Ragman puffing along behind.

'Are you OK?' JD asked Aqua.

'I'm scared. I never did see your friend so how can I say where they took him?'

'They went towards the tall building. See that one with the smoke comin' out of it?'

'Are you sure that's where they landed?'

'No, but say that anyways. When we get there I'll point to two of the buildings and when it comes to your turn, say it was the one with the smoke.'

'If you say so,' Aqua said then lapsed into silence.

JD looked up, squinting into the bright light. Above the other buildings the tower with the smoke stood high, pointing into the sky. JD made his way towards it, crossing main roads and side streets, some small, some just narrow alleys. At the entrance to one of these Aqua poked JD with her elbow and looked down.

'Look,' she said out of the corner of her mouth.

JD looked and there at the base of the building he saw a deep crack, broad at the corner and narrowing into the alleyway. He shuddered; it was the gap through which Aqua had pulled him that night he'd been chased by the Silver Men. Shards of broken concrete lay on the ground. It seemed too long ago for that to have been left from JD's visit and he wondered if somebody else had found the place, but when he looked at Aqua and her wistful smile he understood that it was she who had been there. Just because he'd been taken to the Pits, she hadn't stopped her secret night forays. She was a tough kid, there was no doubt about that, and he felt proud that it was by his efforts she was back from her despair, back some way towards being the old Aqua, the brave little Aqua who roamed the City streets at night. If they stuck together he hoped they could somehow still get out of this place and away to freedom. He didn't know how but he hoped.

'Well, boy. Are we anywhere near?'

JD looked up. A latticework walkway linking two of the tallest buildings arched above his head.

'It's hard to tell. Let's walk on for a bit.'

They walked on down the road. A large transparent bubble descended the side of one of the buildings. It stopped close to them and two people dressed in pale blue atmosphere suits stepped out, followed by a Silver Man. JD shivered but neither the Leaders nor the Silver Man gave them so much as a fleeting glance. They moved away, deep in conversation. The Ragman turned to watch them go, which gave JD the opportunity to speak to Aqua.

'Are you ready? It's this building here,' he said, nodding towards the tower on his left.

'OK,' Aqua said, drawing herself up and putting her shoulders back.

'I'm pretty sure this is the place,' JD said when the Ragman turned back. Squinting up towards the square of sky between the buildings, he said, 'I reckon they flew in here. I recognise this big shack.' He nodded towards the tower from which the trail of smoke rose. 'It's a bit darker than most of the others, that's how I know,' he added for good measure.

'Did they go to the tall tower?' the Ragman said. 'You reckoned it was one of two.'

'That's right. It could have been that one or it could have been the one those people just came out of. I couldn't tell. Aqua will know.'

The Ragman looked at Aqua. 'Well, girl. Which one was it?'

Aqua decided to make a story of it just the way JD had.

'I was back there at the corner. That place where the concrete is cracked. They came in over there,' she said, nodding her head towards a patch of bright sky. The Ragman turned away to look and Aqua grinned at JD. She was beginning to enjoy herself.

'Yes. I remember now,' she said. 'The Silver Men came swooping in around that building, their jet-packs trailing smoke. Two of them held this old man, his arms outstretched, his feet waving in the air.'

The Ragman was looking up as if trying to picture the scene for himself. JD glared at Aqua, warning her not to overdo it. Convincing was good but she was getting carried away. Aqua hunched her shoulders to her ears and grinned. She was having fun.

'Yes,' she went on. 'I can see it. They flew over that see-through arm thing then they all came together as if they were talking. Then they rose up, their jet-packs buzzing, and flew right up to the top of the tallest tower and landed. Right up there,' she said, her voice rising in excitement. 'Right onto the top they went and then they disappeared. They must have landed up there because I didn't see them again.'

The Ragman turned towards Aqua and frowned. 'Are you sure?' he asked, his eyes suddenly alive.

'Yup,' was all she said.

The Ragman stared at the top of the building. 'Hmm,' he said. 'It's possible, I suppose.'

JD was relieved. He'd been worried that as neither of them really knew where the Silver Men had taken Godrum they might have said something silly.

The Ragman stood for some time staring at the tall

251

building, his eyes scanning up and down. Then he smiled and turned back to the children.

'Come on,' he said, shaking their ropes like reins. 'Come with me.' He guided them into one of the tiny alleys, herding them through the shadows until they reached a narrow dead end. JD looked around and shuddered. Tall walls streaked with dirt rose all around them and once more he began to feel the old panic gripping him. He hated being closed in and had to fight hard to think of something, anything to keep his mind off where he was. To distract himself he studied the Ragman's coat, picking out individual strips of material and following them with his eyes as they wove their way in and out of the tangled mass. But then the Ragman walked away and broke the spell. He strode to the end of the narrow close and banged on the wall with his fist.

The children looked at each other and wondered if he'd lost his senses. The Ragman banged again, striking the wall hard with the flat of his hand and muttering under his breath. He raised his hand again but before he could strike the wall again a metal door, clean and shining on its inside yet clad with concrete outside, began to swing out. A face appeared and JD blinked in disbelief. It was the sour-faced woman, Chatelaine. He was sure they'd left her behind at the dome so how could she be here? Now it wasn't only the buildings that seemed to be closing in on him.

With a tug on their ropes the Ragman drew the children to him and shoved them through the doorway into a small square lobby. He shooed them towards a doorway opposite, past a dark stairway that led off to their left. JD was glad they hadn't gone down there. Beyond the doorway they found themselves in a broad, white corridor, clean, high and cool, and they felt as out of place as they looked. JD glanced up and down, searching for something that might tell him where he was but there was nothing, just a long, clinical, white tunnel.

'I've never seen anything like this before,' Aqua whispered. 'Have you, JD?'

JD shook his head. He went to take a step forward but the Ragman held him back. He was deep in conversation with the grey woman, their voices animated as if they were arguing.

'I need to see him and quick. Is he at his post?' the Ragman growled.

'I don't know,' Chatelaine said. 'I guess he must be, but when are you going to hand over those brats? You made me look so stupid back there. Mustering all the kids, telling them to watch what happens to insolent brats, then you just waltz off. How do you think that made me look?' Chatelaine threw her arms up. JD could see she was real angry.

'Never mind all that,' the Ragman said, turning away. 'I've got more important things to attend to right now.

I ain't got time to worry none about your finer feelings.'

He turned away. 'I'm going down now. You just stay here and make sure nobody comes.'

'And when do I get to hurl these filthy brats into the Pit?' Chatelaine shouted at the Ragman's back. 'You tell me that. I'm not going to stand on guard for you just so's you can humiliate me any time you choose. These things,' she spat, pointing at JD and Aqua before running around to face the Ragman once again. 'They go off the top before the sun sets. Yes or no?'

'OK, OK,' the Ragman said. 'You be sure no one comes and I'll see what I can do.'

The Ragman pushed Chatelaine aside and only JD saw the poisonous look she gave him.

'Come with me,' the Ragman said and turning his attention back to his captives, he led them across the lobby, leaving the grey woman shivering in her rage.

'Down there,' he said, pointing to the dingy steps.

JD hesitated. 'Down there?' he said hoarsely, staring down at the dark stairway. He didn't like the look of it one bit, and when a deep echoing groan came up from somewhere far below the blood froze in his veins.

'What's that?' he said, turning back but as if in answer the sound grew louder.

'Just get yourself down there,' the Ragman said impatiently. 'Go on.'

254

'It's dark. I can't see,' JD said, backing away, pressing his back to the wall.

And all the time the noise grew and intensified; a groaning, tortured creaking like heavy wheels grinding against each other. Then something squealed and screamed.

'Oh!' Aqua made a tiny noise and struggled in vain to free her hands. Her eyes were wide and fear was written across her face.

'What's wrong?' JD asked, but Aqua could only stare, unable to speak.

'Aqua. What is it?' JD said again, but he knew it was a pointless question. The noise grew and swelled, filling the air all around them. The ground under their feet shook as if some gigantic creature was climbing the steps towards them.

'What is it?' he shouted above the terrible sound. 'What's that noise?'

But the Ragman said nothing; he just smiled his knowing smile.

'Oh, JD,' Aqua managed to say at last, her voice breaking and tears squeezing from the corners of her eyes. 'It's the Grinder. Now we've told him what he wanted to know he's going to feed us to the Grinder.'

Twenty-seven

The Wheel

A cold hand seemed to close around JD's spine. When Aqua had told him about the Grinder he hadn't believed her, but with the awful machine clanking away just a few paces below him it seemed she'd been right. There really was such a thing.

'What's goin' on?' he shouted, turning and glaring at the Ragman. 'You said –'

'Just get down those steps,' the Ragman cut in, raising his voice above the clatter.

'Don't go, JD. It's the Grinder.' Aqua was beside herself, her eyes wide with terror. 'It's the Grinder. It's the Grinder,' she said over and over again, screwing up her face. 'I can hear them. I can hear kids being fed into it.'

JD listened. Above the crackling and banging he could hear low, grumbling voices. They were human for sure but they weren't making the kind of sound he'd have expected from kids being fed into a Grinder. Surely they would shout and scream?

'Stupid child,' the Ragman said. 'You don't know what you're talking about. Just get down below and stop whining.'

But JD still refused to move. 'Is it the Grinder?' he said, looking into the Ragman's eyes. 'Is this our reward for showin' you where they took Godrum?'

'I don't know what you're talking about. What is this Grinder?' the man said.

'Don't pretend you don't know,' JD spat. 'The Grinder; the machine that mangles kids into food.'

The Ragman had been angry at being disobeyed but in a moment his wrinkled face split into a broad, gap-toothed grin.

'The Grinder? Ho, ho! You kids make me laugh with your funny ideas. There is no Grinder here, you stupid boy, get down those steps and you'll see.'

The Ragman's laughter made JD feel foolish but Aqua was still not convinced. Her body wracked with sobs and her thin, bare legs shook beneath her tabard. She was convinced they were about to be reduced to little piles of bloody food.

JD wasn't so sure but still he hesitated, staring into the darkness. 'I . . . I can't see,' he stuttered. 'It's dark.'

The Ragman harrumphed and strode across to where

JD hovered. Reaching up to a little square box on the wall, he flicked a switch and in an instant, pale yellow light flooded the stone stairway.

JD blinked. He could see the steps curling away in front of him just as if the whole place was lit by rows of candles. But there were no candles. The light came from bright strips that hummed and glistened along the roof. JD stared. Light without candles, without flame; he'd never seen anything like it. Then he remembered the corridor. That too had been light but there were no windows and no candles. He turned to the Ragman.

'How . . . ?' he asked. 'How did that happen?'

'Fireless, boy. You never seen it before?'

JD shook his head.

'Well, get down those steps and maybe you'll learn something.'

JD still wasn't sure, but the smile on the Ragman's face reminded him a bit of Godrum when he'd shown him how to make a still so slowly, keeping his hands and body pressed against the wall, he began to descend.

The steps spiralled down, the turns so tight that JD could never see more than a few paces ahead. Behind him he could hear the Ragman's heavy coat brush against the wall and the shuffling patter of Aqua's little feet. The lower JD went, the louder the clanking and grinding grew. He was frightened but curiosity drove him on.

At the bottom of the steps JD found himself in a big round room dominated by an enormous wheel built of hundreds of round poles all lashed together, vertically, horizontally and with cross-braces everywhere. It lay on its side and in its centre, a thick, shiny pole extended from floor to ceiling. But what amazed JD was not the wheel, or the pole from which smoke and sparks crackled and spat, it was all the people. Ranged around the rim of the giant wheel, leaning their weight onto long spars that extended out almost to the rock walls, were rows and rows of boys. Boonies, Farm boys, some short, some tall, but all grunting and groaning as they heaved the enormous wheel around. Spaced out around the edge of the room older boys stood on raised platforms, Seniors who shouted and cursed if the wheel began to slow, and for no reason other than that they could, they cracked long whips which snaked out across the shoulders of the toiling children who were lashed to the heavy spars. JD had thought the Pit had been bad enough but this was a nightmare.

'There you are, Boonie,' the Ragman said. 'This is what you could hear. No Grinder, you see, no awful machine into which naughty children are fed. Although I guess most of these kids would happily settle for a quick if messy end.'

'Who are they?' JD asked. 'And where did they all come from?'

'Take a good look, boy. These are all kids who escaped

from the Pits or who answered back, were rude or disrespectful. These are the clever ones, the smart alecs. You know the kind, always got an argument, always asking questions. These kids, young Boonie, all of them, each sweating, straining one of them is exactly like you.'

JD stared. 'But why?' he asked. 'What are they doin'? Is it just some kinda punishment, pushin' that heavy wheel around?'

'You could say that, but they are at least doing some good.' He pointed to the strip light that glowed on the ceiling above his head. 'The light that so intrigued you. And all the power that drives the City. Everything comes from here. It's called Fireless power. The wheels turn and the pole passes through a generator and that makes Fireless power. It lights the buildings, runs the elevators; anything that needs power, those kids make it.'

'Is there no other way?' JD said, still horrified at the sight before him.

The Ragman looked away. 'There used to be,' he said as if talking to himself. 'In the old days machines did the work. They drove generators all over the planet; Fireless power was everywhere. But the machines ran on oil and after the Big War the oil was all used up.' The Ragman turned back towards JD. 'So,' he shrugged, waving a hand towards the countless, ragged children trudging and straining at the wheel, 'we had to think of something else.'

JD did not have long to dwell on what the Ragman had said before he was jostled towards another stairway, another steep spiral to the floor below. And there, exactly like the one above, was another great wheel with more rows upon rows of sweating boys all straining to turn it. The shining pole he'd seen on the floor above came down through the ceiling and passed through the hub of this wheel too and JD wondered whether there was another floor below this and another below that where more kids were lashed to more spars, all plodding around, all wearing grooves in countless floors in their ceaseless toil.

The Ragman took JD's shoulder and guided him and Aqua around the edge of the circular room. Most of the slaves kept their heads down, locked into their own private hell, but one or two looked at them as they passed. But it was just the briefest glance before they traipsed onward, ever onward, going nowhere except round and round in circles.

At the far side of the room the Ragman pushed JD towards a rickety wooden ladder which led up to a kind of round nest made out of wood, frayed rope and old pieces of trash. It hung from the ceiling and looked, JD thought, like an indoor version of the Ragman's dome.

The Ragman took the ends of the children's rope tethers and tied them tightly around the ladder.

'You two wait here and don't try any of your silly tricks;

if you do I'll get you each a place on the Fireless wheel straight off. Understand?'

JD nodded but then, instead of climbing the ladder as he'd expected, the Ragman walked back to one of the raised platforms where a Senior stood with his whip. He spoke to him and after a few moments the Senior boy turned his head towards the children and grinned broadly before the ragged man shambled back to the ladder.

'You may think I don't trust you, Boonie,' he said as he arrived. 'And you'd be right, so I've told that boy he's got two more workers for his wheel if either of you steps out of line. And I won't tell you what he said when he saw your girlfriend here,' he added with a leer, 'for fear of upsetting your delicate nature.'

JD felt anger course through his body and struggled to pull his hands free, but they were held fast and before he could think of something to say, something to release his pent-up fury, the Ragman heaved himself up onto the lowest rungs.

He climbed heavily, making the ladder creak and crack under his weight. At the top he paused before an opening in the trash ball.

'Yo,' he called. 'Yo, my bro. Are you home to visitors?'

He received no reply that JD could hear but the Ragman clambered up the ladder and climbed in through a hole in the side of the high nest.

'What's going on, JD?' Aqua whispered, her voice trembling. 'How are we ever going to get out of here?'

'We'll find a way,' JD said and smiled at her. 'We'll be fine. He needs us to help him find Godrum. He won't let us come to no harm, despite his threats.' JD tried hard to sound confident but it was tough. Inside, he was as scared as she was.

He leaned his head towards Aqua's, trying to think of something reassuring to say, but as he did so a crack rent the air and a sharp pain shot through JD's shoulders.

'No talking, you two,' the Senior called, raising his voice above the grinding of the mighty wheel. 'No talking or it'll be the worse for you.'

JD heard the cruel swish of the whip above his head as the boy flicked it out again.

'Can't see how it can get much worse than it's going to be already though, but I'll think of something,' the Senior cackled, and he cracked the whip in the air one more time. 'Yep,' he laughed. 'I'll think of something.'

JD kept his head down. He reckoned it might be smart to stay quiet for a while.

Lashed to the ladder, the children could only watch the giant wheel grind around, all the while trying not to attract the attention of the boy with the whip. From time to time they heard the lash snake out, picking some random victim from among the mass of kids tied to the spars. JD noticed they hardly seemed to care whether the whip hit them or not, they just trudged on, keeping the wheel turning, keeping the blue-white sparks crackling around the central column.

JD was just wondering how the sparks came to be there when he felt the ladder shake once more and looking up, saw the dirty soles of the Ragman's feet coming down towards them. JD watched in silence as, back on the ground, his captor set to untying the ropes that held them to the ladder. He glanced towards the Senior and found him watching too, wondering whether he was going to have two more kids to persecute any time soon.

When their bindings were free the Ragman nodded towards the ladder. 'Go on up, you two, there's someone wants to talk to you.'

JD set off quickly, scampering up the rungs, keen to get out of range of the Senior on the podium, and before long he was at the circular hole in the ball of trash. He peered in. It was pretty dark, but there was no time to hesitate, Aqua was close up behind him with the Ragman just below. JD crawled through the hole and hauled Aqua in too.

The sparks from the Fireless pole flashed and flickered through the doorway, lighting up the dark space, but when the Ragman climbed through he drew a shutter across the opening, cutting out the sight and most of the sound of the grinding wheel.

In the yellow light of a few strategically placed candles JD could see the familiar lattice of shining wooden staves reaching up and over the roof and there were fine rugs on the floor too, just like in the Ragman's dome. But there was no furniture, just a mesh of staves and strips of cloth, woven into a circle, right in the centre of the place. JD felt Aqua press up close against him and heard her whimper.

'Stand up straight, Aqua,' JD whispered. 'Look straight, don't let him see you're scared.'

JD also pulled himself erect and put his shoulders back, but pretty soon he wanted to run and hide too. From the tangled mass in the middle of the room, the circular nest within a nest, there came a groan like a heavy weight being moved. Then an enormous dark shape began to rise up in front of JD's eyes.

It was like something was erupting into the room.

Twenty-eight

Fireless the Giant

JD and Aqua stood transfixed. Their eyes were wide and their mouths hung open as a great sinister shape grew and grew right in front of them. It seemed to JD that if it didn't stop soon it would grow so big it would burst right out of the whole nest, shattering it into pieces and sending them all crashing to the floor below. But in the candlelight he saw that the shape was just a man, a very large man rising to his feet.

The giant turned to face the newcomers and sniffed loudly. Controlling his fear, JD stood straight and studied the man. He was big and broad, his face flushed and wild. JD saw he wore bib dungarees the same as his own, except you would have to sew more than ten pairs of his together to get one to fit this guy. And hair seemed to grow from everywhere. A great ginger mane covered his head and poured down his back. His beard, matted and twisted as a patch of sawgrass, was thick with scraps of food, some fresh, running with moisture, some old and putrefying. JD reckoned he could have survived for many days on the food in that man's beard.

The giant's bare arms were as thick and meaty as a big man's legs and bristled with a kind of auburn fur which extended beyond his wrists and down each meaty finger.

'Is this the kid?' the giant boomed.

'Sure is,' the Ragman said.

'Come here, kid,' the enormous man said, turning his flint-sharp eyes onto JD.

JD glanced at the Ragman, who nodded, so JD stepped up to the edge of the ring of sticks and looked inside. Staring over the edge, he couldn't believe his eyes, for ranged all around and piled one on another were basket after basket of food; thick slices of red meat draped over great hunks of white bread, brown-topped pies, some whole, some with bites taken out of them and cast aside. JD was horrified. Just outside, hundreds of emaciated kids trudged around the wheel, their lives draining away for lack of food and drink, yet here, just a few steps up a ladder, there was enough grub to feed them forever.

The food baskets were stacked right up around the big guy's legs but JD could tell that the floor on which the giant stood was way below where he, Aqua and the Ragman were. Even so, the big guy towered above them.

'Well, come on, Boonie,' the man boomed, picking up a pie, taking a huge bite and crushing the remains between his fingers. 'Let's have it. Let's hear what's got my brother so excited.'

JD opened his mouth to speak but something seemed to have stuck his tongue to the roof of his mouth. He just stood and gawped. Could this really be the Ragman's brother? He could see similarities – their eyes, their twisted beards and fleshy noses –and they lived in the same kind of homes but could this great hulking guy, this grub-spattered mountain of a man, really be kin to the Ragman?

The giant seemed agitated that JD did not reply right off and turned to glare at the Ragman, who almost shouted at JD, 'Come on, boy, tell him what you told me. Tell him about Godrum.'

JD swallowed, trying to unstick his tongue.

'Godrum,' he choked, not sure what it was he was meant to say. 'Godrum was very kind to me.' The words came from nowhere but seemed to sum up everything JD knew or remembered about the old man and by good fortune they also loosened his tongue.

'I found him one mornin' in the Scrubland,' JD went on. 'He was sittin' by a tree and he gave me a drink of

268

water. Then he showed me how to make my own water with a membrane and a hole in the dirt.'

'How did he do that, boy?' the hairy man asked, his great voice a little softer.

JD looked at his feet. 'He dug a hole and put a membrane, a piece of old plastic, over it. Held it down with stones around the edge,' he added, sketching in the details. 'Then he put a little stone in the middle to make the membrane sag. Water came that night and dripped into a tin container he'd put down the hole.'

'He showed you that, eh? Anything else?' the man asked.

JD remembered the decoy rocks but decided that their secret was something precious between Godrum and himself.

'No. Just that. He said folks called it a Godrum Still after him.'

The giant swayed from one great foot to the other, making the floor creak under his weight. 'And did he tell you that everybody curses his name because of it?' he said.

JD nodded, but by doing that he felt he'd somehow agreed with the accusation and it stung his conscience. He drew himself up and looked the man straight in the eye. 'If people curse him then they are stupid,' he said in a bold, clear voice. 'Godrum is a kind man. He gave me water and helped me when I needed it.'

'Yeah, sure,' the man said and turning towards the

Ragman he added: 'So your kid finds an old guy out in the Scrubland who says he's Godrum. Is that it? Is that what's got you so riled up?

'Tell me, young man,' he said, turning back to JD. 'Apart from him saying his name was Godrum, why do you think this old guy you met out there really was the man who ruled this planet for so long?'

JD didn't know how to answer the question and looked towards the Ragman.

'Tell him what he looked like,' the Ragman said.

JD shrugged. 'He was old, very old. He had long straggly grey hair and his mouth was sewn shut with a leather string.' JD made a criss-cross sign in the air with his finger. 'And,' JD remembered, 'he had kind eyes.'

The big man had just stuffed a thick strip of red meat into his mouth and almost choked.

'OK,' he said and when he'd recovered he turned towards the Ragman. 'So there we have it. An old boy with his mouth sewed shut who has kind eyes and, oh,' he added sarcastically, 'and he says he's Godrum. Is that it? Is that what you're here for? Because some Boonie kid who's never seen the Evil One in his life, probably never even heard of him, tells us he's seen him out in the Scrubland? And, just for one moment let's suppose he's right and his,' he pointed a finger at JD, 'his old tramp really is Godrum. What does that prove apart from he's somehow managed to survive out there all this time? Where does that get us? Is that going to get us the code?'

The Ragman stepped up and banged his fist on the giant's nest. 'Now, look here. If you'd just shut your big mouth for a moment and listen to what the boy has to say you might find out where it'll get us.' He turned towards JD and pointed. 'Now, tell him the whole story. Tell him everything that happened and what you saw here in the City.'

The Ragman's face was bright red and his fists were clenched. JD half-expected a fight to break out, there was so much anger in the air. But the hairy man was unmoved. Leaning a great arm across the pile of twigs, he put his face right up against JD's and smiled a fleshy smile. JD knew he was only trying to rile the Ragman but nevertheless thought he'd better get on with his story.

Carefully, he told the whole tale, from the days in the Scrubland right up to how he'd seen the Silver Men flying overhead carrying a ragged figure up to the top of a tall shack in the City. Then he repeated how he and Aqua had seen them take Godrum to one particular building.

At the end of his account JD looked down at his feet.

'That it?' the giant said.

'Yes, sir,' JD said. 'That's it.'

The Ragman and the giant both stood quiet as if thinking. At last the Ragman spoke again.

271

'Well, Fireless. You've heard what the boy has to say. Is he right? Was the old guy he met Godrum and if so could he really be right here in the City? I've been into the street and he showed me where he says the New Leaders took him and . . .' the Ragman paused for a long time before he added: 'I believe him.'

'Hmm,' Fireless said in as quiet a voice as he could manage. 'And just where was it the kid says the New Leaders took the Old Man?'

'Now that,' the Ragman said, smiling as if he'd just enjoyed a real cool drink of water, 'is what really is interesting. If that boy is right, they landed right plumb on the top floor of this very building. Right over your head.'

As if joined by some invisible cord, all four pairs of eyes in that strange room turned upward and stared at a point on the ceiling.

Twenty-nine

The Secret

'Right,' the giant said quietly, munching rhythmically on a handful of grub. 'Let's suppose they really have got the old man up there.' He pointed a finger at the roof. 'Has he told them anything, do you reckon?'

'Who knows?' the Ragman said. 'I'd guess not though. I haven't seen any ship take off. Have you?'

'Don't see nothing from down here. Don't see many folks neither, but I ain't heard nothing.'

'OK,' the Ragman said. 'So let's assume they haven't got the secret out of him yet. That gives us a chance.'

The giant spluttered. 'You reckon? He wouldn't tell us before so what makes you think he'll tell us now?'

'He might. We're still his kin.'

'You're fooling yourself. After you sewed his mouth up and all.'

273

JD's mind was reeling, listening to what the men were saying. He couldn't believe his ears.

'Are you sayin',' he blurted out, unable to contain himself any longer, 'are you sayin' that Godrum is kin to you?'

'Sure,' the Ragman said, smiling a sickly smile. 'I thought you'd have guessed that by now. He's our Pa.'

'But he said it was you sewed up his mouth. You can't do that. Not to your own Pa!'

'Well, we did because you see he wasn't only our Pa. He ruled the place. He was the Leader of Leaders. He had all the power and he wouldn't give it up. By rights we should have taken over, by rights . . .' But there the Ragman stopped. It was as if a signal had been given and when JD looked at Fireless he thought perhaps it had. The giant was frowning at his brother, his eyes swivelling between JD and Aqua, then back to the Ragman.

'What?' the Ragman said.

'Nothing. Just . . . where did you say this kid come from?'

'He's a Pit kid, just a Pit kid who tried to run away.'

'That right?' the giant said directly to JD. 'It's just you put me in mind of someone.'

The giant leaned right over the edge of the wall of sticks and put his great hairy face right up to JD's and stared hard.

274

JD felt his hot breath on his face, smelled the smell of sweat, dirty flesh and stale grub. He swallowed hard. Something bad was coming. He didn't know what it was but he was pretty sure it was coming. JD tried to think about how he might get away.

'Yeah,' Fireless said. 'You sure do remind me of someone. Who are you, kid?'

'JD,' JD said quietly.

'JD, huh? And where do you come from, young JD? You ain't a Farm kid, that's for sure. You look a bit like a Boonie but you ain't got Boonie eyes. Who are you, Master JD, and where did you come from?'

JD shrugged his shoulders and looked down. 'I come from the Dry Marsh,' he said.

'From the Dry Marsh, eh? I thought it might be some-place like that.' Fireless turned and smiled at the Ragman. 'You know what I think we got here, bro?' he said.

'No, the Ragman said. 'What have we got here?

'I think,' Fireless said real slow, 'I think we might just have a ticket out of here.'

In the long silence that followed JD looked at Aqua. She was as puzzled as he was. Then he looked at the Ragman, who was rubbing his chin and staring hard at JD. Then he looked at Fireless, the great giant standing in his hole surrounded by dry wood, rope and trash. He was smiling.

It was the Ragman who broke the silence. 'What are you saying, bro? How's a Boonie kid going to do that?'

'I got an idea about how, with the help of this kid, we might just persuade the Old Man to tell us the code.'

'How's that?' the Ragman said.

'Just look at him, bro, just look. I think I can see why old Godrum befriended him like he says. Gave him water and taught him how to make a still. Why, that old goat wouldn't do nothing for nobody, you know that, yet some kid turns up out of the blue and he looks after him, treats him like . . . treats him like . . .'

'Look up, JD, look me in the face,' the Ragman said and JD did as he was told. He stared at the ragged man.

'You know, I think you might have something, bro. Do you reckon, assuming they actually have got the Old Man up there on the top floor, if we took the kid to him, do you really think the old guy might tell us what we want to know?'

'He might,' Fireless said and laughed a deep, rumbling laugh. 'But what I'm thinking is not that he'll tell us. I'm thinking he'll tell him,' he said, pointing a great finger at JD.

'All we gotta do then is find the Old Man,' the Ragman said. 'And if you're right, d'you know what? We could be off this godforsaken planet and away by sundown.'

'We could too. All we have to do is work out exactly how we're going to do it. Now, this is what I reckon –'

'Hold it there, bro,' the Ragman cut in. 'Let's keep the detail to ourselves. Let me get these kids out of here while we work it out. I won't be long, then we can get right down to it. C'mon you two,' the Ragman said, picking up the ends of the children's tethers and leading them to the door. He pointed at the ladder. 'You kids get yourselves down there and wait at the bottom. And remember, don't try nothing. Our friend with the whip is still looking out for you.'

The Ragman waved to the Senior on the platform and he waved back. Above the rumbling and grinding of the Fireless wheel the Ragman indicated to the boy to keep an eye on JD and Aqua. The Senior gave a thumbs up and cracked his whip for good measure as the children climbed down.

As soon as the Ragman's excited face disappeared from the doorway, JD turned to Aqua, untied her hands and took the rope from her neck.

'Did you hear what they were saying?' he said. 'They're going to take us to Godrum.'

'No,' Aqua snapped. 'They're going to take *you* to Godrum.' She untied JD's hands and lifted the noose over his head. 'Nobody mentioned me and anyway I don't want to see your precious Godrum. I want to go to the Dry Marsh like you said, build a shack and live free. That's what I want and I thought that's what you wanted too.'

'I do want that, Aqua, but –' JD said, but in that moment he realised that Aqua had stopped listening to him. Her eyes were wide and she was staring over his shoulder.

'What's up now?' JD said.

But Aqua said nothing. It was if she had been struck dumb. All she could do was raise a trembling hand to point.

JD turned, wondering what she had seen, but when he saw he understood. His throat went bone-dry and his blood stopped pumping.

'Silver Men,' he gasped. 'Silver Men, here.'

Thirty

Massacre

There were five of them, all in their shining suits, their long gloves and thick-soled boots. The dark tinted visors on their helmets were tipped up and each Silver Man carried a shining steel wand. JD stared, transfixed, as they stepped down into the chamber. And it wasn't just Silver Men. Behind them, screaming, waving and pointing, her arm stretched out, aimed straight at JD, was the evil Chatelaine.

As one man, the Silver Men flipped down their dark visors and set off around the edge of the chamber, the grey woman close behind, urging them on.

'Oh!' was all JD could say, and his breath caught in his throat.

Aqua tugged at his dungarees. 'We've got to get out of here, JD,' she said. 'They're heading our way. C'mon, we've got to get out.'

'But they'll see us. Where can we go?' JD whined, turning his head from side to side. To get out of the chamber they'd have to go past the oncoming Silver Men. They couldn't run back up the ladder 'cos they'd be trapped there too. Anyways, the Ragman and Fireless would be sure to hand them over.

'They're coming,' JD said, his voice trembling. The memory of those mean, silver figures swooping out of the sky back at the shack, the air alive with the sound of jet-packs, brought all his pent-up fears flooding back. He could see Pa scraping in the dirt, as desperate to hide then as he was now. 'Oh no. Oh no,' JD said again and again.

'Stop it, JD. Stop whining,' Aqua said, pulling at JD's arm. 'We've got to run.'

But JD's gaze was fixed on the tops of the shining helmets bobbing above the wheel, coming closer and closer, all the time coming closer.

'Come on, stupid. Don't just stand there,' Aqua shouted, pulling hard at JD's arm. 'We've got to get out of here. Quick, follow me.'

To JD's surprise Aqua dropped to her knees and crawled in among the slaves but, surprised or not, he followed. She worked her way to the centre of the capstan, urging JD along after her, ducking between the heavy bars, the great machine groaning and creaking around them.

'This is no good,' JD said as Aqua searched for a way

past the central column. 'We'll never get out of here. Never.'

'Get a grip, JD,' Aqua said. 'Don't be such a wimp. Think. We could find a way out if only you'd stop whining. You stupid boy,' she scolded.

But JD could see no way out. Crouched in the dirt hard up against the central column, sparks crackling all around, the heavy spars creaking overhead, it seemed hopeless. But then Aqua grabbed his arm.

'I've got an idea,' she shouted in his ear. 'Just do as I do.'

Aqua waited for the next bar to pass over their heads then stood up and put her hands onto it, joining the line of ragged boys pushing it forward. 'Come on,' she said. 'Stand up.'

But JD sat in the dirt until Aqua reached down and hauled him up by the straps of his dungarees. Grabbing one of his hands, she placed it onto the bar next to hers and together they tramped around, each step taking them further away from the Silver Men.

At the farthest point from the Nest Aqua dropped to her knees again and JD followed suit. They let the capstan bar leave them and scrambled out to the side of the chamber. Neither said anything but both turned to watch the ladder where the Silver Men were climbing higher and higher.

'Come on, JD. Let's go,' Aqua said and without waiting for him she ran to the winding steps that led up and out of the chamber.

'Hold on,' JD said. 'Just a moment.'

281

He ran to the next capstan bar. The boy at the outer end looked up as he approached. JD grabbed the rope that bound his hands to the bar and, finding a loose end, started to untie the knot. Tramping along next to the startled boy, he tore at the binding, pulling the end through, easing the knot loose until, grabbing the boy's arm, he pulled his hand free. 'Now,' he shouted. 'Untie your other hand and when you've finished, do the same for your mate.' The boy just gazed at him and continued on his way, his free hand back on the capstan bar.

JD stepped back. 'I cain't do no more,' he called. 'You'll have to help yourself now.'

The boy turned his head and looked at JD but tramped on.

JD's shoulders slumped. 'I cain't do no more,' he said quietly. 'I just cain't . . .'

With a deep sigh, JD turned away and set off to follow Aqua up the stairway. As he put his foot on the first step he heard the sound that had been imprinted on his brain ever since the day he'd crouched beneath the floor of the shack. Above the grinding and rattling of the great capstan he heard a long swish followed by a sharp crack. Then another: Swish . . . crack. Then another and another, swish . . . crack, swish . . . crack, one after another then some together. It froze the blood in his veins. He didn't know what caused that sound, he only knew he'd heard it the day they killed his Pa. Pa had never made a sound, yet from the stick nest high up against the roof of the chamber came cries of agony and screams of pain. There was shouting and yelling then another crack, another yell, a scream, the sound of pleading, some more cracks then silence. Somehow JD knew what had happened and just for a moment he thought about the Ragman and wondered whether the final, penetrating scream had come from his fleshy, water-drenched lips. But any fine feeling he may have had for the ragged old man was quickly driven away by the memory of little Three-Seven-Seven and the emaciated body he'd carried out of the Pit; the Pit that the disgusting old creep had ruled over, the Pit where no pity had ever been shown to any of the countless other Three-Seven-Sevens who'd lived out their short, brutal lives there.

'JD!' Aqua screamed from the steps. 'Come on.'

JD tore himself away and ran up the stairway. Aqua scampered ahead and was soon out of sight. JD leapt up the steps, desperate to be away before the Silver Men finished their work. In the upper chamber JD wondered whether there was time to untie another boy but Aqua was gone, the patter of her footsteps already fading away. JD turned and followed.

At the top, he found Aqua in the square lobby, running her hands over the shiny surface of the outer door, searching for some way to open it.

'Help me, JD. I can't see how this works,' she said,

trying to force her tiny fingers around the edge of the massive steel slab. 'Open, you stupid door,' she hissed under her breath. 'Come on, JD, we've got to find how this works. We've got to get out.'

But JD turned away and walked to the archway which led into the lighted corridor. He put his hand to his mouth and furrowed his brow, thinking hard. Then he grunted as if he'd made up his mind and took a step to his right.

'Where are you going?' Aqua called. 'The door's over here.'

But JD didn't move. He just looked up and down the long, white corridor.

'Come here, JD,' Aqua hissed. 'Come here. Don't you want to get out?'

'Not right now,' JD whispered. 'I've gotta find Godrum.'

'What?' Aqua almost exploded. 'After everything we've done, after getting that horrid old man to bring us here in the first place. Risking our lives to get away, and suddenly you don't want to go? What about our plan?'

Aqua's cheeks were flushed and her eyes burned with anger. 'What about our shack?' she shouted. 'Forget about Godrum, what about us, what about me? Come on, JD, you gotta help me. I could have got away on my own, remember? I could have run but I didn't. I came back for you.'

'Aqua, I'm sorry,' JD said, real quiet, 'but I've gotta find Godrum.'

'Why?' she interrupted. 'Why have you got to help some

old guy who's had his day when we could be out of here, having a new life in the Dry Marsh? Ever since you told me how great it is there I've done nothing but dream about it. About getting away from the City, the Farm, the Pits and all . . . all this,' she spat, waving her thin little arms in a broad arc.

'I will take you, Aqua. I will, but I have to do this thing first.'

'What do you mean you have to? What's so special about this Godrum? You don't owe him anything, JD. It's time to look after yourself, to look after us and help me get this door open.' But her anger was nearly spent. Her shoulders drooped and her arms dropped to her sides. 'Come on, JD,' she pleaded.

'I'm sorry, Aqua. I don't know why but I have to find Godrum. I just know it's the right thing to do. Help me find him, then we'll get out of here and I'll take you wherever you want to go. I promise.'

The two children stared at each other across the lobby, Aqua rooted to the spot, tears shining in her eyes. JD wanted to go over to her but he was afraid. Afraid that if he took those few, small steps his resolve would break, so he stayed where he was and reached out his hand towards the stubborn little girl.

'Come on, Aqua, don't run away. I need you to help me find Godrum.'

Thirty-one

Silver Man Down

JD and Aqua looked at each other. Neither wanted to give way but the sound of heavy boots on the steps behind them spurred JD into action. Grabbing Aqua's hand, he pulled her into the corridor and began to run.

Hand in hand, JD and Aqua sped along the corridor, running hard, their bare feet pattering on the bright white floor, which shone with a dazzling sheen. The corridor stretched ahead in a shallow curve, bending away to their left, and JD hoped against hope that they could get out of sight by the time the Silver Men emerged. On they ran, the sound of their little feet echoing back from the stark white walls.

JD's heart was in his mouth; he knew that any moment the Silver Men would be after them and there was nowhere to hide. They couldn't even try one of the doors because there were no handles, no keys, nothing to show how to get in. Running was all they had, so run they did.

Glancing over his shoulder, JD saw the two Silver Men standing side by side at the end of the corridor, one with his visor up, silently pointing; the other, his visor down and his arm raised. In his heavy, gloved hand he held out one of the shining steel rods that JD feared so much. The children heard the crack but ran harder. Putting their heads down, they sprinted for all they were worth, their breath rasping in their throats.

Then, above the sound of his own panting, JD heard a swish, the swish that came from the Silver Men's weapons, the swish that had brought death to Pa. The swish he reckoned had just done the same to the Ragman and his brother back in the Fireless Room. From the corner of his eye he saw Aqua sprawl headlong onto the glistening floor. She slid past him face down and instinctively he tried to catch her. That simple action saved his life for as he bent to grab hold of Aqua, a tiny barbed ball zinged through the air just a hand's breadth above his head and embedded itself into the wall in front of him.

JD watched in horror as four or five other barbed silver balls sprang out of the first one and threw themselves at the concrete surface, swirling and grinding away, cutting deep grooves into the solid wall. They dashed right and left, up and down, cutting and gouging eyelessly, devouring

287

everything they touched. JD swallowed and shook his head. The thought of what might happen if one of those silver balls and its vicious satellites should hit flesh made him feel sick.

Aqua had come to rest with a bump against the bottom of a flight of stairs, the impact bunching her body into an untidy bundle. JD was sure she was dead, brought down by the Silver Men, but then the collection of thin arms and legs began to untie itself and a frightened little face emerged.

'Oh, Aqua, I thought they'd got you.' JD said, tears of relief springing into his eyes. 'Come on,' he gasped. 'We've gotta get out of here.'

Aqua tottered to her feet but then she fell back, her hands grasping air.

JD stepped forward to pick her up but a movement from down the corridor caught his eye. Both Silver Men, their dark visors covering their faces, were coming towards them, their weapons held out and pointing directly at them. JD froze, his hand stretched down towards Aqua, hers reaching out towards him. Their fingers were just a touch apart. JD looked from side to side. The Silver Men were so close but there was still time, he could still escape up the stairway. He could make it, he knew he could, but in his heart he knew what was right. JD set his face, stretched out his arm and grasped Aqua's shaking fingers. Whatever was going to happen was going to happen to both of them.

They looked into each other's eyes and JD managed a tight-lipped smile. Aqua grimaced back, but when they heard the crack they both screwed up their eyes and cowered down.

Whether it was the sound of the evil little ball grinding itself into the ceiling, the clatter as the Silver Man fell forward or the shouts of the ragged bunch of kids who swarmed over the two men that made them look up they couldn't tell. But JD and Aqua watched open-mouthed as perhaps a dozen or more kids jumped and kicked at the Silver Men, who writhed on the floor under them. Their helmets were ripped away and in no time they were spread wide, their arms and legs pulled out like stars. One of the kids shouted at the men to lie still. He held one of the shining wands in his hand and pointed it at the prostrate Silver Men.

'Hey, you guys, come here,' he called.

JD pointed to himself and mouthed, 'Who, me?'

'Yes, you. Come on. Join the fun.'

JD pulled Aqua to her feet and together they ran towards the laughing kids.

'How did you get here?' JD asked

The leader laughed. 'Because of you,' he said. 'You untied me. Remember?'

JD noticed the livid red marks around his wrists, the

dishevelled hair and dust-streaked face. 'Was that you? Back there on the wheel?'

'Sure was. As soon as I realised what you'd said I untied some of the others and before long most of us were free. I'm Twelve-O-Two by the way. Who are you? I ought to know the number of the guy who set us free.'

'I ain't gotta number. I'm JD and this is Aqua,' JD said, putting his arm around Aqua's shoulders and drawing her to him.

'Well, I'm sure happy to meet you, whoever you are,' Twelve-O-Two said.

'Where are the others?' JD asked.

'Back there,' the boy said, pointing towards the stairway. 'They're busy, come and see.'

Twelve-O-Two handed his wand to one of the other kids, but JD reached out and took it from him and as his fingers closed around the weapon something in his head seemed to snap. He narrowed his eyes and, gripping the silver wand tightly, he walked up to one of the Silver Men stretched out on the floor in front of him. Slowly and deliberately he pointed the shining, steel weapon at the helpless man's throat. In his mind's eye he saw Pa, the Silver Men aiming their wands at him just like he was now pointing his at this man. He'd have known, just like the Silver Man cringing in front of him now knew, just what was going to happen when the trigger was pulled. The man on the floor squirmed and tried to get away. He twisted and writhed his body in a vain effort to shake off the kids who held him down. But they hung on tightly, their young faces set hard, memories of their years in the Pits then on the Fireless wheel tightening their grip.

JD tensed his arm and sneered down at the helpless Silver Man.

'Please,' the man said, sweat running down his face. 'Please don't. I'm sorry. Please . . .' He screwed up his eyes and started to cry. 'Please,' he said again, choking on his tears.

JD curled his finger around the trigger. In an instant he'd have his revenge for everything he'd gone through, for all that had happened. For Pa too, even for Ma. Despite what she'd done, even for Ma. For everything, all the fear and pain, all the disappointments, all the hopeless days and nights, but most of all, this was for Pa. JD pursed his lips and looked down one last time.

'This is for you, Pa,' he said through his teeth. 'This is for you.'

But what he saw at the end of the wand was not an evil Silver Man, not a hard-faced bully. It was just a man, just like Pa. Just a frightened man in a silver suit.

JD really wanted to pull that trigger. He wanted to see this man die. He wanted to see the fear in his eyes the way there must have been fear in his Pa's eyes. He tensed his arm and pressed the end of the silver wand right into the man's throat. He saw the fear in the man's eyes but then, without another thought, JD hurled the wand away. It clattered across the floor and crashed against the wall.

JD stood in silence. He felt completely drained. It seemed that everything he knew, everything he'd ever known had changed.

The kids around him stared at the thin boy in the dungarees standing over the prostrate Silver Man, quietly sobbing at his feet. Nobody seemed to know what they should do until, in an instant, JD raised his head.

'Come on then,' he said to Twelve-O-Two. 'Wasn't there somethin' you wanted to show me?'

'I thought you were going to kill him,' Aqua whispered as they followed Twelve-O-Two along the corridor. 'Why didn't you?'

'What good would that have done?' JD said, his eyes fixed ahead, and he marched on.

Back in the Fireless Room, JD laughed out loud. 'Hey,' he said. 'Look, Aqua, look what they've done.'

JD had expected the capstan to be stopped and to see kids sitting around rubbing their wrists but instead the wheel was still turning, sparks still crackling around the spindle just like when he'd first seen it. Sure, the kids were massaging their sore arms, but lashed to the bars, tramping around sweating and straining, were the Seniors, their short ponytails bobbing up and down as they heaved the bars around.

'Gotta have power,' Twelve-O-Two laughed. 'And we reckoned if the wheel stopped someone might come so we thought these guys might like to have a turn. Don't seem like they're enjoying it much, does it?'

One of the Seniors looked at the kids as he passed. His face was running with sweat and pain was written across his face. He scowled. 'Enjoy it while it lasts, you scum,' he growled. 'We'll get you. They'll soon come to set us free. You wait. Your lives won't be worth living.'

Twelve-O-Two aimed a kick at the Senior as he plodded away and it caught him fair and square on the butt. The Senior winced and Twelve-O-Two laughed.

'Heave away, my friend. We don't want no slackin' now. Gotta have power, you know?'

JD smiled a grim smile. It was great to see the kids enjoying themselves but something bothered him. Looking around, he said, 'What about the other Silver Men? Where are they?'

'Two of them went after you, as you know, and the other three are taking some exercise. A pile of kids just leapt all over them then lashed them to the wheel downstairs. Man, those silver suits sure make a guy sweat.' Twelve-O-Two laughed. 'What a sight! And those kids are having such a great time. Last I saw they were up on the Seniors' stands, whipping those silver guys for all they're worth and drinking their water while they're at it.'

'What about Chatelaine? The woman who brought the Silver Men here?'

Twelve-O-Two looked puzzled. 'I haven't seen any women,' he said.

'Never mind,' JD said. 'I don't suppose we need worry about her right now.'

He smiled. He dearly wanted to stay there forever, soaking up the atmosphere, but when Aqua touched him on the arm he knew what was coming.

'This can't last, JD. Someone is sure to come, just like that Senior said. Either that or Chatelaine will get help. Then we'll be in trouble. I'm scared.'

JD knew she was right. It couldn't last.

'Aqua's right, Twelve-O-Two. We've gotta sort ourselves out. Can you get these kids into some sort of order? Set up a guard or somethin'? Make sure nobody comes down here.'

'How do I do that, JD?'

'You've got the Silver Men's wands. Set some kids on guard by the stairs. Fetch the two Silver Men you caught and lash 'em to the wheel but don't put all the Silver Men together. They might hatch up some plan. Spread 'em out.' JD thought for a moment. 'And better send some kids out to search for water. There's enough grub in the giant's place. Gather it all up and bring it down here. When you've got the water, dish out a bit of food and a drink all around but not too much. I've got a feelin' we might have to make it last. Got that?'

Twelve-O-Two looked puzzled. 'OK,' he said slowly. 'That mean the fun's over?'

'Just for now,' JD said. 'But if we do things right there'll be plenty of time for fun later.'

'What about you?' Twelve-O-Two said. 'And Aqua? You gonna stay here with us?'

'Not right now,' Aqua said. 'JD wants to find Godrum.'

Twelve-O-Two frowned. 'Can we say that now?'

'You can say what you like,' JD said. 'Nobody's goin' to stop you. But if I hear anybody callin' him The Evil One, they'll have me to deal with. That clear?'

'Sure is, but why do you want to find him? Why don't you just stay here with us?'

JD looked away. Aqua had asked the same question. Why did he have to find Godrum? OK, so he wanted to save him from the Silver Men, and right up 'til that moment that had seemed enough, but now there was somethin' else. These kids were lookin' to him to tell 'em what they should do and he had no more idea than they did. He only knew one person who was likely to have the answer to that kind of problem. JD thought for a while then turned back towards the others.

C'mon, Aqua, let's leave these guys to get organised. We've gotta find Godrum.'

Thirty-two

Captain Hidalgo

JD and Aqua climbed the stairs and set off along the white corridor. They hurried to the stairway where Aqua had fallen, where the concrete was broken away and was gouged deep. Without a pause, JD sprang up the steps two at a time and Aqua followed in his wake.

At the top, a long enclosed walkway arched upwards and outwards and JD ran across it. The walkway was bright – sunlight streamed in through tall windows which lined either side. Below them the City was stretched out like a plan. Long, straight roads criss-crossed each other, tall buildings stood in line on either side, men and women like tiny moving dots strolled, unaware of the drama playing out so close to them. JD slowed down to look and seeing the people and all the buildings made him wonder if a bunch of kids was ever likely to change anything so big.

There was so much to do, so many things were wrong, but inside he felt excited. If they did things right, perhaps there was a chance they could make things better.

As soon as he reached the far side of the walkway JD swung left into another curving corridor, the radius perhaps tighter than the one they'd just left, the floor narrower. This corridor had no doors; the inner wall was completely smooth without a single blemish or opening. A few paces along and they came to another short stairway leading up to the left and this led onto another high walkway arching back into the building they'd just left. JD climbed the steps and set off. Looking down to his left, he could see the bridge they'd just come across way below and it made him realise how high they'd come. He smiled. The men had said Godrum was at the top of the building so the higher they went, the closer he was to the kind old man. With Aqua at his side, he ran to the far side of the walkway and, pausing for just a moment, turned right into another long white corridor, just like the one on the ground floor.

'Is this the right way?' Aqua said.

'As long as we're gettin' higher we must reach the top. We'll keep goin' and anytime we find stairs, we'll go up them,' JD said and strode off along the curving, white hallway with Aqua pattering along beside him. She noticed that the doors were back, set out at regular intervals to their left and she wondered what was behind them. She hoped that JD would stop soon, open one and find what he was looking for. But on they went, passing door after door, JD pushing at them, hoping one would open and lead him up to Godrum. But none moved. Then, just as JD was trying another door, a gruff voice called from behind them:

'Hey, you kids. What are you doing? Stop there.'

They stopped and JD felt all his excitement drain away.

'What are you up to?' the voice growled.

JD turned slowly but somehow he knew what he was going to see. He just knew.

'Silver Men,' he whispered.

Two big guys in silver suits open at the neck stood not ten paces behind them, but the panic that had seized JD previously seemed not to hold him quite so tightly this time. Now that he thought of them as just men in silver suits JD found his mind was clear, and he looked coolly back at the two men. He noticed they carried no weapons nor wore their helmets; these truly were just men in silver suits. He knew they could move only slowly in their heavy uniforms so, confident he and Aqua could outrun them when they needed to, he smiled innocently as the men approached.

'C'mon, Aqua,' he said through his teeth. 'We're goin' to run. Ready?'

Aqua grunted.

'Right. Go!' JD said and as one the two children turned and ran as hard as they could away from the Silver Men.

'Hey, you kids. Come back here,' one of the men shouted but they were gone. Pretty soon they were away and out of sight around the curve in the corridor and as they scampered along, leaving the clumsy men far behind, JD felt liberated. This was great. He had no fear and he was happy and they were on their way to find Godrum. He felt nothing could stop them now; all he had to do was find a way up. He pushed at as many doors as he could as he ran. Surely one of them would lead him to Godrum.

Aqua drew ahead as JD tried each door but his longer legs soon brought him back to her shoulder. But suddenly, Aqua found she was running alone. JD had gone.

'JD, where are you?' she called, turning back. She felt a cold sweat on her neck. Had someone been behind one of those doors? Had they grabbed JD and were they even now calling the guards to take him away? Her mind was in a whirl as she crept back along the corridor.

She had only gone about ten paces when she saw an open door. Aqua put her hand to her mouth and, staying close to the wall, tiptoed towards it. Dreading what she might find, she eased her head around the doorpost.

And there he was, free and apparently unconcerned, looking around a bare landing where a flight of concrete stairs spiralled upwards to his right and another downwards to his left. She must have run right past without seeing him.

'JD,' she said, almost stamping her foot. 'Why didn't you say? I thought I'd lost you.'

'Sorry, Aqua, I was goin' to call you but look at this. I reckon this is what we're lookin' for.'

'Oh, JD!' Aqua said. 'I was so scared. I thought –' But before she could vent her anger and frustration the sound of heavy, pounding footsteps came from outside in the corridor.

'Quick,' she whispered. 'Down will be the way out.' She grabbed JD's hand and began pulling him towards the stairs.

'Yes, and that's where they'll be expectin' us to go,' JD said. 'Come on,' he hissed and set off up the stairs. He took the steps two at a time with Aqua close behind and only when he'd gone far enough for the curve of the staircase to hide them did he slow down. He put a finger to his lips and, treading the steps as gently and as silently as he could, crept higher.

When they heard the scuff of boots from below they stopped and held their breath. If they'd made the wrong decision this time it would be all over. Below them they could hear the Silver Men talking.

JD screwed up his eyes, hoping against hope that they'd chosen right. He could hear the men arguing and he willed them to choose the downward stairs. After a long silence one of the Silver Men shouted, calling once more for them to stop, but when this was followed by echoes of heavy boots clumping down the stairs, he knew that, for a while at least, they were safe. He waited until the sound of the Silver Men faded out of earshot then breathed out.

'That was close,' he said.

'Too close. Let's hope they don't come back,' Aqua said.

Still treading carefully, the children climbed upwards. On the next landing the stairs came to a stop against a big steel door, covered with bolts. All of the doors JD had seen before had been clean, white and spotless but this one was something new.

Avoiding the great bolts and rivets that studded the door, JD put his shoulder against the steel plates and pushed hard. The door opened a crack, then thudded back into place. JD tried again and by heaving steadily he eased the door open far enough for Aqua to get through. He squeezed through after her and let the door go. It fell back with a deep boom that echoed into the bare concrete space beyond.

In the dark, shadowy corridor the only light came from an irregular row of flickering orange candle flames set in niches high in the walls, which curved away into the distance. It reminded JD of the Pits and made him shudder. As his eyes became used to the meagre light he saw a jagged crack like a streak of dead lightning climbing the wall next to where they stood and below it a pile of broken rubble lay on the floor. There were no clean painted walls here; the whole place had a cold, abandoned feel.

Taking Aqua by the hand, JD set off along the corridor, his eyes searching right and left. He touched the rough concrete walls with his hands and noticed how the sound of their every movement echoed in the darkness. After a while they came to a heavy gate set into the wall on iron hinges. JD went up to it and peered through the bars. Behind was a space as dark as death while on the wall next to the grille a stub of candle guttered.

'Come on,' JD whispered, trying to sound confident. 'Let's get on.'

Aqua pushed up to his side and huddled close. 'I don't like this place,' she said. 'It frightens me.'

'Don't be scared,' JD said, covering his own fear. 'We must be nearly there. There don't seem to be any more stairs. This must be the top.'

Staying close to each other, they crept through the darkness, past two more sets of heavy gates until they came up against another solid steel door with a candle stub burning next to it.

'This is different,' JD said. 'I wonder what's behind this one.'

'Might be more stairs,' Aqua whispered. 'It looks a bit like that first door we came through.'

JD stepped up to the door and pushed but nothing

302

moved. He pushed harder but the door stayed firmly shut.

'What's that, JD?' Aqua said, pointing to the wall.

JD looked up. Below the candle, a square box was set into the wall. He thought it looked a bit like the thing the Ragman had shown him on the stairway down to the Fireless Room but instead of a switch there was a round, red button.

'Shall I push it?' JD whispered.

'I don't know,' Aqua said. 'If you think it's OK.'

JD reached up and pushed the dome-shaped button and at once a bright Fireless strip flashed on overhead, bathing them in a harsh, white light.

'Oh!' Aqua said, putting her hand over her mouth, and when a deep rumbling sound began to shake the ground where they stood, she slid in behind JD and hid her face. He could feel her bunched-up fists pushing into his back and when a long, jagged crack like a set of pointed teeth appeared in the door, he felt her cower down behind him.

JD wanted to hide too but he stood firm, watching the crack widen more and more, the interlocking teeth slowly grinding open until by the time the rumbling stopped there was a space between them as wide as a man. Shielding his eyes, JD tried to see inside but it was pitch dark.

When the sound of shuffling footsteps came from the darkness, JD backed away and Aqua held onto him tightly.

The footsteps came nearer and nearer until, there in the opening, his suit shining in the floodlight, stood a Silver Man. Aqua gasped and JD instinctively glanced along the corridor, checking his escape route. Turning back, JD forced himself to look at the Silver Man and it gave him quite a shock.

To JD, Silver Men had always been big and powerful, strong and stern-faced, and even though he'd seen the Fireless kids overpower two of them, his first inclination was still to run. But faced with this new Silver Man it was all he could do to stop himself laughing. This was one very old Silver Man. His head was bare and he was completely bald right down to his lack of eyebrows. And his suit! Silver Men had bright, metallic suits, belted and reinforced, bristling with weapons. They wore big gauntlets, their fingers studded with black metal strips, but this man's suit was tarnished and where it had split along some of the creases it was held together with sticky tape. Dirt and grime streaked the whole worn outfit and in place of the fearsome gloves this poor old Silver Man's gnarled fingers poked out from cut-off mitts. JD couldn't hold back his laughter any longer and had to hide his face as the imitation Silver Man peered out through the jagged hole.

The apparition blinked. 'What's this?' he growled. 'It ain't grub time. What are you doing here?' he said, peering short-sightedly at JD and Aqua. 'Who are you?' he said.

'Domestics,' JD said, thinking fast. 'There's to be a big

clean-up; important visitors coming. We've come to clean out your rooms.'

'I don't need no help,' the man said. 'I keep this place spotless. You won't find no dirt in here. Years in the force does that for you so you can take yourselves off. They can bring anyone they like up here any time and they could eat their food off the floor if they wanted. No, sir, I don't need no domestics up here.'

'But,' JD muttered. 'They said –'

'I don't care what they said,' the old Silver Man almost shouted. 'Go on, get out of here.'

He waved his hands at JD and in a rustle of tin foil turned away. Putting out his hand to one side, he pressed a button on the wall, there was a clunk followed by a whir, and the jagged teeth began to close.

JD watched helplessly. His hastily thought-out plan had failed and he could only stand and watch as the doors ground slowly shut.

Just before the gap closed completely Aqua poked her head out from behind JD and spoke. 'Don't you think we should have told him about the coup?' she said, almost calling out, her voice so loud and shrill the Silver Man could not fail to hear.

JD was aghast. What was she saying? Tell him about the coup? Did she mean the boys in the Fireless Room? He turned and glared at her.

'I think he ought to know,' Aqua said. 'That man said so, didn't he, he said to tell him.'

'What?' the old man said and put his hand up to the switch. The door stopped and in an instant he was at the narrow opening, pressing his face against the jagged teeth.

'Who said that and what did they say to tell me?' The wizened face, distorted as it pushed into the gap, was both stern and puzzled at the same time.

Aqua slipped past JD and stood there, a tiny figure bathed in the light. She looked up.

'There's been a plot, a coup,' she said. 'The Old Leaders. Fighting. There's lots of fighting.'

JD was amazed that Aqua was so calm, face to face with a Silver Man, even this imitation Silver Man. Just moments before, she'd been shaking with fear and now look at her. She was so brave. He stepped back into the shadows, leaving the stage to her.

The Silver Man frowned, his skin wrinkling from above his eyes to the top of his head. 'A coup, eh? And I missed it stuck up here guarding this old fool. Why didn't they call for me? I'd have got among 'em all right.' The scruffy Silver Man stepped back and struck a pose, sniffing loudly and flexing long-disappeared muscles.

The rumbling started once more and the jagged crack began to open out until the man stood filling the space between the teeth. He turned his head on one side and

306

peered down at Aqua. She stared back, looking him straight in the eyes.

'And what was it they said about me?' the old guy said at last.

'They said we were to tell you that you could go down and join the fun,' Aqua said without a moment's hesitation. 'They said there's still plenty of killing to do.'

The wrinkled man stood tall. 'There. I knew they'd need me. I'll sort 'em out. I bet they said old Hidalgo would sort them out. I bet they said that, didn't they?'

'That's exactly what they said, Mr Hidalgo. They said they need you down in the Fireless Room right now.'

The tatty Silver Man beamed but then the smile faded from his face.

'Wait a moment,' he said slowly. 'Just wait a moment.' He narrowed his eyes and studied Aqua suspiciously. 'I can't desert my post. That's against regulations. If I go what's going to happen here? I've got a really important job, you know. I'm guarding a very valuable prisoner. I can't just up and leave. Even if there is fighting to be done.'

'They know that, Mr Hidalgo. That's why they sent the boy to keep an eye on the prisoner while I'm cleaning and while you're away,' Aqua said. Then, quick as a flash, she turned and called: 'Boy!' with all the authority she could muster.

'Where is that boy?' Aqua snapped, looking directly at

307

JD. 'Boy,' she called again. 'Get over here. Stop skulking in the shadows. Captain Hidalgo has things to show you before he can leave. Come here right now or he'll be seeing to you too.'

JD edged forward. Did she mean him?

'Here, boy,' she snapped. 'Come here.'

JD stepped forward and to his complete surprise, as soon as he was within reach Aqua swung her arm and smacked the back of his head.

'Ow!' he said.

'I'll give you *Ow*,' she said, pushing JD towards the opening. 'Now get in there and help the Captain before he gives you a good thrashing.'

JD stumbled past the tarnished Silver Man and into a narrow passageway. He was amazed at Aqua's presence of mind. What a girl, he thought to himself, not for the first time. What a girl!

JD walked ahead while Aqua followed, talking all the time to the Silver Man, not letting him get a word in or question her story.

At the end of the narrow passage JD found himself in a stark, white room, high, wide and empty except for one thing. And that one thing made the hairs on the back of his neck stand up. In the middle of the floor stood a long steel table with sturdy legs and on it, strapped down with heavy belts, was a figure. It lay perfectly still. There was no sign of life. The only indication that this was anything other than a corpse was a rubber tube which ran from a water container on a stand into the taped-over face.

JD's heart skipped a beat. There were no ragged clothes or papered legs, no kind face or jagged cut in the throat but he knew straight off who it was lying on that steel table. He only hoped he hadn't come too late.

Thirty-three

Family

The body on the table lay completely still. The chest did not rise or fall, the bare, strapped-down arms did not twitch or move in any way. JD stepped forward but before he could see if there was any life in the corpse, the ageing Silver Man was next to him.

'That's the Evil One, that is,' he said, full of his own importance. 'I'm the only one they trust to guard him. He won't get away from me.'

'Strapped down like that he couldn't get away from anyone,' JD said under his breath. 'Is he alive?'

'Oh yes. They've got to keep him alive until they've learned the secret.'

'What secret?'

Hidalgo glared at JD.

'Never mind what secret. That's not for the likes of you.

Now, you wait here and don't touch nothing while I fetch my battle helmet and exterminator. Then I'll show you what you have to do.'

JD stayed by the body while Hidalgo scuttled off, his worn suit flapping as he moved. JD wanted to reach out to Godrum; he wanted to talk to him, tell him he was there and that everything was going to be OK, but he knew he had to be patient. Aqua understood to leave JD alone. She moved away, leaving the thin boy with his head bowed, standing next to the man who meant so much to him.

In a few moments Hidalgo reappeared, wearing a Silver Man's helmet and carrying the dreaded steel wand. For the first time JD began to think of the old fool as a real Silver Man. That was until he saw that the helmet was as battered as the suit, the visor cracked and stuck together with tape. And the wand, that evil weapon that all Silver Men carried, was just a silly painted stick. Nevertheless, Hidalgo brandished it angrily, swishing it through the air and growling to himself.

'Grr,' he said. 'I can't wait to get back into battle.'

He flashed his painted stick above JD's head. JD thought it wise to duck and cower down but inside he smiled. What an old fool, he thought.

'Grr,' the old man snarled again. 'You wait. When they see old Hidalgo coming, those rebels will be quaking in their boots.' He waved his stick again and bared a row of broken and stained teeth. JD had to keep his head low to hide his grin.

When Hidalgo had finished swishing and posing he took JD by the shoulder and guided him back towards the door.

'Come, girl,' he called to Aqua. 'You seem to be the brains around here. You come too. Let me show you how the door works.'

Aqua followed them. At the end of the passage the old man pushed JD against the wall and pointed to a big domed button by his shoulder.

'That's the control,' he said to Aqua. 'When the light goes on and the buzzer sounds that means someone's outside. You press the control and let the door open a crack so's you can see who's there,' he said. 'If it ain't me, shut the door again. The only person allowed in here is me. Understood?'

'What about letting myself out when I've finished cleaning?' Aqua said.

'No,' Hidalgo snapped before she had finished speaking. 'You don't leave until I get back. There has to be a proper handover, just like when I was in the guard. Anyway,' he said, poking JD with his stick, 'he's too stupid to be left alone. No. You're in charge, understand? And I want you both here when I get back. I want this place shining and you two standing in line, ready for my inspection.'

Aqua snapped up straight and gave a salute. 'Understood, Captain Hidalgo. You can trust me. I won't let you down.'

Aqua thought the old man was going to burst out of his suit. He raised his painted stick to his helmet, sprang to attention and stamped one foot next to the other.

'Very good,' he said, clipping his words. 'Close the door behind me, girl. I've got some killing to do.'

'Yes, sir,' Aqua almost shouted and saluted again.

The ersatz warrior spun on his heel and marched off. Aqua poked her head out through the gap and watched him go.

'Captain Hidalgo,' she heard him mutter. '*Captain Hidalgo . . .*'

Aqua pressed the control and the door began to close. Grinning from ear to ear, she hugged JD. 'What an old fool,' she said, but just as the teeth in the door began to mesh a voice called from outside and her heart stopped.

'Hey you, girl! Stop the door.'

Aqua leaped out of JD's arms and spun around. Peering through the zigzag was the face of the jailer. Surely he couldn't have realised he'd been fooled. Not so soon. They were so close. With a trembling hand she reached up, pressed the control and the door stopped.

'Ye . . . es, sir?' Aqua said.

'Where did you say this battle was?' the old man asked.

Aqua breathed out. Suited and booted and armed for

the fray, he'd forgotten where he was meant to be going.

'The Fireless Room,' she said. 'Down where they keep the great Fireless wheel.'

'Right,' the tattered Silver Man said uncertainly. 'The Fireless Room.'

'Just keep going down as far as you can go,' Aqua said, trying to put some urgency into her voice. 'Quick, Mr Hidalgo, they need you down there and anyhow, you don't want to miss all the fun.'

'Right,' the man said again and his face disappeared from the crack. Aqua pressed the button and with a satisfying clunk the teeth locked together.

Alone again, standing in the shadows, listening to the silence Aqua began to tremble from the top of her head to her little bare feet. She'd kept up the pretence for so long but now it was over she felt utterly drained and began to cry. JD pulled her close and held her tight.

'Come on, JD,' she sighed, easing herself out of his embrace. 'Let's go and rescue your precious Godrum.'

'Thanks, Aqua,' JD said, his voice husky with emotion. He wanted to say more. He wanted to say how great she'd been and how he could never have got so far without her but he was afraid, afraid of letting go. If he allowed his feelings to take charge he wasn't sure he could keep going and there was still so much to do. So he turned away, leaving it all unsaid.

Back in the big room, he and Aqua stood close to the table, looking down at the silent body swaddled in bands of dirty white cloth, with pipes leading to the bandaged face. JD reached out and gently touched the bandages. The body quivered.

'Mr Godrum,' JD whispered. 'It's JD. I've come to help you.'

It could have been his imagination but JD thought the head turned a fraction. He touched him again and this time he was sure. The head moved.

'Quick, Aqua, he's alive. Let's get this stuff off,' JD said and began picking at the bandages, searching for somewhere to start.

Aqua ran to the far side of the table and began tugging at a piece of cloth. Soon both children were pulling at bandages, unwinding them as gently as they could. Some long strands of wispy grey hair appeared, then a bald pate then a deep furrowed, sun-burned brow. When JD eased the last piece of cloth away from the eyes he stopped, expecting them to open but nothing happened.

'Mr Godrum,' he said. 'Can you hear me?'

One of the eyelids flickered. 'Mr Godrum, it's me. JD.'

The eyelid flickered again. Creased from the bandages, it opened a fraction then quickly screwed up tight.

'It's the light,' Aqua said. 'And anyway it's no good talking to him; he can't answer until we've unwrapped his mouth.'

'I can,' a deep belching croak said from further down the encased body.

'Yes, he can,' JD said excitedly. 'He talks through his neck. Don't you remember? I told you. This *is* Godrum.'

The children unwrapped Godrum's head and neck as fast as they could. Aqua winced when JD peeled the bandages away from the man's mouth. The leather thongs were gone but they'd left angry red holes and horrible twisted bunches of skin, and the lips, sealed for so long, had been cut apart, leaving two ragged edges of livid flesh.

After a few more attempts Godrum managed to open his eyes a little and JD smiled when he saw the two narrow slits shining gold, just like he remembered them.

'Mr Godrum,' he whispered. 'Do you remember me?'

'I remember you, JD,' Godrum croaked. This time he spoke through his mouth, although the tattered lips barely moved. 'I knew you'd come.'

'I knew I would too, Mr Godrum. Why is that?'

'It would take too long to tell, but right from that time in the Scrubland I knew you were the one.'

'He was the one what?' Aqua butted in.

'It's a long tale but as soon as we met, I saw it.'

'Saw what? What did you see?' Aqua sounded impatient.

'The future,' Godrum croaked, closing his eyes again.

JD began to pull at the straps that held Godrum down

316

but as he did so the old man opened his eyes and said, 'Don't bother with those, son. I ain't goin' no place.'

'But, Mr Godrum, we've gotta get you out of here.'

'Too late,' Godrum rasped. 'It's too late for me. I've been here too long. I can't walk no more and you sure can't carry me. It's all up for me, JD.'

JD stopped fiddling with the straps and dropped his arms. Tears came to his eyes and all he could say was: 'Oh, Mr Godrum.'

'Mr Godrum,' Aqua said in her clear, matter-of-fact way. 'If you can't leave, why did you say you were waiting for JD?'

Godrum turned his head. 'Who are you, little one?' he said.

'Aqua,' she said, and JD noticed she no longer quoted her number.

'Farm girl?' Godrum asked.

'Yes, but I'm a domestic now, or was 'til JD came. We are running away to the Dry Marsh. We are going to build a shack out there and live free.'

'Ah,' Godrum said. 'Runnin' away.'

For no reason he could figure JD was suddenly overwhelmed with guilt. He felt ashamed but didn't know why. Looking at his bare feet, he wiggled his toes.

'Mmm,' he said. 'I'm takin' Aqua away from the City.'

Godrum sighed heavily. 'My eldest son did that. He ran away.'

'How many sons do you have, Mr Godrum?' JD said, looking up.

'I have three.'

Three sons? JD knew of two and they were both horrible, but neither the Ragman nor Fireless had said anything about a brother.

Godrum coughed. 'Two of my sons plotted against me.' He paused for a long time then swallowed hard. 'And the other one ran away. He took his wife and my grandson and it broke my heart.' Godrum coughed again and JD saw he was having difficulty speaking.

'Would you like a drink, Mr Godrum?' JD said, and nodded to Aqua who lifted the water bottle from the stand and brought it to the table. She pulled out the pipe, unscrewed the top and held it out. Godrum began to raise his arm and lift his head but as soon as he started to ease himself up, he flopped down again and his head fell back. He lay with his chest heaving and his breath coming in short, painful gasps.

When the old man's breathing had subsided, Aqua held the container over his lips and poured a thin trickle of water into his mouth. At first Godrum coughed but after a few more drops he closed his eyes and lay back. JD felt his pain. A lump began to form in his throat and his eyes stung with dry tears.

'Mr Godrum, why are they doin' this to you? Why do they call you names and treat you bad?'

For a while Godrum said nothing.

'I don't know, JD,' he breathed, then swallowed hard as if summoning up all his strength. 'I did my best. I thought I was helpin' when I showed folks how to make water but they cursed me for it. Then, when I said if they'd only change their ways I'd take 'em to a new home where they could start again, they sewed me up and cast me out.'

'Who did, Mr Godrum? Who did all that?'

'My own sons, mainly. The very ones I thought I could trust. Two of 'em led a coup to throw me out. They took over the council and their brother ran away. And when I wouldn't give 'em the code to fly the ships they sewed up my mouth and left me out in the Scrubland to die.'

'Why wouldn't you give 'em the code, Mr Godrum? They are your sons, after all.'

'They were greedy and cared only for themselves. They didn't care what happened to others as long as they got what they wanted. If I'd let 'em fly off to a new planet they'd have wrecked that just the same as we've done here.'

The old man gasped for breath and shook his head from side to side. 'But it didn't do 'em no good. Now they've been overthrown by their own guards.'

'Are they the Silver Men? Those guys who fly around and kill people.'

319

'Yes. They tell me they punished my sons by puttin' 'em to work. One has to run the Pits and the other the Fireless wheel.'

'Oh . . .' JD said. He was going to tell the old man what had happened down in the Fireless Room but something stopped him. He looked at Aqua and frowned, urging her not to say anything. Poor Godrum was going through quite enough. He didn't need to know right now that his sons were dead.

Aqua nodded. She understood.

'JD,' she said in an urgent whisper. 'We have to get on. If we are going to get Godrum away we need to get on.'

Godrum tried to raise his head again. 'It's a kind thought, young lady, but you can't take me anyplace. I couldn't even make it to the door.'

'Whether we go with you or without,' Aqua said, 'we have to go. If we get caught here we'll never get away.'

She walked around the table and pulled at JD's arm but JD stayed put.

'Hold on, Aqua. I can't just go.'

He looked down at Godrum stretched out on the table and, despite the livid, misshapen slit he had for a mouth, JD thought he looked kind of content. When the old man opened his eyes they twinkled, like he was smiling.

'You go if you want, JD. You run away if you want but I can give you and the girl somethin' better than a short life in the Dry Marsh. I can give you the chance of real happiness.'

'What do you mean, Mr Godrum?'

'What do you think I mean? Ain't you been listenin' to me? Ain't it occurred to you that the reason I was deposed and disfigured, the reason I'm lyin' here endurin' daily torture is because I know somethin', a secret so great men will do anythin' to get it?'

'I did hear some folks say somethin' about that, Mr Godrum. You know some kinda secret code. But how can a thing like that be any use to us?' JD said. 'Will it help us get away? Will it give us freedom?'

'No, JD. Not in the way you expect anyways, but it could get you someplace better than your old Dry Marsh. Someplace where the air is cool, where plants grow from the ground and creatures fly in the air; a world where water runs free and food is all around. A place where living trees soar to the blue sky, where everything is beautiful and there ain't no wars, nor Pits, no Cities nor any baby Farms.' Godrum paused and breathed out deeply. 'What do you say, JD? Wouldn't you rather be in a place like that? Ain't that better than scratchin' in the dirt out in the Dry Marsh?'

'Is there really such a place?' JD said, trying to keep any disbelief out of his voice. 'My Pa used to tell stories like that but I didn't believe him.'

'But would you like to believe in such a place?'

321

'Sure. Who wouldn't?'

'Listen to me, JD. I am old and weak. Every day they come and torture me, hopin' I'll tell 'em the secret. They believe in it. Before that, my sons believed in it. These people may be cruel and they may be evil but they ain't stupid. They know I'm right, they know it exists.' Godrum paused. His face was drawn; the lines around his eyes and mouth had grown deeper as he struggled for breath.

'I don't mind what they do to me,' he said at last. 'All I care about is stayin' alive 'til I can pass the secret on to someone who will respect it. Someone who has seen what misery wars and pollution can bring and how this whole planet is doomed because of it. And,' Godrum swallowed hard, 'from the first time we met, JD, right from when you tried to steal my water tube, I knew it was you. I felt it, I saw it. And when you drew out that figure five in the dust, it was like a great weight had lifted from my shoulders.'

JD furrowed his brow. 'I don't understand Mr Godrum.'

'When you drew that figure five for me out there in the Scrubland, when you finished it with that curl, I guessed then who you were. I showed all my kids to write like that and when you told me it was your Pa who showed you, I knew.'

'I still don't understand,' JD said. 'What's my Pa gotta do with all this?'

'I told you one of my boys run off. He run off with his

woman and I guess they must have settled in the Dry Marsh. You'd have been a tiny baby back then but now you're growed and well . . . here you are.'

'I'm not sure I know what you're saying, Mr Godrum. And anyways, if you knew all this why didn't you say somethin' back then, when we were out there in the Scrubland?'

'I wasn't sure and anyways, you were dead set on findin' your Ma.'

'No, I wasn't. It was you told me I was. Don't you remember?'

'Yeah? Well, I guess I did too, but you needed to learn, to find out for yourself what this old world is like and what folks are like so's you'd understand. But I knew you'd come back. I knew you'd find me and now you have it's your time, you and your friend's. Unless . . . unless you are goin' to run away too.'

Aqua watched and listened, her face still, her eyes like deep pools. Her dream of the Dry Marsh was gone and she knew it. But if JD wasn't going back then she didn't want to go either. She walked to where JD stood and touched his hand.

'We won't run away, Mr Godrum,' she said calmly, and the deep valleys in the battered face seemed to shrink and fill.

'I knew you wouldn't,' he smiled.

323

Thirty-four

JD's Choice

The rasp of the door buzzer made JD jump.

'It's Hidalgo,' Aqua gasped. 'He's come back. Now what do we do?'

'It might not be him,' JD whispered.

'Who else would it be?'

JD shrugged his shoulders. 'Better have a look. You never know.'

'OK,' Aqua said and disappeared into the corridor leading to the door. The buzzer went again. 'Whoever it is, they're sure in a rush about something,' JD said to nobody. He turned back to Godrum, who lay quite still with his eyes closed, the gentle smile still fixed across his battered face. 'OK, Mr Godrum, where is this place you're talkin' about? This place with them trees and water and all. How do we get there?'

'You want to go?' the old man breathed.

'I guess.'

'You're not sure?'

'I don't know what to do, Mr Godrum. Aqua wants to go to the Dry Marsh, build a shack and live easy. You tell me there's some wonderful new place where there's water all around and no wars or nothin'. I don't know what's best. Anyways, don't I need some kinda code to get there, this secret everybody wants from you, Mr Godrum?'

'You already have it.' Godrum whispered, his voice growing fainter every time he spoke.

'No, I don't,' JD said. 'I don't even know what a code is.'

Godrum sighed gently. 'Tell me your figurin', JD,' he breathed. 'Just like you did way back.'

'One, two, three . . .' JD began, unfolding one finger for each figure he called to mind. '. . . eight, nine, ten . . .' He slowed down. He had to think hard to get the new ones in the right order. 'El . . . ev . . . en, twelve, thirteen, fourteen, fifteen, sixteen.' He finished with a flourish, rushing the last few figures almost into one. 'There, Mr Godrum, that's right, ain't it?'

'Sure is, son. You got 'em dead right. Now, do you still have the membrane?'

'What membrane?' JD asked.

'The one I gave you; the one with the code on it.'

325

JD's heart jumped. The membrane. So much had happened since the Scrubland but in an instant he remembered. They were near the Old Road, Godrum had shown him how to make a still and then just before they went to sleep the old man had given him something, a piece of folded plastic he said to use when he needed water. But he'd never used it, never much thought about it. He put his hand inside the bib of his dungarees and in the flat pocket that Ma had sewed, among all the dirt and grit from the Pits his fingers touched the close-folded sheet of plastic.

'You got it, son?' Godrum whispered. 'Have you got it?'

JD drew the plastic from his pocket and held it out. 'Yes, sir. I've got it.'

'Good, good,' Godrum said, the words floating out from his ragged lips on laboured breaths. 'Now, listen real close, I ain't got the strength to say this twice.'

JD leaned over the old man and put his ear close to Godrum's lips. He felt the warmth of his breath and heard the gasping rattle in his throat.

'You go up the steps over there.' He swivelled his eyes and JD looked behind him. 'That's right. You go up 'em, through the walkway beyond, and when you get inside, you'll find a big door. Go through and close that door real tight behind you.'

Godrum swallowed. His breath was coming short and his chest began to rise and fall as he fought for breath.

'Take it easy, Mr Godrum, take it easy,' JD said. He could see the old man was getting agitated and was trying to raise his hand. It brushed against JD's arm but fell away, back onto the table by his side. He grunted and tried again. This time JD took the old man's hand and held it. Godrum closed his fingers around JD's and his face relaxed. A weak smile spread across his battered features.

'Spread . . . the membrane over . . . the panel. Then . . .' It was all he could do to get each word out. JD leaned as close as he could, his ear almost touching Godrum's mouth. 'Do your figurin' in order. Don't matter where the numbers are, do 'em in order. You got that? Tell me . . . you . . . got . . . that . . . JD?' JD felt a long breath escape from Godrum's ragged lips, and his head fell back onto the table. But at the same time his hand tightened around JD's and held on.

JD put his mouth right up to Godrum's ear. 'I got that,' he whispered. 'I got it. But what happens then?'

'Then you go. The . . . ship . . . will . . . take . . . you.'

JD could hardly hear the old man's words, each one was fainter than the one before, but the grip on JD's hand grew tighter and Godrum's body tensed.

'If you want to go, JD, go. Take your friend and go. Leave all this behind.'

No sooner had he said the words than the old man's fingers loosened and his arm fell away. JD looked down.

The breathing had stopped but the remains of a gentle smile lay folded into the creases of the craggy old face.

JD felt tears welling up in his eyes and through the mist he smiled a grim smile at Godrum's frail, still body.

'Thanks, Mr Godrum,' he whispered, but the words caught in his throat. He dared not say any more and reached out to brush away a wisp of long grey hair that lay across the battered face. One more word and he would break down and sob his heart out but that wasn't what Godrum would have wanted. That wasn't why the old man had waited for him, just for him to cry like a baby. JD knew why the old man had held on and understood too what had driven him all this time. He couldn't escape, he knew he would never fly his ship to that better place, that place where the green trees grew and water fell out of the sky. And even if he had, what good would it have done? No, he'd waited, he'd waited so's JD could have that chance.

JD straightened up. Godrum had told him what he had to do so now he'd better get on and do it. He'd take Aqua. They only had to climb those steps and walk into the ship. He knew the code and reckoned he knew how to use it. Together they'd fly off to a new place and build a new life. A life with no wars, no pollutions and –

A small sound made JD look up. He blinked the tears from his eyes and turned towards the doorway where Aqua stood quietly. She'd been watching and listening.

'What?' he said.

'I found who was at the door,' Aqua said.

'Who?'

'Come here,' she said, turning away, and from the corridor four small, ragged boys shuffled forward in a tight group, jostling together for courage.

They looked up at JD and in a split second that vision of Three-Seven-Seven flew straight back into his mind. These kids looked so like the wasted, frail little boy he'd buried out by the Pits. They seemed so young and thin, their round eyes staring up at him.

'Who are you?' JD said but he knew the answer before they spoke.

'We've come up from the Fireless Room,' one of them said his voice like a small bell. 'The boy Twelve-O-Two said to come. Said we should ask you what to do. We've caught two more Silver Men and we've got some grub and water but what do we do now?'

'How should I know?'

The little boy who had spoken looked at his feet and JD looked at them too. They were covered in dirt and scratches. The toes were splayed out from days and nights tramping around the Fireless wheel. The boy looked up again.

'Twelve-O-Two said you'd know what to do. He said for you to come back. He said you'd know.'

329

JD stared at the ragged boys then turned his eyes up to meet Aqua's. She smiled and walked over to where he stood next to the body of his precious Godrum and took his hand.

'C'mon, JD,' she whispered. 'They're waiting for you.'

'But, Aqua. What about the Dry Marsh?' But he wasn't thinking about any Dry Marsh. He was thinking about a place where critters flew and water fell from the sky.

'He told me, Aqua. Godrum told me the secret. I know what to do and we could go now. If we just go up those steps into his ship we could fly away to a fabulous place. We'd have all the water we want and –'

'Sure we could, JD, any time we want. But right now we've got things to do,' Aqua said and gently led him away.

JD gripped her hand. 'I know,' he sighed. 'I know.'

She led him past the four little boys, who fell in behind them, and together they went out into the concrete corridor. At the top of the stairs, by the heavy door, JD stopped.

'You know, Aqua, I've had an idea. If we could gather in the Pit kids and the Farm kids and bring 'em all together with the boys from the Fireless wheel, if we all got together and tried real hard, do you reckon we could change the way things are around here? Make it better.'

Aqua smiled.

'Yes, JD,' she said. 'I reckon we could too.'